KISS HER GOODBYE

e for Allan Guthrie's *Two-Way Split*:

lis first two books remind me in their way of a wry vers   *t Carter*, novel and movie alike ... There's an offhand vi   id downscale amorality that give Guthrie's books the kind   ck charm and smirky melancholy his people need to s   *The Guardian*

'Allan Guthrie has a bright – or should I say dark? –   crime fiction.' Bill Pronzini, author of *Blue Lonesome*

'A tight little mood piece whose mood, like Rank   lack and blue.' *Kirkus Reviews*

'I was ... riveted by this stripped down, breathless, all-at-one-sitting read – a tough, fast-moving, funny novel with the kind of energy that's so compelling in a lot of the best mid-century American noir.' Lee Horsley, *Crime Culture*

'A straight-up bona fide classic, no messing ... it's the speed, the economy of the style that got me.' *Bullet Magazine*

'A memorable, stunning and pitch-perfect debut ... one you should grab forthwith. I can't remember a first novel this good in a long, long time.' Ed Gorman, *Mystery Scene*

'Quite simply, superb.' *Crime Scene Scotland*

'One of the five best crime novels I've ever read.' Ken Bruen, author of *The Guards*

'All the beauty of *Blue Velvet* and all the insanity of *Wild at Heart*.' Ray Banks, author of *The Saturday Boy*

KISS HER GOODBYE

Allan Guthrie

This edition published in Great Britain in 2006 by
Polygon, an imprint of Birlinn Ltd
West Newington House
10 Newington Road
Edinburgh
EH9 1QS

www.birlinn.co.uk

ISBN 10: 1 904598 77 3
ISBN13: 978 1 904598 77 0

British Library Cataloguing-in-Publication Data
A catalogue record for this book is available
on request from the British Library

Typeset by Hewer Text UK Ltd, Edinburgh
Printed and bound by Thomson Litho, East Kilbride

PART ONE

ONE

The day he found out his daughter was dead, Joe Hope was at Cooper's flat watching horse racing on Channel 4. Joe's filly was a couple of lengths off the pace with less than two furlongs to go. He yawned and cupped his hand over his mouth. They'd been working late. It was early afternoon, Joe had had hardly any sleep and by now the adrenalin of the previous night had all but drained away. He was hot and tired and thinking about saying goodbye and going home.

When the phone rang Joe glanced towards his old friend. Cooper's gaze didn't shift from the television set – one of those new flatscreen LCD jobs he'd bought just last week for two grand. Two grand for a fucking TV! Joe hadn't said anything, and maybe it was just his tired eyes, but the picture seemed to have a permanent ghost and watching it was making him dizzy.

Joe yawned again. He was too old to get away with missing a night's sleep.

Last night they'd visited one of Cooper's clients, a mouthy young twat by the name of Billy Strachan. Billy was well behind on his repayments, and seemingly not too bothered by the fact. He had been overheard in his local calling Cooper a wanker and boasting that he had no intentions of paying back another penny. He advised Cooper, so the source had claimed, to come and make him, if he thought he was hard enough.

Cooper was a loan shark. Joe worked for him.

First rule of debt collecting: if you want to improve the odds on your client being at home, visit him at night when he ought to be curled up in bed, asleep. Second rule: always carry a weapon.

Joe and Cooper, each carrying a baseball bat, had called on Billy Strachan at two in the morning. Although the noise of his front door being kicked in woke him up, by the time they'd burst into the sitting room, Billy had managed to stagger only as far as his bedroom doorway. With one hand he rubbed his eyes, while with the other he clutched a floral patterned quilt to his chest. He blurted out, 'The fuck?' as Joe ran towards him, then turned and was plunging back through the doorway when Joe placed a foot on the dragging end of the quilt. It tore out of Billy's grasp and fell to the ground. Naked, he stumbled towards his empty bed and looked around, now wide awake.

'Nowhere to run,' Cooper said. 'Nowhere to hide, Billy. Eh?'

'Maybe you're thinking that this is just a bad dream,' Joe said. 'But you're not asleep, Billy.'

'Not yet,' Cooper said.

Billy stood by the bed, protecting his balls with his hands.

Cooper raised the index finger of his left hand and flicked it from side to side. 'That's what your eyes are doing. Know what I call that? Panic flicker.'

Joe took a step towards the bed. Cooper was about to launch into one of his rants. Joe took another step, fully expecting Cooper to start on the stillness thing any minute. Billy was shaking like he'd been stuck in a freezer for a week. His eyes jumped from Cooper to Joe, back to Cooper.

'Where's all your tough talk now, Billy?' Cooper said.

Joe breathed in the smell of stale smoke. A heaped ashtray sat on a bedside table, sandwiched between a book on origami and a packet of Marlboros.

'You can judge a man,' Cooper said, 'by his stillness.' He closed his eyes and stood perfectly still.

Joe watched him for half a minute. Cooper remained motionless and would continue to do so until Joe interrupted him in another three or four minutes. Nothing moved. Not a twitch from any of the overdeveloped muscles in Cooper's five-foot-six-inch frame. He appeared to have stopped breathing.

Billy Strachan read books on origami, for fuck's sake. Any minute now the poor bastard was going to piss himself.

Joe adjusted the grip on his bat and slammed it into Billy's knuckles. With a grunt, Billy crumpled to the floor just like the quilt had done. Joe hit the boy's ankle, kneecap, elbow in quick succession. Quick double-handers. Not too much power. Probably didn't break more than a couple of bones.

Billy screamed.

Cooper opened his eyes and glanced at Joe. 'That was nowhere near five minutes.' He gave a quick shake of his head and marched towards Billy Strachan. 'We're going to kill you now, you little tosser.'

'That isn't necessary.' Joe put his hand on Cooper's elbow.

Billy was sobbing. He started screaming again.

Cooper said, 'Two minutes at most.'

'He's got the message.'

Cooper shook Joe's hand off and took a swing. Something crunched when the bat hit Billy's face and Billy stopped screaming. Cooper said, 'Now he's got the message.'

Joe nodded. Billy had got the message, all right. He was probably dreaming about it. If he could, he'd pay. If not, Joe and Cooper would be back. Quietly, Joe said to the unconscious figure, 'You don't want to fuck with a man's reputation.'

He didn't think Billy would be slagging Cooper down at his local for a while. At least, not until he got his teeth fixed.

Joe and Cooper left Billy lying on his side on his bedroom floor and drove to a classy brothel in the New Town. The Real Gentleman's Club was decorated like a Victorian bordello. Rumour had it that the curtains alone had cost eleven grand. In the waiting room, Cooper chose a slim young girl called Yvette and Joe went for a slightly chunkier and considerably older whore who called herself Annabella.

They climbed a flight of stairs. Cooper disappeared down the corridor with Yvette. Joe and Annabella climbed another flight. 'In here,' Annabella said. She opened the door and turned on the light. The room stank of incense. A parrot in a cage by the window squawked once, then was quiet. It obviously knew when to shut up.

At eight o'clock in the morning, six hundred quid poorer, Joe and Cooper left the Real Gentleman's Club and spent the next four hours at the Phoenix on Broughton Street sinking a few pints with whisky chasers. Winding down.

Beating people up wasn't easy.

The ringing phone in Cooper's sitting room reminded Joe that he'd switched off his mobile last night in case Ruth phoned while he was working and he hadn't turned it back on yet. He dug it out of his coat and pressed the power button. The phone was several years old, chunky, with a dark grey plastic exterior. Cooper kept telling him it was about time he got a new one. It rang after a couple of seconds and Joe dialled his voice mail. A sexy electronic middle-class English voice told him he had sixteen messages. Fuck, Ruth had excelled herself. Normally she didn't leave more than ten. She must have had a slow evening. No way was he trawling through that lot now. He turned the phone off and slipped it back in his pocket.

Cooper's phone was still ringing. Joe might have answered the bloody thing, if this were his house. Probably some twat trying to sell double-glazing. But it certainly wasn't Joe's place to answer Cooper's phone, even if the incessant ringing was becoming really irritating.

Eventually, Cooper glanced round the room and said, 'Where is the little bint?'

Assuming Cooper was referring to Sally, his seventeen-year-old girlfriend, Joe told him, 'She went out for a walk with the baby.'

Cooper twisted his neck to look over his shoulder, somehow managing to keep his left leg draped over the arm of his olive green armchair. He shouted, 'Sally?'

'I saw her go out,' Joe said. 'During the last race.'

Cooper obviously didn't believe him. 'Sally?'

Joe had a headache. At the brothel he'd lain awake, hands clasped behind his head, listening to Annabella's throaty snores. He guessed he'd slept for no more than an hour.

He closed his eyes and did his best to ignore Cooper's shouts and the phone's persistent ringing. Yellow lights strobed behind his eyelids. Tiredness muffled the various background noises. He could fall asleep now, if he wanted.

'Sally?'

Joe's eyes snapped open. 'I saw her leave, Cooper.' His friend was a right fucking twat sometimes. 'You think I'm making it up?' On the TV screen Joe saw his horse move from third to second. Only half-a-length behind the leader and gaining all the time. 'Come on,' he muttered. Under a furlong left.

Cooper tapped a fingernail against the side of his beer can. 'She could've told me.'

The ringing stopped. Joe breathed out, only then aware he'd been holding his breath. Almost immediately the phone began ringing again. He stopped breathing. After a few seconds he inhaled with a sucking sound and said, 'You going to get that?'

'Keep what's left of your hair on.' Cooper picked up the phone from the table inches from his hand. Didn't say a word. A puzzled expression creased his forehead. He passed Joe the receiver, gripping the phone so hard his knuckles were white. 'Ruth,' he said.

Joe filled his lungs, then exhaled through his nose. 'Can't you leave me alone?' he said to his wife. His horse was challenging for the lead. 'Come on.'

She sounded hysterical. Her words ran together. He couldn't make out a damn thing she was saying. For Christ's sake. He'd been out all night before. 'What's the big deal?' he asked her.

In reply she made noises that sounded like an unmusical child singing a difficult melody.

Was she jealous? Did she think he'd been sleeping with someone? He interrupted her. 'Take it slowly.'

Once, a long time ago, she'd said, 'Fuck whoever you want, cause it won't be me.' When was that? Ten years ago?

The noise stopped. Joe heard her catch her breath. She said, 'Gem.' She wheezed. Tried to speak. Choked. Tried again. Broke down, whining.

Jesus Christ. 'Come on,' he said. 'Come on.'

She thought he was talking to her. She managed to say, 'Home. Please.'

'Quick as I can.' Joe hung up. 'Ruth's flipped.' He asked Cooper, 'What did she say to you?'

'Didn't catch much of it.' Cooper's fingers drummed on the beer can. 'Passed her on to you, eh?'

'She mention Gem?'

'Might have. Couldn't really tell.'

'I have to go.'

'Well done,' Cooper said, tilting his beer can at the TV. A hundred quid at four-to-one. Not bad for sitting on your arse drinking beer, Joe thought. Not bad at all.

TWO

Joe drove halfway across Edinburgh wondering what his little girl had done this time to upset her mother. Gemma was nineteen. A bright girl. But with only a year of university under her belt, she'd decided to chuck it in. Announced one day that she was leaving Edinburgh to stay with Adam Wright, a distant cousin of her mother's, for a while. When Adam's parents died in a car crash a few years ago, he had inherited a stack of money and bought an ugly old warehouse of a building on the outskirts of Kirkwall in the Orkney Islands. Entirely founded on having had a few stories published in women's magazines back in the early nineties, he set up a writers' retreat, and installed himself as a sort of literary guru. Ruth couldn't stand him. Probably because he'd once spilled red wine on her dress at a wedding reception. Gem, who had notions of becoming a poet, thought Adam was wonderful. And Adam was fond of her, too.

'You can't give up university just like that,' Ruth had said the night Gemma told them of her plans.

Gem had an old school atlas open across her knees. She pointed to Edinburgh, then, with her finger, drew a line directly north. Beyond the Scottish coastline, she hit the group of islands where Adam's retreat was located. She looked up. 'Further east than you think.' She smiled at Joe.

Ruth stormed out of the room.

'I'm sure you'll love it in Orkney,' Joe said.

She closed the atlas. 'I better go see if Mum's okay.'

Joe called Adam a few days before Gem left and told him to

take good care of her. Adam promised she'd be well looked after. Really, he said, she was in extremely capable hands. Orkney was a lot safer than Edinburgh. Hardly any arseholes running around with baseball bats.

He hung up when Joe told him what would happen if any harm came to her.

Joe's fingers were tingling as he got out of the car. He locked it. Fumbled for his flat keys. Dropped them. He swore and picked them up off the pavement.

He ran up the stairs. Couldn't help himself.

Ruth opened the door the minute his key scratched in the lock. She was a mess. Her eyes looked like she'd scooped them out, dipped them in a tin of tomatoes and put them back in. She sniffed. Wiped her nose with the back of her hand. She said, 'Gem.' She turned her head. Wisps of dyed brown hair shrouded her face.

He grabbed her hand. Snot slid around under his fingers. 'Tell me.'

Her hand slipped out of his grasp. She looked at him, lips stretched, gums pink and fleshy. He could have sworn she was grinning. Left of centre, a single strand of saliva bridged her lips. She said, 'She's dead.'

He formed a fist. Slammed his knuckles into his open palm. He kicked the door. Let his hands drop. Ruth's shoulders were shaking. Her jaw quivered. She looked hideously old.

'Piss off.' Joe wiped his hand on his trousers. 'You're a lying cow.' He turned his back on her.

'Don't go.' She grabbed his sleeve. 'I need you.'

He swatted her hand away. Bile coated his tongue. He went to the bathroom. Locked the door. Spat in the sink. He felt dizzy. His armpits itched. He sat on the toilet and shouted through the door, 'When did this happen?'

'Come out.'

The smell of urine made him want to retch. He lurched towards the door.

He grabbed a fistful of hair and pulled. His scalp hurt. He pulled harder. The pain was satisfying. He yelled. Then he caught sight of himself in the mirror. He let go. He looked ridiculous. A thirty-eight-year-old man trying to pull his hair out by the roots. Fucking ridiculous. 'When I'm ready,' he muttered.

He leaned against the sink. The cold tap dripped. He tightened it. No difference. Needed a new washer. Bugger it. He'd been meaning to get it fixed for a while. He watched drops of water explode against the grey enamel. Fascinating little liquid bombs. When he looked up at himself in the mirror he felt sick. Felt like he'd swallowed a bucket of phlegm.

Hands clammy, he turned the doorknob and pushed the door open. Ruth was huddled in the corner, facing him. 'What happened?' he asked her.

She didn't look at him. 'Pills.'

'Pills,' he said, nodding. 'Pills. What kind of pills?'

'Paracetamol.'

He stared at the swollen veins on the backs of his hands. Putting on a bit of weight, maybe. His wedding ring was too tight these days. He cleared his throat. He couldn't say it.

After a while Ruth said it for him. 'She killed herself.'

Standing on the finishing line, clutching the hare to your chest – and you can't let go – as a thirty-five kilo greyhound sprints towards you. The dog rams you in the stomach. Bam. Joe struggled to get his breath back. Then, still panting, he said, 'She wouldn't do that. Not Gem. Not my daughter.'

Ruth looked at him, her red eyes squeezing tears down her face. 'The police said there were no suspicious circumstances.'

He stuck one of his knuckles in his mouth and bit it. It tasted salty.

'She was depressed, Joe.'

He took his finger out of his mouth.

Ruth said, 'They have to do a post mortem.'

'Why, for fuck's sake?'

'Don't get angry. It's the law. They're doing it as soon—'

'I don't want to know.' He caught himself grabbing a handful of hair again. Stopped just in time. He shoved his hands in his pockets where they couldn't do any damage. His legs were shaking. He'd have to sit down. 'When did it happen?'

'Last night.'

His hands sprang out of his pockets, fingers splayed. 'And you didn't tell me?' Fingers so rigid they hurt.

'How could I?' She pressed her back against the wall. 'I tried.' She put her head in her hands and spoke into her lap. 'Your phone was turned off.' She lifted her head, screamed. Joe raised his hands. Fucking racket. She stopped after a while. Took several rapid breaths. Then, quietly, she said, 'I didn't know where you were.'

'Could have tried Cooper's.'

'Nobody answered.'

'What, all night?'

'Nobody answered.'

'Could have left a message.'

'I left hundreds of fucking messages on your fucking mobile.' She screamed again. Then took a long wheezy breath.

Joe said, patiently, 'You could have left a message at Cooper's.'

'Oh, yeah. Right. Hi, Sally. If you see Joe could you tell him his daughter's dead? Brilliant, Joe. Where the fuck were you, anyway?'

He shrugged. 'Out.'

'What, all night?' She was mocking him.

'Happens. You know it happens.'

Now she was definitely grinning. 'Young, huh? Was she? Pretty?'

'Don't start, Ruth.'

'Dark-haired? Nineteen? Blue eyes? Remind you of your daughter, Joe?'

'Stop it.'

'Remind you of Gem, eh?'

He shouted. 'Stop it.' He stepped towards her. 'You're fucking disgusting.'

'Was she good, Joe? Was she?'

He shouted, 'Shut the fuck up.'

She pushed her face towards his. 'Answer me. Was she a good fuck, Joe?'

He opened the door and hurried downstairs. Last thing he wanted was to batter the fuck out of Ruth. It wasn't her fault her daughter was dead.

That was the fault of the fucker who swore he'd look after her. Adam Wright had broken his promise. And now it was Joe's turn to break something.

THREE

Joe didn't know what happened to the rest of the afternoon. He'd needed a drink while he decided what to do about Adam, so he went to a few bars in the Grassmarket and had a couple of whiskies in each. Then he headed up Victoria Street and along the High Street. He had another couple in The World's End and was feeling relaxed until a very short man tried to pick a fight with him. Worried he might kill the little twat, he left.

Twat. Twatt.

He remembered Gemma telling him, 'Dad, you'll love this. There's a village in Orkney called Twatt.'

It was getting dark outside when he made his way back to his car. He fumbled for his keys. The damn phone was in the way. He took the phone out of his pocket, opened the car door and climbed inside. He turned on the phone and sat for a while thinking about the messages Ruth had left. Messages he had not yet heard. Fuck them. Fuck her. He started the engine and headed for Leith.

Rain dotted the windscreen as he crawled along Restalrig Road. Still early yet. The telephone kiosk at the bottom of the road was empty. Give it an hour or two, there'd be a huddle of whores round what Tina called 'the fuck box,' hiding whatever sexual transaction was being conducted inside. Further along, a skimpily dressed trio tottered on high heels towards the car as he drove slowly past. One of them, an unlit cigarette dangling from her glossy lower lip, looked about fourteen. The other two were older, smoking for real. Ten feet away their pimp stood under an umbrella, a Rottweiler crouched at his feet. Joe drove on. No sign of her. Maybe she wasn't here yet.

Since the police abolished the tolerance zone back in November of last year, she'd been a little harder to track down. She now moved in a random pattern around Leith. Normally he rang her mobile. If she was busy he left a message and she called him when she could. But . . . Fuck, he didn't want to wait tonight. He'd drive down to the Shore. Try there.

He was about to put his foot down when he spotted Tina's shiny white handbag gleaming in the headlights. He looked up, peering at her face, making sure it was her. He blasted his horn. She recognised the car and smiled. She was probably thinking her luck was in. Only eight o'clock and Bob was here with the readies. Yeah. Bob. That's how she knew him. Her little half-wave made her blouse rise and the flash of bare stomach made Joe shiver.

He pulled over. Reached across to open the door.

She beat him to it. 'You're early.' She tugged at her skirt. Lifted her arse. Tugged again.

'If your skirt's uncomfortable,' he said, 'you can take it off.'

'That'll be a first.'

He didn't reply. After a while, still wearing her skirt, she leaned back in her seat and sighed.

'Nice and warm in here,' she said. 'Snug.'

He drove in silence, trundling past Victorian tenements, a couple of newsagents, a pub.

She shifted in her seat. 'Problems?' she asked.

'Could say that.'

'Wife?'

He said nothing.

'Why don't you leave her? Nice guy like you. Why stick around?'

'Not that simple.'

She put her hand on his thigh and kneaded his leg. Her fingernails, what was left of them after she'd finished biting them, were green. 'You smell of booze,' she said. 'You drunk? You shouldn't be driving, you know.'

'I've never been more sober in my life.'

She squeezed his thigh. His leg trembled under her fingers. 'You're early tonight,' she said.

He was about to tell her he'd be away for a while when a couple of drunken twats stepped off the pavement ten feet in front of the car. One of them pointed his finger and tried to look threatening. Joe pointed right back at him. Didn't brake. Why the fuck should he? The bumper clipped the imbecile on the side of the leg. Joe saw him collapse in the mirror, spinning when he hit the ground. He clutched his knee. His friend gesticulated angrily.

'Stop the car.' Tina reached into the back. 'You still keep the bat here?'

Joe slowed to a halt. 'Leave them, Tina.'

'Won't be a minute.' Tina grabbed Joe's baseball bat from behind the driver's seat and leapt out of the car. Joe opened the door on his side and got out and leaned against the roof. The uninjured man was shouting obscenities, ignoring his friend. Tina strode up to him and jabbed him in the gut with the end of the bat. As he bent over, winded, Tina stepped back and took a swing at his jaw. The bat shuddered on contact. He fell over on his side and shut up.

His friend looked at Tina, both hands clasping his knee. 'Jesus,' he said.

Ignoring him, Tina grabbed his unconscious friend by the trouser leg and dragged him partially onto the pavement. Joe walked away from the car. Approached her slowly. She was struggling with the dead weight. He placed his hand on her elbow. 'Let me do it,' he said.

She shook his hand off. 'Take this.' She gave him the baseball bat, then grabbed the other leg and hoisted the rest of the poor fuck off the road. Tina offered her hand to the unconscious man's friend. He shook his head. Scrabbled to his feet. He waddled onto the pavement, tucked his head under his arm and started to cry.

'Okay, now?' Joe held out his hand and Tina's fingers brushed against his. 'Let's go,' he said. They went back to the car. She insisted on driving. He sat back and closed his eyes, listening to the hum of the engine.

'You going to put that away?' she asked him.

Opening his eyes, he saw her glance at the baseball bat lodged between his knees. He picked it up and lobbed it over the back of the seat.

She ran her left hand through her hair. She had thick hair.

Not like Ruth, whose hair was so thin that in places you could see her scalp through it. Probably from dyeing it all these years.

He put his hand on Tina's bare leg. It was cold and smooth. He let his hand ride up her skirt.

'You want me to stop the car and blow you? You pay for it, Bob. You ought to try it some time.'

He shook his head. He felt like going home to his bed. Cuddling up to his crazy wife. Falling asleep. But he could hardly do that, could he? What he wanted was to speak to somebody who knew Gemma. Tina was okay, but she didn't know his daughter. Cooper, maybe? Cooper knew her as well as anybody. Cooper and Joe had been friends since their schooldays. Yeah, he'd go see Cooper in a bit. Joe rummaged in his pocket, extracted his wallet and opened it. He counted a thousand pounds in twenties.

'I'm not going to be around for a while,' he said.

'I might miss you.'

'Might?' He laughed. 'You say the nicest things.' He started counting the money again. Exactly one thousand. Gently, he prised her left hand off the steering wheel and pressed the money into her palm.

'What's that for?'

'Being so fucking kind,' he said.

She leaned across and kissed him on the cheek.

Tenderness. You get it where you can. Even if you have to pay for it.

She drove to her flat, saying she wanted to bury the money he'd given her. She probably meant it literally. Under the floorboards or somewhere.

She invited Joe in. He accepted. Cooper could wait. Joe had only been to Tina's flat once before and he'd been so drunk he remembered her bedroom, but not much else.

In the hallway she flicked on the light, then hiked up her skirt and started to walk towards the sitting room with her arse jutting out.

'Don't,' he told her.

She gave him a look he couldn't classify. Push him and he'd say she was disappointed, but she couldn't be, could she? After all this time. Anyway, she was a whore. She wriggled back into her skirt. He followed her into the sitting room. Too tidy. It looked unlived in. A fitted kitchen was crammed into the right-hand third of the room. The surfaces were spotless and he couldn't smell the slightest trace of cooking. Maybe she never cooked. Dined out every night. A different punter each time.

'Drink?' She was bending over the fridge, holding one of those baby bottles of Stella. He nodded. She closed the fridge door and investigated a few random drawers before she found what she was looking for. 'Got the bugger.' Joe smiled when she brandished the bottle opener. She levered the top off the bottle and the beer fizzed. Joe slumped onto the settee. She put the bottle opener back in the drawer and handed him the bottle. She said, 'Just going to put the money somewhere safe,' and disappeared from the room.

Joe pressed the chilled bottle to his cheek and stared at the blank television screen in front of him. Before long, Tina returned and joined him on the settee. He yawned. 'Want me to open a window?' she said. 'Fresh air might keep you awake.'

He shook his head. 'Got a fag?' He took a mouthful of beer.

She snapped open her handbag and dug out a packet of Silk Cut. 'Didn't know you smoked.' She offered him the packet.

He took one of her cigarettes and put it between his lips. He'd given up more than two years ago. 'Light?'

She pointed an orange disposable at his face. He leaned closer. Sucked. The smoke bit the back of his throat. He coughed, eyes watering. He coughed again. She was laughing at him.

'Fuck it,' he said. 'Been a long time. Too long. You have it.'

She took the cigarette from him and pasted it to her lips. 'This is how us pros do it.' She tilted her head back, puckered her mouth and launched a smoke ring towards the ceiling.

His throat felt like it was stuffed with sandpaper, but at least he'd stopped coughing. He wiped his eyes and took a long swig of beer.

'What's the matter?' she said. 'Wish you'd tell me.'

'You got more beer?' He wished he could tell her, too. He'd have to go soon. Speak to Cooper. About Gem.

She fetched another beer from the fridge. Got the bottle opener. Brought both items over to him. She sat down and kicked off her shoes. The straps had left welts on her feet. Her toenails were green like her fingernails. 'Well?'

'I saw a kid back there. When I was looking for you. Looked like she should be at school. Or doing her homework.'

'That'll be Jacqui.' She spelled the name for him. 'Runaway from Dundee.'

'I've never seen a kid soliciting, Tina.'

'Showed up last month. Three of them.' Smoke trickled out of her mouth. She licked her lips. 'Don't know the other two. They claim they're sixteen.'

'Not the ones with her tonight. They were old enough to know what they were doing.'

'No, the other two look like schoolgirls. I think they're local.'

'Shit,' Joe said. 'What's going on?'

She leaned her head back and took a deep drag. 'The older girls say it was almost unheard of before the police closed down the tolerance zone.' She blew smoke at the ceiling. 'You couldn't work underage in a monitored zone. Couldn't get away with it.'

The police introduced the tolerance policy in the early eighties. You wanted a shag, you went to Leith's Coburg Street. Worked beautifully for nearly two decades. Then, last year, local residents forced the police to designate a new tolerance zone in Salamander Street. For Joe, it was a fucking nuisance. It lasted little more than two weeks before the police shut down the zone permanently. Which, for Joe, was an even bigger fucking nuisance.

Still, he coped. The more pernicious consequence was that the city, virtually free of child prostitution for nearly twenty years, was in danger of reintroducing something that made Joe's stomach turn.

'Kids,' he muttered. He faced Tina on the settee, suddenly feeling depressed enough to cry. He changed the subject before he embarrassed himself. 'When my wife told me she was pregnant,' he said, 'I was angry.'

'Not surprised,' Tina said. 'No offence, but you're getting on a bit.'

'I'm talking twenty years ago. Round about the time the police introduced the original tolerance zone.'

'My mistake.' She grabbed his beer and took a swig. Handed it back. 'Go on.'

'I didn't want a baby,' he said. 'Too young to be a father, you know. Too irresponsible. Too busy having a good time.'

'Down Coburg Street.'

'Piss off. Not then.'

'Piss off yourself,' she said. 'Baby wasn't planned, I take it?'

'Hardly.'

'Were you married?'

'Nearly a year.'

'Was it good?'

He looked at Tina. He'd enjoyed her company at least once a week for the last couple of years, but he'd never studied her face before. Glossy orange lipstick thickened her lips. Her nose was too big and had been broken in a couple of places. Dark blue mascara hooded her eyes. She was hardly what you'd describe as pretty. Pretty girls worked the lap dancing circuit if they could. The Fantasy Bar, Bottoms Up, Hooters. Best of the lot was the Western Bar, where the girls got to keep all the money they made. He studied Tina. No, maybe not so pretty, but she could handle herself, though. She'd been simply stunning with that baseball bat.

'Stop staring.'

'Piss off,' he said. 'Any more beer?'

'You're fucking delightful company tonight.' She got up again. Opened the fridge door. 'Last one.'

'Sometimes I wonder why Ruth married me,' he said as she brought him the beer.

'More to the point, why did you marry her?'

'That would be telling.' He gulped down half the contents of the bottle.

'Why do I bother asking?' She put her arm round him and he let his head fall against her neck. 'You can't even tell me your real name, Bob.' She smelled of cheap perfume and smoke. 'Even though you know mine.'

He sat up and drank the rest of the beer. 'I prefer Tina.'

'And what's wrong with Ruth?'

'You wouldn't want to know.' Ruth, he thought. He should talk to Ruth. Not Cooper. If he wanted to talk to someone who knew his daughter, he should talk to his wife. Maybe, he thought as he stood up, he was just a little bit drunk.

FOUR

Ruth, his wife, his delightful wife, was in the kitchen. Ah, bless her, the wee bundle of joy, she'd changed her clothes. She was sitting at the table, slouched over like she was suffering from stomach cramp, a mug of tea cradled in the bosom of her black dress. Man, could she suffer. Her eyes were crimson. She didn't look up at him. Scattered on the table in front of her were half-a-dozen travel brochures. Joe could make out the covers of only three: Andalusia, Morocco, Tunisia. Her favourite holiday locations. Time to run away, was it? Her daughter was dead and Ruth was planning a holiday. She never faced anything. Fuck. Give her a break, you twat.

He dragged out a chair, sat down opposite her and tried to be kind. His tongue felt thick. 'You shouldn't be on your own.'

Slowly, she lifted the mug to her mouth. She slurped, gasped, set down the mug. Her gaze drifted towards him. 'You're so considerate.'

He waited a moment, then said, 'What happened to Gem?'

Her eyes held his for a couple of seconds. Then she looked into her mug. 'I don't believe you.' She lowered her head and he noticed she was developing a cracker of a bald patch at the crown. Her head jerked upright. Spit flew out of her mouth when she said, 'I don't fucking believe you.' Her face was screwed up, old, ugly. 'You're a fucking' – her hands flew into the air, fingers spread – 'bastard, Joe.'

He put his head in his hands and rubbed his eyes. When he took his hands away the overhead light seemed unnaturally bright. He looked up at it and winced. When he looked back down again she was staring at him, her upper lip curled. Her face was still old and ugly.

She said through quivering lips, 'Don't you care that your daughter's dead?'

'I'm asking,' he said. 'What happened?'

'You've got a cheek. You know it's your fault.'

He waited a moment. 'I was nowhere near her. How can it have been my fault?'

'She left because of you.'

'Bollocks.'

'Why do you think she left, then?'

He stood up. 'I don't have to listen to this shit.'

'You wish, Joe. You fucking wish.'

'What do you mean, she left because of me?' He sat down again.

'She was unhappy. You didn't talk to her about it.'

'I would have.' He ran his hand through his hair. It felt thin, more like Ruth's every day. 'I would have. What do you mean? Talked to her about what? The fuck're you on about? I didn't know she wanted to talk. She didn't say anything.'

'How could you not know?'

He tapped his fingers against his brow. 'Why – why didn't she say? Why didn't you tell me?'

'Why do you think she left university? Why do you think she left home and went to live on some godforsaken island with a relative she hardly knows?' Saliva gathered at the edges of her mouth. 'Because she was happy?'

Joe turned away. 'What was upsetting her?'

'I don't know.' Ruth squeezed her mug between her hands. 'Something happened. She wouldn't tell me what.'

'She wouldn't have—'

'She would. You fucking dumb bastard. You know she would have told you anything.'

'If she didn't tell you—'

'Joe, she loved you.' Ruth banged her fist against her heart. 'God knows why, but she loved you.'

He felt as if all the blood had drained from his body. 'Why

didn't she say something? If there was a problem.' He swallowed. 'She should have said.'

'You never asked.'

'I didn't know. Fucking hell. I didn't know anything was wrong. Why would I ask?'

'You should have.'

'Well, I fucking didn't, you dozy bitch. How many times do I have to tell you?'

'If you'd fucking paid attention, maybe she wouldn't be dead.' Ruth jumped to her feet and slung the mug at him. It missed, crashed into the cooker behind him and exploded. The side of his face was wet. He stretched his tongue towards his cheek. Cold, strong, black tea. Veins of dark brown liquid trailed across the pine table, bunching at the bottom edge of Ruth's travel brochure for Morocco. He looked sideways at the floor. Puddles of tea swelled on the linoleum.

'Was that a full cup?' he asked. 'Or don't I deserve that much wastage?'

Her shoulders rocked up and down, the only indication that she might be laughing. Of course, she might equally be crying. 'Actually,' she said, 'I'd drunk hardly any of it.'

He still couldn't determine her mood. Nothing new there. Now she was staring at her fidgeting hands. He wiped his cheek with his palm.

'I saw this TV programme once.' She looked at him, eyes shiny. 'This woman lost her daughter. Car accident. She said her biggest fear was that she'd never stop crying.'

Joe waited. Finally he said, 'What are you trying to say?'

'Never mind.' She lowered her head. 'You weren't there for Gemma.'

'What was I supposed to do?' Joe stamped his foot and was annoyed with himself at the childishness of his gesture. He grunted, steadied himself. 'I didn't know anything was wrong.'

'You could write a book about the things you don't know.' She turned her head to the side and stared at the wall.

He bent over and squeezed her chin between his fingers, forcing her to face him. She lowered her eyes. Refused to meet his gaze. Her face was grey, tear-streaked. Quietly, he asked her, 'What else don't I know?'

'I'm being mean,' she said, looking at the floor. 'Take no notice.' Her jaw moved between his finger and thumb. 'Shouldn't be too hard for you.'

He let go of her. 'I'm going to Cooper's.'

'Fine,' she said. 'Off to your boyfriend's loving arms at the slightest excuse.'

'Fuck your jealous bullshit.' Joe came very close to hitting his wife. If he stayed any longer he wasn't sure he'd be able to control himself.

'I assure you I have nothing to be jealous of,' she said. 'Believe me.'

''Bye, darling,' he said as he slammed the door.

FIVE

If he pressed any harder he'd push the damn buzzer right through the wall.

A light drizzle dotted the illuminated name panel, which was casting an orange glow over the back of Joe's hand. Just about enough light for him to read his watch. Early yet. One twenty. What was Cooper doing in bed? He released his finger from the buzzer momentarily to wipe his damp forehead. He'd left the car at home and walked over here. Like Tina had said, the fresh air had done him good.

He felt fine. Clear-headed. Calm. The row with Ruth almost forgotten.

He stabbed the buzzer a couple more times and then held the fucker down.

The buzzing added a bass accompaniment to the drunken singing coming from just around the corner. Hearts supporters expressing contempt for their city rivals. *If you hate the fuckin' Hibees clap your hands.* Judging by the steady increase in volume, they were heading this way. Pretty hard, these football fans, daring to wake up the whole neighbourhood. Joe watched them swagger into view. He counted six of them. Five wore maroon and white scarves. The other carried his scarf scrunched up in his hand. The only thing hard about them was their consonants.

The one with the bare neck spotted Joe. 'Clap your fucking hands, Dad.'

Joe didn't take his finger off the buzzer.

Another one grabbed both ends of his scarf in his fist and stretched his arm above his head. He stuck his tongue out of the side of his mouth, leaning his head to the left. Joe reckoned he could snap the skinny fuck in two and toss one half into Broughton Street, the other into Leith Walk, without drawing breath.

The rest of the gang dutifully laughed. Then the joker let go of his scarf and started chanting: *You're going home in a fucking ambulance.* Ah, Joe thought, they'd managed to learn two songs. Immediately the others joined in. *You're going home in a fucking ambulance.* They pointed at Joe, belting out their tuneless one-line chorus.

Cooper's voice crackled out of the speaker. 'Who the fuck is it?'

Joe said his name.

'What's that racket?'

'Hearts choral society.' The latch buzzed and Joe pushed the door open. He closed it behind him, muffling the roar from the street as the gang, seeing their opportunity disappearing, charged. Too late. The chance of a bit of sport had gone. He gave the wall a gentle rap with his knuckles and strode forward. One of the little twats pounded on the door behind him. Joe thought about going back, slamming his fist into the noisy fucker's face. But he let it go.

Cooper lived towards the rear on the ground floor.

Joe found him framed in his doorway. He was wearing only a pair of black boxers. Not uniformly black. The word 'HUNG' was written in yellow. He was smoking, the thumb of his free hand tucked under the elastic of his pants. 'The fuck you want this time of night?'

'I need to talk.'

'Since when?' Cooper flicked ash onto the floor. 'You read too many fucking books.' He raised his eyebrows. When Joe didn't respond, he added, 'Fucking pansy.'

'It's Gem.'

Something like concern flickered over Cooper's face. Then he steeled himself, as if remembering who he was, and his face once again adopted its usual bored expression. He took a drag of his fag. He removed his thumb from his waistband and stuck his hand down his pants. For a moment or two he scratched his balls. It seemed to help him make a decision. He said, 'You better come in.'

Joe followed him through to the sitting room. 'Hope I didn't wake up Gary,' he said to Cooper's back.

'That kid'd sleep through a gang bang.'

'Takes after his dad, then.' Joe wrung his hands together. He felt nervous.

'Run that by me again.' Cooper flicked on a lamp and slumped in his usual seat. He dangled one bare leg over the arm of the chair. 'Sounded like you were questioning my sexual potency.'

'Wouldn't dream of it.' Joe had come here to talk. The problem was, he didn't know where to start. He sat down and said, 'Bloke told me about these gadgets I thought you might like.'

Cooper looked interested.

'Pussy snorkels, they're called. They have these bits that go up your nostrils.' Joe demonstrated with his hands. 'And these legs that clip over your ears.' He touched his ears.

Cooper looked bewildered.

'They help you breathe,' Joe explained. 'When you're muff diving.'

Cooper's face lit up. 'Pussy snorkels.' He banged his hand on the arm of his chair. 'Fantastic. Pussy snorkels. For muff divers.' He roared with delight. 'These things genuine?'

'Believe so. Got an address. I can get a couple to try out.'

'Sure,' Cooper said. 'Fuck me. Have to give them a shot, eh?'

'Thought you'd be amused.' Joe reached over and lifted the glass ashtray Cooper had nicked from the Boundary Bar a few years ago off the table. He held the ashtray towards Cooper.

'That what you woke me for?' Cooper glanced at the wilting ash hanging from the filter poking between his fingers, and stubbed out the cigarette with a couple of turns of his wrist. 'To tell me about pussy snorkels?'

Joe placed the ashtray back on the table. The cigarette butt still smouldered. 'I didn't think you'd be asleep yet.'

'Hard work being a father, Joe.' Cooper yawned. 'You should know. I mean, Gemma must have—'

'Gemma's dead.' Joe spoke so quietly he wasn't sure Cooper had heard. But Cooper had stopped speaking.

When Joe looked towards him, Cooper said, 'You're shitting me.'

Joe said nothing and looked away.

Cooper said, 'You're not shitting me.'

Joe stuck his head in his hands. When he looked up, Cooper was standing in front of him. Joe stared at the word, 'HUNG' and said, 'You want to get your crotch out of my face?'

'I'll get changed. You want a drink or something?'

'Bring a bottle.'

'I've got some Bunnahabhain.'

Joe stared into his hands. A moment later he heard the sound of clinking glasses. When he looked up Cooper, still in his underpants, was twisting the top off a whisky bottle.

'I'll do that,' Joe said. 'You go make yourself decent.'

Cooper shrugged.

A girl's voice, thick with sleep, said, 'What's going on?'

Joe turned in his seat and raised his empty glass to Sally. 'Fancy one?' Cooper's girlfriend was standing in the doorway, wearing only a t-shirt.

'Hi, Joe.' Sally gave him a forced smile. 'Give it a miss, thanks.'

Cooper said, 'Come on back to bed.'

'You coming?'

Cooper grabbed her arm. 'Just to get changed. My enormous pecker's embarrassing Joe.'

On her tiptoes, she leaned her head against his shoulder. 'I'm tired, Chicken.'

Joe coughed and began pouring himself a drink. The whisky-glug was a magnificent sound. Full of warmth. Cooper led Sally back to bed.

When Cooper returned, wearing a pair of black chinos and a faded t-shirt bearing the legend 'FILTH' with an accompanying picture of a pig in a policeman's uniform, Joe said, 'What's the matter? Couldn't find a chicken t-shirt?'

'Get fucked.' Cooper plunged into his seat. 'Pissed off because nobody has a nickname for you?'

'What's with "chicken," anyway?' Joe poured a dram for Cooper and handed him the glass.

'Fucked if I know.' Cooper sipped his Bunnahabhain. 'She's decided she wants to call me Chicken.'

'Anybody else called you that, you'd nut them.'

'Sally wants to call me Chicken, she can call me Chicken. It's a term of endearment, Joe. That's what it is.' He took another sip. 'Matter of fact, she can call me what she likes. One of the benefits of being my son's mother.'

'Fair enough.' Joe knocked back his whisky and poured himself another. He offered Cooper the bottle. Cooper stretched out his arm and Joe topped up his glass.

'So,' Cooper said. 'What happened?'

Joe leaned back in his chair. His jaw felt slack. 'You know Gemma as well as anybody.'

'Practically her uncle.'

'She wouldn't kill herself, right?'

'Who knows what makes them unhappy, Joe.'

Sadness swam through Joe's veins, mixing with the whisky. Even his best friend had realised Gemma was unhappy. Joe's fingers tightened around his glass. When it broke, he didn't move, just sat staring at the dribble of liquid, the shards of glass, the small piece stuck in the flesh of his palm. He was amazed at how sharp it was, how little it hurt.

'I'll bill you,' Cooper said. 'That's bloody expensive whisky you just wasted.'

Joe plucked the glass out of his hand and dark blood leaked out. He put his hand to his mouth, sucked.

Cooper picked up the remote control and turned on the TV. 'Bet there's nothing on,' he said.

Joe got up, staggering a little as he went to the toilet. He held his hand under the cold tap. The cold water numbed his hand. Penetrated to the bone. It felt pretty good. He flexed his fingers. The bleeding had slowed. He dried his hand on toilet paper to avoid getting blood on the hand towel, then rummaged in the overhead cabinet. He found a box of Mickey Mouse plasters. Nothing else. Fuck it. Who cared? He stuck a plaster on and plodded back to the sitting room.

Broken glass still lay on the table. Cooper was watching a car advert. Channel 5. You could tell by the poor reception. 'Henry,' Cooper said. 'Some player.' He chuckled. 'Va-va-voom,' he said.

Joe trudged through to the kitchen, grabbed some kitchen roll and returned to the sitting room with it. He picked up the glass fragments and wrapped them in several sheets of kitchen roll. He mopped up the spillage, carried the parcel of glass through to the kitchen and dropped it in the pedal bin tucked inside the walk-in cupboard.

It occurred to him that he knew this house almost as well as his own. Straight to the walk-in cupboard. Didn't have to think about it. Scarcely a day passed when he wasn't here. Where was the bin at home? It was a moment before he remembered that Ruth kept it under the sink. He thought maybe he should go home. But he felt too weak. Like he'd lost pints of blood. He glanced at his Mickey Mouse plaster. Home seemed like a major journey, a huge undertaking that he really wasn't capable of. Not now. And why should he? That crazy bitch would just yell at him and accuse him of being a queer. Anyway, Cooper had two spare bedrooms. Shame not to use one of them. Or Joe could just sink into one of those comfy armchairs and nod off.

When he stepped into the sitting room, Cooper looked up and stabbed the remote control with his thumb. The TV screen went blank. 'You okay?'

Joe lowered himself into his seat and paraded the plaster to Cooper.

'Lovely,' Cooper said. 'So, what happened to Gem?'

It took Joe ten minutes to relate the facts. All the while he peppered his statements with threats against Adam. Talking to Cooper clarified where the blame lay. Adam was supposed to look after her. Adam had fucked up.

Surprisingly, Cooper didn't agree. He said, 'Leave it.'

Joe's hand felt stiff. 'That your best advice?'

'There was nothing you could do, Joe. Gemma was un-happy. Nothing anybody could do about it.'

'If I'd spoken to her, found out what was troubling her—'

'Leave it alone. It's done.'

'Maybe I could have stopped her.'

'You weren't there. You couldn't have known.'

'Adam was. He's to blame. Yeah?'

'You're drunk,' Cooper said. 'You're not thinking straight. Get some sleep. Hey, look, we'll talk in the morning.'

'It'll make more sense then, will it? That what you're saying?'

'Deal with it, Joe.'

'That your best advice? Anything happened to your kid, anything happened to Gary, that's the advice you'd want from me? Fucking "deal with it"?'

'Probably not.' Cooper shook his head. 'Fact is, I'm really shite at this sort of thing.'

'Really?' Joe paused, then he said, 'More drink?'

An hour and four whiskies later Joe left Cooper watching TV and went to bed in the spare room. When his head hit the pillow, he closed his eyes and realised with an overwhelming intensity that his only child was dead. Deny it all he liked, and he would when he was sober again, the loss was incompre-hensible.

He could not allow it to have happened. Jesus, he was sounding like Ruth, for Christ's sake. Adam was the one who shouldn't have let it happen. The man was a fuck-up. Shouldn't be allowed to live.

Before he fell asleep, it occurred to Joe that maybe Gem had spoken to Adam. She liked him, so it was possible she'd confided in him. Maybe Adam knew why she'd taken her own life. Maybe Joe should speak to Adam before killing him. A couple of questions wouldn't hurt. Yeah, a couple of questions, then he'd kill him.

SIX

Joe woke with a sour mouth and a headache a student could brag about for months. He sat up, dangled his legs over the side of the bed and wriggled his toes. His insides felt delicate. Maybe some food – then again, maybe not. The thought alone made his stomach lurch. A drink, then? No adverse reaction this time. Exhaling slowly, he got to his feet, moaned, hauled on his trousers, slipped his shirt on without fastening the buttons and, several minutes later, staggered into the hallway.

Having managed that, climbing Everest ought to be a doddle.

He plodded towards the kitchen. Sally was at the table feeding Gary. She jumped when she saw Joe.

'Oh,' Joe said. 'I didn't . . . sorry. I'll go.'

'It's okay,' she said. 'I didn't know you were still here. Thought you'd gone.'

'Yeah,' Joe said. 'Yeah. Got some bad news. Got drunk. Crashed out.' Explain it away like any normal day. 'You know.'

'Cooper told me about Gemma,' she said. 'I'm so sorry, Joe. Sit down. I'll fix you some breakfast when Cheetah's finished.'

'Couldn't eat a thing.' Joe pulled a face and patted his stomach. 'But thanks.' He watched the baby suck Sally's nipple. 'Cheetah?'

'Look.' Sally slid her forefinger under Gary's earlobe. Joe took a step closer. Dark fuzzy hair grew all over the cartilage of the little man's ear. 'Remember Tarzan?' Sally asked him.

'Ah, the chimp.' Joe chuckled. 'Cheetah. Like it.'

Sally moved her hand and stroked her baby's head, smoothing the jet-black hair across his scalp. 'My pet name for him, Joe. Don't tell Cooper. He won't find it amusing.'

'You don't say.' After a minute, Joe asked, 'Both ears like that?'

She nodded. 'Apparently it's quite common. He'll lose the hair as he gets older. He's only ten months.'

Joe said, 'Extraordinary,' because he didn't know what else to say. He stood in front of her for a moment, realised he was staring and probably shouldn't be, given what he was staring at, and took a step back. He turned towards the sink. 'Just get myself a drink, if that's okay.'

'Course it is. How you feeling, Joe?'

'Like I headbutted a wall.' He took a glass from the drying rack. 'Guts feel like they've been through a shredder.' Filled the glass with tap water. 'Apart from that, I'm raring to go.'

'I meant, you know . . .'

For a moment he was confused. Then he said, 'Oh, yeah. See what you mean. I'm okay.'

'Yeah?'

He noticed the Mickey Mouse plaster and remembered crushing the glass last night. He peeled off the plaster. The skin round the cut was pale and spongy. 'I'm fine.' Joe stuffed the plaster inside an empty milk carton sitting on the work surface. A bit of fresh air and the cut would soon scab over.

'How's Ruth taking it?'

Glass of water in one hand, milk carton in the other, Joe walked over to the bin. He crushed the carton and disposed of it. 'I better go.' He raised his glass to his lips and swallowed a mouthful of tepid water. 'Cooper around?'

'Went to the hospital.'

'What's wrong?'

'Visiting.'

'Doesn't sound like Cooper. Who's ill?'

'Somebody Strachan, I think he said. Billy, maybe? Do you know him?'

Joe hesitated. Last night's memories were hazy, but his recollections of the night before last were clear enough. The quilt falling to the floor. The book on origami. Joe swallowed the rest of his water. Why was Cooper visiting the hospital? Couldn't he leave the poor fuck alone? Billy had taken a beating. He didn't need to be tormented as well.

'Name doesn't ring any bells,' Joe told Sally. He returned to the sink, refilled his glass and gulped the water down in one. He felt sick. He shivered. 'Gotta go,' he muttered.

The smoke was thick enough to taste. Joe coughed and put his hand to his mouth. He was reminded of the fag he'd had last night. Only a single puff. Fortunately, he still felt too ill to consider having a second drag.

Rattling his pocket, he approached the drinks machine in the corner. He counted his change, deciding between Irn Bru and Coke. As he spun the money in the slot, a wave of nausea forced his eyes shut. He swore, opened his eyes and pressed the Coke button, expecting as always that nothing would happen. He'd lost count of the number of times these bastard machines had ripped him off.

A can of Coke clattered to the bottom.

There you go. It knew well enough not to mess with him today.

He reached in, removed the can and pulled the tab. He took a long swallow. Could be colder. He looked around him. The place was rumbling like a minor earthquake. Not that he'd experienced one first hand, but he imagined this wee bookies sounded similar. Race commentary on the 12.20 at Folkestone blasted out of the loudspeakers. The mile and a half race was reaching the seven furlong stage. Getting interesting. More interesting, though, if you had money staked on the outcome.

Dotted around the room were about twenty men. More than half were standing by now. As he watched, another few got to their feet. Almost all those still sitting were old enough to be pensioners. The volume rose. Listening carefully, you could pick out individual layers. Roars of encouragement, shouts of annoyance, wails of anger. Each separate, distinct. Clenched fists waved, winning or losing. All eyes, apart from Joe's, fixed to the bank of overhead screens, faces intense with a passion rarely seen by wives or girlfriends. Looking at one bloke in particular, sporting a skinhead, tight white t-shirt (at this time of year), jeans and white socks, Joe thought: or boyfriends, if you wanted to be p.c. with the poofs. At which point Gemma's voice yelled in his ear: 'They're not poofs, Dad. They're *gays*.'

He put his hand on the drinks machine and hoped to fuck he wasn't going to burst into tears. *It's the smoke, lads. Making my eyes water.* He took another swig of Coke and set the can on top of the machine. He rested his forehead on his arm, apologising to his daughter under his breath. She didn't answer.

She was somewhere in Orkney. He couldn't imagine her naked, cold, stiff, stuck out of sight in a big fucking drawer. God, he wanted to hear her voice. He wanted to see her.

Over the din of the last furlong of the Folkestone race he became aware that his mobile was ringing. Reaching into his pocket, he made for the exit, the relative quiet of the street. 'Hello.'

'Finally turned your phone back on.'

Relative was the right word. It was Adam. Traffic crawled

along both sides of the road. A motorbike dodged between the cars. Hardly a deathly silence. He put his little finger in his left ear and said, 'Listen, you bastard—'

'No, you listen. How could you do that, Joe?'

'Adam, I've been meaning—'

'Don't bother denying it. I have proof.'

'You were supposed to look after her.'

'You can talk! I know all about your little secret, you fucking animal.'

'I don't know what you're talking about, Adam, and I don't fucking care. Start running.'

'Give me a reason why I shouldn't tell the police.'

About what? Joe was silent for a moment.

'You can't, huh? Didn't think so.'

'You let Gemma die,' Joe said. 'You're going to pay for it.'

'You fucking arrogant cocksucker. You know fucking well that you're entirely to blame.'

'Now you're taking the piss.'

'Your fault, Joe. If Ruth wasn't so cut up already, I'd tell her what I know. Your fault.'

Joe whispered, 'Taking the fucking piss.' His shoulders were shaking. An explosion of rage shattered his self-control. He shouted into the phone, 'Taking the fucking piss.' He yelled once again into the phone, pulled back his arm and threw the phone as hard as he could against the nearest wall. The casing broke, scattering plastic over the pavement. A couple of passers-by looked at him and he felt suddenly embarrassed. He bent down, picked up the bigger pieces and ambled to the bin twenty feet down the road. Casual as you like. As if phone hurling was a traditional Scottish sport. One at a time, he fed the bits of broken phone into the mouth of the bin, Adam's voice still echoing in his ear. Joe looked at his watch, wondering if he could get a flight to Orkney today. Then they'd see whose fault it was.

SEVEN

When Joe looked at his watch again it was seven minutes past seven and British Airways Flight 8899 had just landed at Kirkwall airport. After the plane came to a standstill Joe complained to the stewardess that the flight had arrived two minutes late. He didn't mind, of course. A two-minute delay wasn't worth making a fuss about. His complaint was simply a matter of principle. He was still sore at the fact that his one-way ticket had cost him £188.70 (including airport tax, sir). Compounded by the detour via Inverness, it was no wonder the bloody plane was practically empty.

After destroying his phone outside the bookies, Joe had gone home, made the call on his landline and arranged the flight. Ruth was out. No note, no message. No thought whatsoever for anybody else. As per bloody usual. He tried her mobile and got her voicemail. He left a message telling her he was flying to Orkney and didn't know when he'd be back and if she had a problem with that she could get to fuck. He spent an hour tidying up the mess she'd left in the kitchen, pausing over an empty vodka bottle sitting in the centre of the table. Odd. She didn't drink. Making a point, was she? *Well, Joseph, it isn't only you that can get drunk.* Thing is, Joe wouldn't have started on a half empty bottle in the first place. Ruth would be suffering now. She wasn't a drinker. A couple of shots and she was anybody's. He snatched the bottle off the table, poured the dribble that was left down the sink and chucked the bottle.

He packed a bag in under five minutes. A book, underwear, shirts, pair of trousers, washbag. He wasn't going to stay long. He added another book. For the journey. Take his mind off other things. Maybe. No harm in being optimistic.

As he stepped off the plane at Kirkwall airport, having read only a single sentence, albeit a dozen times, he suffered a moment's hesitation. The wind whipped his face, clacked the lapels of his overcoat, flattened his trousers against his shins. He could turn round right this minute and go straight back home. Did he want to do this? Well, it hardly mattered. The plane probably wasn't going anywhere else tonight. Apart from which, wimping out would set him back another hundred and eighty quid. Forget it. Turn to the front and face the Orkney music.

With each step, gusts of wind lifted the bag – his only item of luggage, small enough to be allowed on board as hand luggage – away from his side.

Anyway, he reasoned, he had to see Adam. Had to make the man face up to his responsibilities. Joe owed it to his daughter.

This was a business trip. Joe had a job to do and he was going to fucking well do it.

Fighting a steady headwind, he staggered towards the terminal building. Once inside, he found an unexpected bounce in his step. There was no security and he had no luggage other than his bag, so he headed directly for the exit sign, stepped outside and found a taxi rank with a solitary waiting taxi.

The driver folded up his newspaper when he spotted Joe. Joe opened the back door, shoved in his bag and ducked inside after it.

The driver said something. Sounded like a question. He said it again. 'Whahr tae?' He was small, bald, over fifty, and when he turned in his seat he reminded Joe of the stiff, mechanical motion of a clockwork toy. It took Joe a moment to penetrate the accent. Then he got it.

Joe asked, 'You know Wrighters' Retreat?'

'Adam Wright's place? Oh, aye. Clever name, isn't it?'

'Just take me there.'

The driver started the engine, licked his lips and drove for a while, saying nothing. A couple of minutes into the drive he cleared his throat and said, 'Come up from Inverness?'

'Edinburgh.'

The driver was silent again. He drove textbook style, both hands on the wheel. Joe unglued his eyes from the driver and stared out the window, eyes sweeping over the expanse of flat green fields leading to a ribbon of grey sea merging with a darkening sky. What little remained of the light at this time of the evening stained the walls of a few scattered cottages the same dull grey as the sea. After a while the driver spoke again. 'Hope you don't mind me saying so,' and continued without waiting for a reply, 'but you don't look like a writer.'

Joe said, 'You just can't tell.'

The driver nodded. A jerky, clockwork nod. 'Girl died there the other day. At Adam's place. Terrible tragedy. Killed herself.'

Joe didn't respond.

'Her folks must be hurting,' the driver said. 'What do you think leads a little girl to do that?'

'The little girl was called Gemma. She was nineteen.'

The driver's eyes stared at Joe's reflection in the rearview mirror, no doubt wondering how his Edinburgh passenger knew the details of this local tragedy. He glanced at the road, shook his bald head and looked in the mirror again. 'I knew you weren't a writer. You're her father, right?'

Joe said nothing.

The driver said, 'Whole life ahead of her. Tragic. Anything I can do . . .' He shrugged.

'If you really want to help,' Joe said, 'you can shut the fuck up.'

EIGHT

'Is there a sports shop in Kirkwall?' Joe asked the taxi driver.

'Thought you wanted me to shut up. In fact, if I remember correctly—'

Joe leaned forward, placed his hand on the driver's leg and squeezed.

The driver winced. 'Aye, in the town.'

Joe removed his hand and glanced at his watch. Too late. If only he'd been able to get an earlier flight. Late night shopping? In this dump? Unlikely. He asked anyway. 'Closed, I suppose?'

The driver didn't require any prompting this time. 'You'll have to wait till the morning.' Quickly, he added, 'Is it golf you're interested in?' Maybe he imagined Joe had interpreted his answer as being a shade impertinent, as if he was telling Joe what was permitted, and wanted to clarify that he was really being helpful, not rude. Or maybe he just liked to hear the sound of his own voice. Or maybe he was just stupid. Or maybe he was really a clockwork device that, once wound up, couldn't stop.

When Joe didn't respond the driver spoke again. 'Fishing?'

Joe waited a moment, then said, 'Baseball.'

'Oh,' the driver said. 'Unusual.' He clammed up again. Probably didn't know what to say. Never met anyone Scottish claiming to have an interest in baseball. Reckoned his passenger was a major nutter. Or taking the piss. Dangerous, leg-squeezing, taking-the-piss nutter. Yeah, Joe thought, that's me.

Several minutes later, the driver said, 'Never met anyone Scottish who played baseball.'

'Never played the game,' Joe said. 'I just like the bats.'

'Grand.' The driver's Adam's apple bobbed up and down. 'Nearly there.' Evidently keen to change the subject. He rapped his fingers on the steering wheel. His left leg was trembling.

'Don't worry,' Joe told him, leaning forward. The driver flinched. 'I don't have an issue with you,' Joe said. 'At the moment.' He leaned back, thinking, what a twat. If he'd planned to snap the driver's neck he'd have done it by now. Joe rested his head against the window and reflected. To be honest, that was all shite about breaking the driver's neck. It was what he would like everybody to think he'd do. Truth was, although he'd come pretty close a few times, Joe had never killed anyone, and he was more than a bit nervous at the prospect of doing so.

He raised his head, sat up, put one hand on his bag and tugged the zip. He felt like he had as a teenager about to lose his virginity. He zipped up the bag again, clasped his hands together and tucked them between his knees. He'd put somebody in a coma once, but the bloke came out of it a couple of weeks later. One time he broke a punter's spine – the man didn't die but he doubtless wished he had. Another occasion, he'd fucked up a client's leg with some tools (this guy really had been a twat) and he'd have died if Joe hadn't called an ambulance before he left the guy's flat. What with the shock and blood loss it was touch and go anyway, even with the paramedics' speedy arrival. But, no, Cooper employed somebody else to take over where Joe normally stopped. Employed, that is, on a contract basis. A man called Park. Joe imagined he wasn't your typical hired killer. Didn't call himself a killer, either. Thought it too undignified. Claimed that anybody could kill. Give a six-year-old girl a handgun with the safety off and she'd manage to point it in somebody's face and pull the trigger. Anybody could kill. QED, as far as Park was concerned. So he called himself an expurgator, which was different, apparently, although the subtle distinction was lost on Joe, even though he had gone to university.

The point was, Park could have called himself a fucking fairy and nobody would have dared bat an eyelid. Joe had met him on each of the occasions some thoughtless prick had annoyed Cooper sufficiently to justify the expense of having him killed. To date, that was three times. And three times Joe had broken out in one hell of a sweat. He hurt people and he could live with that. Killing people, he wasn't comfortable with, and he wasn't comfortable with anyone who was comfortable with it. Cooper said he should work on cultivating more of an inferiority complex. Like Park. Cooper said you could tell a mile off that Park's dick was hardly big enough to satisfy a midget. Maybe so. But whatever the size of his cock, Park's utter disregard for human life was one of the few things that scared Joe.

No, Joe had never killed anyone.

Still, he thought, drawing his hands out from between his knees and flexing his fingers, there had to be a first time.

On the outskirts of Kirkwall, the car pulled into a driveway separating a handful of suburban villas and entered a large parking area. Two cars and a motorbike were parked in front of the entrance to an ugly, brilliantly white L-shaped building that squatted at the edge of an otherwise empty field. Along the length of the entire façade a single window peeped through the concrete. The building looked more like a warehouse than Joe's idea of a writers' retreat. But this was it. This was where Gemma had lived.

The driver asked for the fare.

This was where she had died.

Joe handed over the money and stepped out of the car. The driver passed his change out the window and didn't hang around to wish him luck. Joe watched the taxi's tail-lights disappear, then turned and approached the doorway. Twenty feet high, oak, studded, the door was like the entrance to a fairytale castle. He glanced at the doorbell, but chose to ignore it. Beginning a couple of feet off the ground and extending about four feet upwards, a panel was cut into the oak. A brass handle beckoned at shoulder height. A smaller door. The entrance for mere mortals. He turned the handle and shoved. The little door jerked open. He crouched, lifted his foot over the lip and stepped inside.

He had the feeling he was expected. Nothing psychic. Just a simple deduction based on the fact that someone had just snapped off the lights. Joe dragged his other foot inside. The door banged shut, bounced open again and creaked slowly back towards him. He stood for a moment, listening keenly, while his eyes adjusted to the darkness. Blood pounded in his ears. Adrenalin crackled in his veins. His heart thumped against his ribcage. He threw his bag into the darkness in front of him and heard a yell of surprise. Joe launched himself after the clatter of footsteps, tripped over his bag and went sprawling. He scraped his wrist on the floor. Great fucking start.

The footsteps stopped. A voice said, 'That you, Joe?'

Joe sat up and tried to examine his wrist in the sliver of fading daylight that crept through the still partly open door. He couldn't make out a bloody thing. Tenderly, he touched his chafed skin. Adam's voice had come from fifteen, maybe twenty feet away. 'Got some advice for you,' Joe yelled into the darkness. 'Run. And keep fucking running.' He heard footsteps. Slow and heavy. Getting closer.

'Why did you do it?' Adam's voice sounded no more than ten feet away now.

Joe was giving the stupid fuck every opportunity. Twat wanted to get killed, then so be it. Another footstep. Another. Joe supported his right wrist with his left palm and wriggled the fingers of his sore hand. It felt slightly swollen, but it wasn't broken or sprained. He could still use it to rip Adam's head off. The dumb fuck was getting closer, his shoes clacking on the polished floor like hooves. Joe, wanting to keep him coming, said, 'Do what? The fuck are you talking about?'

Adam's voice quivered. 'Can't even bring myself to say it.' Joe couldn't stand much more of this shit. But he played along. Quietly, in the near darkness, Joe raised himself to his feet. 'You want to tell me what I've done?' Keep the bastard talking. Get him closer. 'I'd really like to know.'

Four resounding footsteps. Agitation apparent in the acoustics of Adam's forward momentum. 'First Gemma,' he said. 'And then Ruth.'

Joe swore. He couldn't help but be intrigued. Adam had his attention. 'What are you talking about?'

A single footstep. Adam was a vague shape only a few feet away. If Joe reached out he could probably touch him. But he wanted him closer still. He wanted to see the whites of his victim's eyes. Which, of course, he couldn't in the fucking dark. So he'd make do with smelling the twat's breath. Then he'd make his move. 'Humour me,' Joe said. 'Remind me what it was I did.'

Unfortunately, Adam never had the chance. At that moment a blinding light burst through the door. Joe screwed his eyes shut. Shielding his face with his hands, he staggered backwards towards the wall. He heard footsteps rushing towards him. Still unable to see, he was attacked from both sides. Somebody yanked his left arm from in front of his face and twisted it behind his back. Somebody else did the same with his right. He yelled as the bastard's grip tightened on his friction burn. He kept his head lowered and twisted to the side, trying to keep his eyes away from the spotlight.

He heard more footsteps entering the building. Adam said, 'I'm okay. Don't worry about me.' Then, a mumbled response

Joe couldn't quite hear since he was yelling again as handcuffs tightened around his wrists.

They turned off the spotlight. After a few seconds Joe opened his eyes. Somebody had flicked the hall light back on and, as his eyes adjusted slowly, Adam came into focus. He looked wide-eyed, angry. He kept wiping his chin with the back of his hand as if he had a serious drool problem. The fingers of his other hand were balled into a fist. A couple of uniformed policemen stood by his side. In front of them was the man in charge. Dark blue suit, tightly knotted dark brown tie. A glance from him and the two men either side of Joe loosened their grip on his arms. Their boss tugged at his jacket cuffs. 'Joseph Hope?'

'Joe, please.'

'We'd like you to come with us.'

'Party somewhere, is there?'

'You do not have to say anything.'

'Silent party, huh? I've heard those are increasing in popularity.'

'But it may harm your defence if you do not mention—'

'I see where this is going. You want me to draw pictures, right?'

'—when questioned, something which you later rely on in court.'

'Wait a fucking minute.' Joe would have scratched his head if his hands weren't handcuffed behind his back.

'Anything you do say may be given in evidence. Do you understand what I've just said?'

'Are you arresting me?'

'Standard procedure in certain circumstances before an interview takes place.

You are not under arrest. Yet. But you are being detained to assist us with our investigation.'

'Investigation into what?' Joe banged his wrists against his spine.

The policeman glared at Joe. 'Into the murder,' he said, 'of Mrs Ruth Hope.'

'What?' Joe's arms flapped behind his back like broken wings. His only other outlet for physical expression was to stamp his feet, which was out of the question. Ruth was dead? 'What?' he repeated.

Adam said, 'You're fortunate I'm not a violent man, Joe. Otherwise, DS Monkman here would have another murder—'

No, there was one other way he could express himself. Joe lowered his head and charged forward, catching almost everybody by surprise. He ploughed into Monkman, knocking him over. He brushed past one of Adam's advancing police bodyguards. Luckily for Adam, the other one stepped to the side, allowing Joe a clear path, then swatted him on the back of the head with his baton as he drew alongside. Joe crumpled to the floor at Adam's feet, tried to get up and sank to the floor again.

After a minute or two Joe rolled onto his side, head throbbing. He'd have a fucking lump the size of an old man's bollock tomorrow. He looked up to see Monkman looming over him, lips drawn tight, face pale and blue eyes bulging. Joe started to laugh. 'Look at you,' he said. 'Happy as a pig in shit.'

Monkman cocked his head and drew back a highly polished shoe. 'Ha,' he said, kicking Joe in the ribs. 'Ha,' kicking Joe again. 'Ha,' once more. He paused, then started again. He said 'Ha' half a dozen more times.

Joe groaned. But it wasn't so bad. He'd had much worse kickings. His ribs hurt like fuck but he didn't think anything was broken. Glad it was over, though.

Monkman crossed his arms and said, 'Did anybody else find that funny?'

NINE

Joe stared at the ceiling. Once they'd removed his handcuffs he was able to hug himself with his right arm. Somehow, it helped. He lay on the narrow bed in his cell, cradling his side, palm warming the spot where the pain nagged most. Purely psychosomatic, he was sure, but the heat seemed to alleviate the constant, dull ache that had spread across his ribcage. He'd discovered over the past hour that the pain burst into life when he tried to sit up. He'd had to learn to lie back and relax. He couldn't relax properly, though. Couldn't take a deep breath without his side hurting.

Still, he'd been lucky. As beatings went, this one had been pretty lenient. At least none of the bastards had kicked him in the head. Which was just as well. His head already hurt enough from the baton blow that had knocked him to the ground. Another blow might have done some serious damage. Yeah, all in all it had been pretty civilized. In fact, apart from Monkman, the policemen hadn't convinced Joe that they had their hearts in their work. They were going through the motions. Had they been auditioning for a vacancy in the collecting business, they'd have failed. No question. Cooper wouldn't have hired them on those performances – mind you, if they hadn't already hospitalised somebody, Cooper wouldn't have granted them an interview in the first place. Still. The point was, Orkney's finest showed no enthusiasm. They were too tentative, obviously holding themselves in check, obviously lacking in previous exposure to perpetrating acts of violence on innocent victims. And far too obviously worried about the consequences. This was a one-off for them.

For Adam, too. He'd surprised Joe. Even if he wasn't violent, and even if he wasn't particularly fond of Ruth, you'd think he'd want a shot. But, no, he'd passed when it was his turn. It wasn't just that, though. Joe remembered at one point, a brief interlude between various identically shod feet driving into his ribs, glimpsing Adam through the ruck of bodies. A pudgy hand covered his mouth, piggy eyes alert, body tensed. He wasn't enjoying the show. In the end, Adam strode forward, said, 'Excuse me,' to the officer currently on kicking duty, bent over Joe's prostate figure and said, 'He's had enough.'

The officer stepped back, happy to be excused from his uncomfortable duty.

Monkman said, 'You know what he did to his wife?' He waited for a reply, unfolded his arms, folded them again. 'Your cousin?' Receiving no response from Adam, Monkman said, 'You know he was planning on doing something similar to you?'

Joe was gasping for breath. He strained to hear Adam's mumbled reply, but he would have taken odds as low as six-to-four on that Adam said, his words spoken so softly they could only have been intended to reach Joe's ears, 'I know what he did to his daughter.' Their eyes met. Adam pursed his lips, nodding. Joe turned his eyes away, looked at the floor, and panted like a beaten dog. Each breath was a stab in his side.

Monkman said, 'Okay.'

Two of the other policemen helped Joe to his feet and half-dragged, half-carried him to the waiting mini-van. He protested as quietly as he could, struggling against his desire to check the damage, see if his ribcage looked as bad as it felt. But, handcuffed, he couldn't check shit. They shoved him into the back of the van. One of the other policemen got in alongside him and, after a while, Monkman joined them.

Monkman sat opposite Joe. Once the copper had made himself comfortable he said, 'Think you'll need to see a doctor?'

Joe said nothing.

Monkman said, 'Good answer.' Moments later he said, 'We'll get you checked out. Get you strapped up.'

Joe said, 'Don't bother.'

The van trundled along. Joe stared at Monkman's shoes. One day, he'd take them off and feed them to the bastard. Pigs ate anything, didn't they? He looked up. What did the fucker expect? Gratitude? The offer of medical attention was just a ploy to save his own skin. If Joe died in custody as the result of a punctured lung or something, Monkman wouldn't look too clever. Maybe he was regretting ordering the kicking. Joe wondered if he should threaten to press charges.

Monkman said, 'You grinning at? You just killed your wife. You got fuck all to laugh about.'

Ice formed at the top of Joe's spine. He kept smiling. It seemed important to keep smiling.

Monkman's eyes opened wide and he shook his head. 'Father like you, no wonder your daughter killed herself.'

'Is that official? Gem killed herself?'

It was official, Joe was thinking now as he clutched his side, no longer smiling, just staring at the magnolia walls of his prison cell. But he knew that. He knew Gem had killed herself, even without a post-mortem report. It still didn't make sense. None of it made the slightest bit of sense.

One day your daughter kills herself. Next day, somebody kills your wife. How can you make sense of that?

What made matters worse was that the police had told him almost nothing. Joe didn't even know how Ruth had died. He knew from Monkman only that she'd been murdered. But what did that mean? Had she been strangled, stabbed, shot? Was she the victim of a hit-and-run? And where had it happened? At home, in the street, while she was shopping at Safeway's? For all Joe knew, a disgruntled employee might have garrotted her in the tinned soup aisle.

Bubbles. Joe saw bubbles.

He closed his eyes. More bubbles. A single yellow, plastic duck bobbing on the surface of the bath water. His fingers drag through the tepid water. She's been in there too long. His hand leaps out. Bam. Her head snaps back. Her eyes widen, dazed. His hand clamps over her mouth, forces her head under. His fingers vibrate with her screams. Her legs kick, splashing a right bloody storm. Over the rim of the bath, soaking his trousers. Her hands claw at him. He lets her up, watching her choke, splutter, gasp for breath. One, two, three. Again. Her limbs thrash. Up she comes. This time pity takes over. One, two, three. He rams the back of her head against the wall. A dull sound. Thwack. Like a smack through wet clothing. Makes him shiver. Like the first whisky of the day. She grunts. Her eyes cloud over. She sinks back into the water, head rolling to the side. He grabs her by the neck and holds her face under water.

Bubbles. He sees bubbles.

He closes his eyes. Can't watch. He counts. One, two, three. He counts to twenty. Thirty. Forty. Opens his eyes. Fifty-two, fifty-three. A single bubble reaches the surface. Pops. Half a minute later – eighty-two, eighty-three – the water is almost smooth. Not a bubble in sight, the plastic duck floats on the lightly undulating surface.

If Joe had killed her that's how he'd have done it. But he hadn't, had he? At the time he was – well, he didn't know where he was. Fuck it, he knew nothing. He didn't even know when she'd been killed, did he? He sat up suddenly, groaned out loud and clutched his side. Sweat beaded on his forehead. Fucking ribs. Getting better, though. For at least five minutes he hadn't noticed the pain at all. He remained seated, and listened to the sound of low voices approaching his cell.

He distinctly heard the shuffle of feet. Soles scuffing

concrete. The footsteps stopped and a key rattled in the lock. The door opened and Monkman stepped into the cell accompanied by a plainclothes detective Joe hadn't seen before.

'On your feet.' Monkman brandished a pair of handcuffs. Joe stood up slowly, grimacing. 'Turn round. Hands behind your back.' Joe did as instructed and Monkman clicked the handcuffs into place. Roughly. Joe turned to face him. 'Time we had a little chat,' the policeman said.

TEN

The interrogation room was windowless and stank of sweat. Each bile yellow wall was completely bare. A long table, with two plastic chairs on each side, was jammed against the left-hand wall. On top of the table, resting against the wall, was a fancy-looking tape recorder, a dual deck with a pair of dinky speakers and a microphone on a cheap plastic stand.

Joe said, 'We having a disco, lads?'

'Sit down.' As if to demonstrate, Monkman dragged a chair out from under the table and sat down. He placed a notepad on the table and wiggled a pencil between his fingers.

'Don't know that I can do that,' Joe said.

Monkman leaned back in his chair. 'Why not?'

'You ever tried sitting down with your hands cuffed behind your back?' Joe said. 'Makes it bloody hard. You can have a go if you like. Borrow these. Warn you, though, you're liable to lose your balance and fall bollock over tit onto the floor.'

Monkman leaned forward and pointed his pencil at Joe. 'Sit your arse the fuck down.'

'No need to get all red in the face,' Joe said. 'Can I speak to you in confidence? I've got these strange pains in my side that I really don't want to aggravate. Fall into that chair with a thump and I'll be howling like a stuck pig.'

Monkman lowered his head. Twiddled his pencil.

'You want to watch your blood pressure,' Joe advised him. 'Your neck's gone red. Pays to take care of your health, you know. Maybe this job's too much for you. You could take up something less stressful. Something more suited to a redneck policeman.' He pretended to think for a minute. 'Pig farming, for instance. I hear—'

Monkman raised his head. Lips bloodless, cheek muscles taut, he inched his torso towards Joe. Without a word the other CID man, young, early twenties perhaps, with a small scar pitting the skin above his left eyebrow, grabbed Joe's elbow and steered him towards the far side of the table. He positioned Joe in front of one of the chairs and pressed down on his shoulders. Joe's arse hit the chair with a thump that jolted his spine and rattled his ribs. The intense pain almost made him pass out. He took a few seconds to compose himself, then smiled at Monkman and said, 'You going to turn that fucking tape recorder on, or do you need some help?'

Monkman tugged at the cuffs of his jacket sleeves. First the right one, then the left. Then he reached over and pressed the record button on the tape deck. He introduced everybody in the room. The silent detective, it transpired, was a mere constable called McGivern.

McGivern joined Monkman at the other side of the table. Monkman said, 'Why did you kill your wife, Mr Hope?'

'Aren't you supposed to lead up to that question?'

'Just answer it.'

Joe took a deep breath, tilted his head back and gazed at the ceiling for a while. When he thought they'd waited long enough, he said, 'She pissed me off.'

'Aha,' Monkman said. 'How did she do that?'

'I had a social engagement.' Joe licked his dry lips. Waited a little longer. 'She refused to iron my shirt.'

Monkman glanced at his colleague. McGivern shrugged. Monkman said, 'You expect us to believe that your wife's failure to iron your shirt was sufficient provocation for you to murder her?'

'You're the detective. Impress me with your deductive powers.'

Monkman picked up his notepad and slapped it against the table. 'You know what worries me?'

'Your personality?'

'You don't seem at all upset that she's dead.'

Joe said, 'No comment.'

'Here we go.' Monkman let go of the notepad so he could pull the left sleeve of his jacket a millimetre closer to his wrist. 'Will you answer this, then? It's a very simple question.' He cleared his throat. 'Did you kill your wife, Mr Hope?'

'You really don't believe in beating about the bush, eh? I like that, so I'll give you an answer. I did not kill my wife, Detective Sergeant Monkman.'

'Do you have any idea who might have killed your wife?'

'I do not have a baldy notion.'

'A what?'

'No.'

'But it wasn't you.'

'Like I said.'

'Mr Hope. What do you do for a living?'

'Ah, I see. Change the line of attack. Disorient the suspect, huh? Very clever. I'm all confused. What was the question?'

'Your job, Mr Hope?'

'Managing Director of IBM Belgium.'

'Mr Hope, you are unemployed. And have been, apparently, since you left university. That's quite a long time.'

Joe shrugged. 'No work around. What can you do?'

'Yet you own your own home.'

'D minus for your homework. Ruth owns the house. Not me.'

'But you do now, Mr Hope. She's dead, if you recall. The house belongs to you.'

'I'd forgotten. Thanks for reminding me.' Joe didn't say anything further. The silence lengthened. Nobody spoke. Was this another cheap interrogation tactic? Most people don't like silence. Makes them feel uncomfortable. So they talk. Say whatever comes to mind. The policemen weren't going to break the silence. Monkman was going to sit there playing with his pencil while his colleague shuffled his feet and made an irritating sucking sound with his teeth. The silence dragged. McGivern started to tap the table gently.

Joe couldn't be bothered with this. He wasn't going to find out what had happened to Ruth by sitting on his arse listening to McGivern's medley of irritating noises. 'Unless you're going to arrest me,' he said, 'you can only hold me for six hours. You left me alone in the cell for an hour. That means you have less than five hours left and you're sitting there wasting it like a pair of useless twats.' He paused, observing their reactions. Monkman looked agitated. McGivern looked bored. Joe said, 'I've been here before. I know the rules. I know the tricks. Why don't we just get the fuck on with it?'

Monkman scratched his ear with blunt end of his pencil. 'Was it about money? Was that your motivation?'

'You think I killed her for the house?'

'I don't know. Did you?'

'To be honest, the house was a bonus. It was mainly, as I said earlier, the fact that she didn't iron my shirts.'

'Very droll,' Monkman said.

'What about Adam Wright?'

Joe turned to look at the man who'd just spoken. 'Constable McGivern,' he said. 'Pleased to meet you.' The policeman didn't respond, other than to emit a sucking noise that sounded a bit like a chirping bird. Joe said, 'What about Adam?'

'You jumped on a plane at a moment's notice and took a taxi straight to his abode,' McGivern said. 'Seems there was a kind of urgency involved in your actions, wouldn't you say?'

'Wanted to ask the man a few questions. No law against that, is there?'

'Why couldn't you ask them over the phone?'

'Rather than at his, what did you call it, abode?' Joe waited a moment, then said, 'Too impersonal. I wanted a face-to-face meeting.'

'The taxi driver who picked you up at the airport said your behaviour was threatening.'

'Spoken to him already? That was quick.'

'Did you threaten the driver, Mr Hope?'

'I'm a well-built guy. I have a substantial physical presence. I can understand how some people might find me threatening.'

'Did you threaten the taxi driver, Mr Hope? Yes or no.'

'Not one tiny hair of his head.'

Monkman said, 'The driver, as you well know, is perfectly bald. Now answer the constable's question. Please.'

'I did not threaten the bald taxi driver. May I also say that I did not threaten Adam in any way. And I did not kill my wife. Anything else you want me to deny? Oh, I know. Just for the tape.' He winked. 'I did not receive a kicking from the local police force. Can I go now?'

'Mr Hope,' Monkman said. 'What would it take for you to be serious about this?'

'Fifty quid.'

'Mr Hope.'

'Take it or leave it. Final offer.'

'Your wife is dead.'

'Totally slipped my mind. Again. Thank you for reminding me, sergeant.'

Monkman jabbed his pencil into the notepad so hard that the point snapped off. 'Fuck,' he said, staring at the half-centimetre-long piece of graphite that had detached itself from the rest of the pencil. He swept it off the notepad and stared at his useless pencil. Then, as if suddenly remembering that he had just sworn on tape, he said, 'Excuse me.' He tossed the pencil onto the table. It rolled towards the edge of the table.

McGivern stood up.

'Leave it, constable.' The pencil fell on the floor and McGivern returned to his seat. Monkman said, 'Okay, Mr Hope. Okay.'

'You know, what with one thing or another, I feel we've become quite intimate,' Joe said. 'I don't mind at all if you want to call me Joe.'

'Thank you, but I'll call you Mr Hope, Mr Hope. Now, let's suppose for a moment that you didn't kill your wife.' Monkman folded his arms. 'As you claim.' He uncrossed his arms and leaned forward. 'Wouldn't you like to find out who did?'

'Let's cut the crap,' Joe said. 'I'll answer your questions on one condition.'

'What's that?'

'You tell me how she died.'

Monkman looked at McGivern. McGivern cast his eyes downwards. Monkman said, 'Supposing I do, what guarantee do I have that you'll cooperate?'

'Turn off the tape,' Joe said.

Monkman leaned over and said, 'Mr Hope asked for the tape to be paused at nine eleven.' He pressed the pause button.

'Police brutality,' Joe said. 'I could press charges.'

'For what?'

'For earlier.'

'Be my guest.'

'You sure?'

Monkman said, 'Positive.'

'Up to you,' Joe said. 'You think I won't win? Maybe so, but I can make it messy for you.'

'Your word against half-a-dozen officers. You wouldn't stand a chance.'

'I have a civilian witness.'

Monkman locked his fingers and placed his hands behind his head. 'You serious? Adam Wright won't talk.'

'You prepared to stake your career on that?'

Monkman glued his eyes to Joe's. 'Yes.'

Joe stared back, then said, 'Shit. You told him something about me, didn't you? He called me an animal. What lies did you tell him? You're a bunch of crooked fucks.'

'Nothing crooked about it,' Monkman said. 'I told Adam that you very probably murdered his cousin. I'd guess that's what he was pissed off about.' He shook his head sadly.

'He was pissed off before he knew about Ruth.'

'Can't help you there.' Monkman shrugged. 'But I can help you with the matter of our little skirmish at Wrighters' Retreat. Let's suppose Adam did have a change of heart. There's the matter of a dead girl on his property. Maybe you heard about it? Could get very messy for someone running a residential business.'

Joe said, 'Turn the tape recorder back on if you want, but I refuse to answer any more questions.'

'You beginning to realise what serious shit you're in?'

'No comment.'

'Up to your neck, Joe,' Monkman said. 'I think it's time you confessed.'

ELEVEN

When DC McGivern tilted his head, Joe pictured Broken Neck. He smiled at the memory that had sprung from nowhere. There she danced, head tilted to the side, white scarf wrapped tightly around her neck. Tassels trailed past her hips, swinging as she danced round her handbag with her girlfriend. What was she called? Lesley, Lindsey? Joe couldn't remember her real name. He always called her Broken Neck. She was Ruth's best friend at university. And for maybe a couple of months after Gemma was born. Then they lost touch. Whatever her name, she wore that white scarf all the time Joe knew her. Fixed around her neck like a plaster cast.

Joe first noticed them as they wiggled their arses in the middle of an uncluttered dance floor at a university disco. Broken Neck looked like she'd been in an accident. The other one writhed with her wrists in the air, as if she was inviting someone to bind them together. Joe was drunk. Bad news. The good news was that they were equally drunk. He strolled up to them and started talking. Spoke to Broken Neck first. Pointed to her neck, asked her if her injury was serious, and laughed. Of course she couldn't hear a word he said. He shrugged and turned to the other girl. He tried hard to be witty and cool, and, not surprisingly, being forced to shout to make himself heard, failed miserably on both counts. He remembered telling her she looked a bit like Sean Connery. Which she did. Still did. Same mouth. Could have been his daughter. Such a statement might easily have been taken the wrong way. After all, it was hardly flattering to tell a young woman she looked like a man, however handsome the man. Fortunately, once she'd established what he was saying (he had to yell, his mouth so close to her ear that his lips brushed her skin), she found the comparison amusing. After a few dances they went outside for a while to cool down. The silence was water to a parched throat. Broken Neck followed them. A turd in the water. They ignored her. In the quiet, they exchanged names. Ruth kept up the joke. Tried to do Connery's lazy accent, exaggerating the trademark drunken "s" in her surname. Shimpshon. She made a fair attempt.

Eventually, Broken Neck got the message. She went to the toilet just after midnight and didn't return. Joe danced with Ruth Simpson until the music stopped at two. By the last dance, they were glued hip-to-hip and Joe had a hard-on the size of the Scott Monument. He invited her back to his flat.

Five other students shared the kitchen and bathroom, but at least they each had private bedrooms.

'Just like mine,' Ruth said as he held open the door and switched on the light. A single bed, a desk and a wardrobe. Roughly the size of his cell in Kirkwall police station.

Joe remembered switching on the gooseneck lamp that was perched on top of a pile of books on the floor next to the bed. Ruth turned off the overhead light. She skipped across the room, knelt on the carpet by Joe's pile of books and started reading the titles off the spine: 'The Revenger's Tragedy,' 'The Changeling,' 'Women Beware Women,' ''Tis Pity She's A Whore,' 'The Malcontent,' 'The Duchess of Malfi.' Maybe a few others. She didn't comment, just read the titles aloud. Joe couldn't tell if she was deliberately slurring her words or if she had just drunk too much. She returned to John Ford's ''Tis Pity She's a Whore,' ran her finger across the spine. 'Is it good? Have you read that one?'

Kneeling on the floor beside her, Joe said, 'They're good for propping up my lamp. If you're really interested, you can borrow any of them, any time, if you really want.' He took hold of her hand and clutched it to his chest. He kissed her forehead. 'But I don't think now's the right time to be discussing plays.'

She leaned against him, her slender frame expanding with a giant gulp of air. 'I've only done this once,' she said.

Joe put his arms around her and pulled her closer. She was shaking. 'Let's get into bed,' he said.

They struggled out of their clothes, flinging their discarded garments on the floor. Down to his underpants, hard-on throbbing like an excited heart, Joe glanced sideways at her, as casual a glance as he could muster. She was sitting on the bed, hands wedged between her knees, wearing only her underwear. She couldn't have looked more terrified if she knew she was facing a firing squad at dawn.

'You'll get cold,' he said.

She pulled back the quilt and slipped into bed. 'Turn off the light.'

Joe did as requested and slid in after her. They quickly realised there wasn't enough room for two people in the bed. After experimenting with various positions they found that lying on their sides, facing each other, was better than anything else. Joe's pants were wet. He announced that he was taking them off. He got out of bed, removed his underwear and climbed back in. Resumed the side-on position. Her hand stroked his leg, moved up his thigh, circled his stomach and moved towards his groin.

He waited, stomach muscles tense as stretched elastic. Hoped. Even considered praying.

'What's wrong?' she asked.

'Not again,' he muttered. The instant she touched his dick he'd gone soft.

Joe rubbed his wrists and stared at the telephone. For someone normally so decisive, he was having remarkable difficulty making up his mind about who to phone. Deciding that the answer wasn't about to spring out of the phone, no matter how hard he stared at it, he looked up. Beyond the vacant seat directly opposite – Monkman had disappeared when the phone was brought into the interrogation room and still hadn't returned – a uniformed policeman, the one that had arrived with the phone and had been responsible for plugging it in, was now stationed at the door, legs spread, arms behind his back, looking like he was waiting his turn on the set of a porn film. He rocked on his heels, anticipating, possibly, a blowjob from DC McGivern. He was going to be disappointed, though. McGivern didn't seem all that interested. The constable was whistling a tune through his teeth and slapping his thighs like a bored teenager. Performing oral sex with a colleague was probably the last thing on his mind. Pity. Having something in his mouth would shut the bastard up. Joe rubbed his wrists again, contemplating how much fun it would be to plant his fist in McGivern's jaw and stop that fucking racket once and for all. Christ, that melody was agonisingly familiar.

Joe clapped his hands together, rubbed his palms, then picked up the phone. He ought to call a lawyer, he knew, but the lure of a friendly voice was hard to resist. If he rang Cooper, Joe reasoned, he might be able to find out what had happened to Ruth. And he could always ask his friend to contact a lawyer for him.

Before he could change his mind, he dialled Cooper's number.

Sally answered.

McGivern stopped whistling and sat still. Interested again.

'I need to speak to Cooper.'

'Joe? Are you okay? Where are you?'

'I need to speak to Cooper, Sally.'

'I'll get him for you.'

He heard her shout, 'Chicken?' In the background, Cooper shouted back. After what seemed like an interminable wait, during which McGivern whistled a few more bars of that damned tune, Cooper's voice yelled in his ear, 'What have you done, Joe?'

For a moment, Joe couldn't think of a reply. His best friend knew already. As had Adam. It seemed Joe was the last person to find out. What knocked the wind out of Joe was Cooper's assumption that he was guilty. Fantastic. A real kick in the ribs. Pain flared in his side at the thought and he closed his eyes.

Cooper spoke again. 'Christ, Joe. You're well fucked. What happened? I mean, why the hell did you do it, eh?'

Joe thought about slamming the phone down. Instead, he said, calmly, eyes still closed, 'Can you get me a lawyer?'

'You'll fucking need one, tell you that.'

Joe's eyes snapped open. 'Get me a lawyer, Cooper.'

'Okay. Keep what's left of your hair on. Want me to represent you?'

'I need a lawyer, not a comedian.'

'I resent that. I spent nearly a year at university studying that shit. Hate to see it go to waste.'

'A lawyer, Cooper.'

'Right. Where are you?'

'The nick. In Kirkwall.'

'That's where Gemma—'

'They're flying me back to Edinburgh.'

'When?'

'That's all I know. Get me a lawyer. Get him to phone here and find out.'

'Yeah. Anything else?'

'Tell the lawyer I'm not guilty. I didn't do shit.'

'Whatever you say. It's your money. Did you at least get the tosser?'

'Who?'

'You know, the bloke who was supposed to be looking after her.'

'Not yet,' Joe said. 'Got some questions I need to ask him first.'

'You looking for somebody else to blame, then?'

'What's that supposed to mean?'

'Forget it. Look, I'll ask around. Get you the best lawyer I can.'

'You do that.' Joe hung up, instantly realising he'd forgotten to ask if Cooper knew how Ruth had died.

McGivern raised his eyebrows.

'Twat,' Joe said to McGivern.

'Nice way to speak about your friends.'

'Got a smoke?'

'No smoking.' McGivern's eyes swept the room for a sign that proved him correct. There wasn't one.

'Come on,' Joe said. 'Put me at ease, won't it. Make me tell you things. Secrets.'

McGivern hesitated, then dug in his pocket and removed a packet of Gitanes. He opened it, offering the half empty packet to Joe.

'Fancy,' Joe said, removing a cigarette, studying it.

The policeman's hand dipped into his pocket again and reappeared with a gold lighter. He flipped the top open and a flame sprang up. He leaned across the desk, holding the lighter inches from Joe's face. 'Hang on,' he said. 'What are you going to use as an ashtray?'

'I'll improvise.' Tilting his head towards DC McGivern, Joe raised his hand – cigarette clamped between his fingers – towards his mouth. His hand stopped moving before the cigarette touched his lips. He leaned back. McGivern lifted his thumb and the flame died. Joe gripped his unlit cigarette at either end and snapped it in two. McGivern's face paled. One at a time Joe tossed each half of the broken cigarette at the policeman. 'Can I have another?' Joe said.

TWELVE

When DS Monkman returned to the interrogation room he insisted Joe's handcuffs be replaced. DC McGivern stood up, walked round the table and fastened the cuffs.

'Can't you at least put them on in front?'

'Can't do that,' Monkman said. 'You'd have a lethal weapon. Fine strong piece of steel in the centre you could bring down two-handed on an unsuspecting officer's head.' Monkman took the spare seat opposite. When McGivern sat down again, Monkman, without any preamble, formally charged Joe with the murder of Mrs Ruth Hope.

'You're charging me?' Joe said when Monkman had finished.

'Want me to repeat it? I thought I was perfectly clear. Maybe I should take elocution lessons.'

'I didn't fucking do it.' Joe banged the edge of the table with his thighs as he stood up. By the time he remembered his sore ribs it was too late. Anticipating agonising stabs in his side, he held his breath. A burning sensation spread across his side. Painful, but not incapacitating. Relieved, he breathed out. If he could jump to his feet like that, it proved that even in the last hour or so there was already a measurable improvement in the state of his health. Maybe his ribs had escaped with severe bruising. No cracks or breakages. Could be, though, that he was just so angry that his body was numb. 'You're wrong.'

'You're going to Edinburgh and I'll enjoy being there to watch you go down.' 'Bet you fucking will.' Then, realising the significance of what Monkman had just said, Joe said, 'What?'

'You didn't think we were going to let you travel back home on your own.'

'But why you? Doesn't require the perfectly honed skills of Orkney's finest detective sergeant to escort an unarmed, handcuffed prisoner. Anybody with half a brain could do it. You ought to be spoiled for choice.'

'Actually, the law requires that you be escorted by two officers,' Monkman said. 'DC McGivern has agreed to accompany us. He'll be flying back tomorrow. I, on the other hand, will be staying.'

'You still haven't told me why. If they want me for questioning in Edinburgh I'd have thought it was their responsibility to come and fetch me.'

'Ordinarily, yes,' Monkman said. 'But I offered my services to my colleagues down south and they said they'd be honoured for me to help with the enquiry.'

'Anything to avoid paying the airfare,' McGivern said. 'Tight bastards.'

'Not too happy with the assignment?' Joe asked him. 'Or is it the fact that the sergeant here is sending you straight back home while he seizes his opportunity to make an impression in the big city that pisses you off?' Joe didn't wait for an answer. He looked at Monkman. 'Tell me something, Orkney boy. Am I nothing more than a small town detective's big chance?'

'I'm not from around here,' Detective Sergeant Monkman said. 'Although my dad was born in Stromness.'

'Where you from?' Joe asked.

'Brora,' Monkman said.

'You have a supermarket there?' Joe sat down while he waited for Monkman's reply. After a while, Joe said, 'I rest my case.'

DC McGivern drove them to the airport. Once out of town only the occasional light glimmered in the distance. Otherwise the night was dark and shapeless. The journey passed in silence. Joe wondered if DS Monkman was sulking. An airline official met them at the airport's terminal building and, scolding them for being late, shepherded them to the aircraft. Apart from Joe and the two policemen, there were maybe a dozen passengers, all warm and cosy. They fell silent as Joe, sandwiched between Monkman and McGivern, was led to the front. Joe could see into the cockpit. Crammed into a tiny space, the pilot turned, nodded to Monkman, nodded to McGivern, ignored Joe. Just another uniformed twat. No sign of a stewardess.

'Hey,' Joe said to the pilot, 'am I entitled to a free drink?'

PART TWO

THIRTEEN

Leaving the chain on the hook, she opened the door and peered through the crack. A short, heavily muscled stranger with an intense look in his eyes. Behind him stood a taller, bored-looking punter. Both were in their late thirties or early forties. Both wore dark suits.

'We have a couple of questions,' the short one said. 'Could you spare a minute?'

'Police?' she said.

The short one broke into a wide grin. 'Jehovah's Witnesses,' he said.

Not the police. Not punters. Jehovah's Witnesses? Was he joking?

She didn't believe him. She pushed the door shut. Didn't take long to realise they weren't leaving, though. A minute later, she could still hear their muffled voices. Persistent buggers. Persistent enough to be genuine. Yeah, that was it. The short one looked serious enough to believe he was in direct contact with God. Tina had a problem with religion. Her childhood had been full of it. When the letterbox rattled she took a step away from the door.

Stubby fingers held the letterbox open and the short man's voice boomed through the opening. 'A minute, Tina. One minute of your time.'

Shit. They knew her name. Her working name. Well, good for them. None of her clients would have any qualms about giving her name to a couple of frigging holier-than-thou, Bible-bashing arseholes looking for sinners to convert. As long as a few quid changed hands, obviously. And once they had her name, it wouldn't be difficult to find out where she lived. Ask around. Hand over a few more quid to one of her fellow sex workers. Damn those whores. She should learn to keep her mouth shut.

'Not interested.' God, her voice had cracked. Jesus help her. 'Go away.' 'We just want to talk to you,' the short man said. 'It won't take long. Couple of minutes. Then we'll go.'

'I'm not buying.' Not today. Not ever. Oh, Christ. 'Fuck off or I'll call the police.' Assertive. That ought to do it.

'Tina,' the short man said. 'I don't believe your relationship with the boys in blue is altogether friendly. You wouldn't want to piss them off unnecessarily, would you?'

'Get to fuck,' Tina said. The letterbox snapped shut and she heard muttering again. After a short while the letterbox creaked open once more and a piece of white card poked through the hole.

'Take it,' the short man said.

She was prepared to make a small sacrifice. If accepting some of their literature was going to get rid of them, she'd take it. Reading a leaflet certainly paled in comparison with crucifixion.

The card tilted in the grip of her fingers and she realised she was holding a photograph. She turned it over and looked at the familiar face of the man pictured in close-up. He seemed uncomfortable having his picture taken. Raising his whisky to the camera seemed like a feeble attempt to hide behind the glass. Which didn't surprise her. For all his posturing, Bob was shy. She gazed at his forced smile, remembered him leaving in a hurry, saying he'd be away for a while. Giving her a grand.

So the pair outside the door weren't missionaries. Praise the Lord.

The short man's voice boomed through the letterbox again. 'You know the guy in the picture?'

'You were joking?' Tina said.

After a moment: 'Huh?'

'About being Jehovah's Witnesses?'

The short man laughed. The sound rumbled in his chest. After a few seconds he stopped and coughed. He said, 'Me and God, we don't really see eye to eye.'

Knowing they weren't religious freaks made Tina more confident. 'What do you want?'

'You recognise him? In the photo?'

'What's it to you?'

'We're his friends. Joe's in trouble. He needs your help.'

Joe. Now she knew his first name. It was a start. Get his surname off these dicks and financial opportunities beckoned. She'd always assumed Bob, whoops, Joe was rich. Nice car, nice clothes. Most of the time, when he wasn't drunk, he smelled expensive. And he chucked money around like he had his own printing press. She wasn't looking to blackmail the poor bastard, but if the opportunity came up to her and tapped her on the shoulder she wasn't going to pretend it wasn't there. Tina hadn't been sentimental since she was six years old.

She could pinpoint the exact time.

Nineteen ninety. Couple of weeks before Christmas. After a month of solid nagging, her mum finally gave in and took her to a cat and dog rescue home. An assistant led them to a sprawl of kennels. Hand in hand, Tina and her mum strolled along the row of cages. Dozens of puppies scrambled over each other to jump at the wire mesh and bark and squeal and yelp and howl at the young girl and her mother. Dozens in each cage. Seven cages later they came to the end of the row. Another three rows awaited them.

Her mum said, 'I didn't know it would be like this. I think we've seen enough.'

Tina's excitement was curbed by her knowledge that the pups nobody wanted would be put down, and, although she didn't know precisely what it entailed, she knew that being put down was a very bad thing. She was crying when her mum said she could only take one puppy home and that she had to choose now. She cried harder. Still crying, she retraced her steps. Stopped halfway along. Backtracked to the previous cage. Pointed.

'A terrier,' her mum said, close behind her. 'Good choice. I like his beard.'

The assistant pranced towards them without unfolding her arms. 'That one's a bitch.'

Tina put her hand over her mouth. She waited for her mum to thump the assistant for her bad word and was glad when nothing happened.

They left the kennels and went to an office where her mum had to fill in some forms before the man in charge of the home would hand over the puppy. By the time she'd finished, Tina had stopped crying and was looking forward to seeing her puppy outside its cage. She was trying to think of a name for it.

'Fraser,' she said, and started bobbing up and down.

'It's a girl puppy.' Her mum passed the completed form to the assistant. 'Fraser's a boy's name.'

As the assistant read the form, a frown creased her brow. She said, 'I'm afraid we can't give you the dog.'

'I don't understand,' Tina's mum said. 'What's the problem?'

'Your income.'

'I don't have one.'

'That's the point. It's standard policy.' She looked at Tina. Tina looked at her mum. The assistant said, 'I'm really sorry.'

'What are you saying?' her mum said.

'You live with your boyfriend?'

'Davie,' Tina said. 'He's in the Salvation Army.'

The girl ignored Tina. 'And neither of you are in employment?'

'At the moment?' her mum said. 'You mean right now?' She shook her head.

'We can't release a dog to a home that doesn't have a stable income.'

'Can we not have Fraser, Mum? What's going to happen to her if we can't have her? What if nobody else wants her? Mum?'

'Shut it, Tina.' Her mum was wearing her angry face. And she was starting to use bad words that she'd have to wash out of her mouth when she got home. 'This bitch would rather let the poor beast die than give it to dogshite like us.'

Tina wet the bed that night. When she told her mum, her mum ordered her back to bed. Tina didn't do what she was told. She slept on the settee. In the morning Davie spanked her for being a dirty little girl. Then he made her change her bedclothes and fling the soiled sheets in the washing machine. After that, he made her lie face down on her freshly made bed while he rubbed cream into her burning bottom.

'That's better,' he said. 'Isn't it?'

Her mum didn't hear him, didn't see what he was doing. She was sleeping off a hangover. Something she did most mornings.

Davie hung around for a couple of years, which presented plenty further opportunities for smacking Tina. And for easing the pain afterwards. Then one day he was gone. Her mother said he'd stolen some money from his church.

Tina was happy. She told her mum she hadn't liked it when Davie rubbed cream on her bum. Her mum cuffed her on the mouth, which made her lip bleed. Told her to wash her filthy mouth out and never mention that again.

Tina hunched over and spoke to the eyes peering through the letterbox. 'Who are you?'

'Cooper,' the man said.

'You got a first name, Cooper?'

'Just Cooper.'

'Who's your friend? He just got one name as well? Sting, is it?'

'That's Mr Park,' he said, eyes glancing to the side. 'Joe's lawyer.'

'What's Joe done?' Tina asked.

'Can't we discuss this inside?'

'You don't like chatting through a letterbox?' Tina straightened up and unhooked the chain.

'Thank you.' Cooper stepped into the hallway, brushing past her.

Mr Park was more courteous. He held out his hand and said, 'Pleased to meet you.'

'Likewise,' Tina told him, then gestured for him to follow Cooper into the sitting room.

Cooper was sitting on the settee, in the same seat Bob – damn – Joe had sat in last time she'd seen him. Mr Park hitched up his trousers and eased into the seat next to Cooper. Tina remained standing.

'What's this about?' she said.

'No easy way to say it,' Cooper said. 'Joe's in a spot of bother. He killed his wife.'

Tina gasped. She couldn't help herself. She knew Joe's marriage was far from ideal, but she didn't see Joe as a murderer. 'An accident?'

'Hard to accidentally beat someone to death with a baseball bat.'

The lawyer spoke. 'Equally hard to stuff a body in the boot of your car. Accidentally.'

'When was this?'

'The night you invited him here,' Cooper said. 'In the early hours of the morning.'

'How come the police haven't been to see me?'

Cooper smiled. 'They don't know about you. Joe hasn't breathed a word.'

'So why are you here? What do you want?'

Cooper said, 'I'm Joe's friend. I want him to get away with it.'

'What's that got to do with me.'

'You're his alibi.'

'But it wasn't that late when he left.'

'He didn't leave,' the lawyer said. 'He was here all night.'

'I'm telling you, he left well before midnight.'

'I don't think so,' Cooper said. 'You understand what I'm saying?'

'I think I'm beginning to get the picture.'

Cooper stood up. 'How much do you want?'

'For perverting the course of justice? That's got to be worth five grand.'

'Easily,' Cooper agreed.

'So make it ten.'

Mr Park chuckled. 'We don't have that much cash. You take a cheque, Tina?'

'One second.' She hurried through to her bedroom and rummaged in the desk. She returned to the sitting room. 'I can take Switch, Delta, Visa, MasterCard, Amex or Diners.' She placed the credit card machine on the desk and looked at their puzzled faces. 'I run a legitimate business under my real name. How would you like to pay?'

Cooper said, 'What's the business?'

'I teach self-defence,' Tina said. 'Mainly to women.'

'You work in a gym?'

She shook her head, but didn't expand on the subject. She held weekly classes in a disused church. The rental was next to nothing, but it had to be. With Cooper's donation, she was thinking she might be able to hire somewhere with heating. Somewhere that didn't have broken windows would be a start.

'A woman of many talents.' Cooper put his hand in his inside pocket, took out his wallet. 'Joe's often commended your blowjobs. You wouldn't like to throw in a freebie? Cement the deal, as it were?'

'I wouldn't suck you off if you paid me.'

'Got plenty spunk already, I see,' Cooper said.

'Let's do this quickly,' she said. 'I want you out of my house.'

'Some people have no taste.' Cooper sat down. 'You pay a percentage on that?' He jerked his head at the credit card machine.

'Four point six percent.'

'Extortionate,' Mr Park said.

'I'll get the cash together for you,' Cooper said.

'Let's get this over with now,' Tina said. 'I want you out.'

'Four point six percent of ten grand is four hundred and sixty pounds.'

'I went to school,' Tina said. 'I can do sums.'

'Can you do logic?'

'What do you mean?'

'You don't want the extra money? You want to end up paying tax on it? I'll get you the cash.'

'When?'

'Maybe today.' She was about to say okay when he added, 'Tomorrow at the latest.'

'Today, or it's no deal.'

'I'll see what I can do.'

Tina pretended to think about it. After what seemed an appropriate amount of time she nodded slowly. 'You strike me as the sort of man who deals in cash a lot,' she said to Cooper. 'I wouldn't imagine my request would present too much of a challenge for you.'

'I like a challenge,' Cooper said. 'Don't mind admitting it.'

Mr Park got to his feet. He held out his hand and said, 'Pleasure doing business with you.'

Tina shook his hand. He had a surprisingly firm grip. 'By the way,' she said. 'What's my story?'

'Keep it simple.' Cooper's knees clicked when he stood up. 'Joe arrived at' – he looked at her – 'whatever time he arrived. When was it?'

'Back of eight. Half past, maybe.'

'Okay. He was drunk, yeah? He'd had some bad news. You went to bed early. You gave him a quick gobble and he fell asleep. In the morning he didn't feel too good, so he stayed here until his head cleared.'

'What time did he leave?'

'Eleven? Doesn't really matter. The important thing is that he was tucked up snug in bed with you when he was supposed to be killing his wife.'

'One thing bothers me.' Tina faced Mr Park. 'Why me? Traditionally, sex workers don't make the best witnesses.'

'Traditionally,' Mr Park said, 'they do favours for money.'

'Come on.' Cooper started to go. He turned mid-step and said to Tina, 'Not a word. You say anything to anybody and I'll cut your face to ribbons. You understand?'

Tina said, 'I'd like to see you try.'

Cooper closed his eyes, clasped his hands in front of his stomach and stood perfectly still. 'You want a taster, just say the word.'

Tina studied the little man stuffed into the charcoal suit. Short hair. Number three back and sides, slightly longer on top. Shit brown peppered with grey. The heavy lines scoring his forehead betrayed his pretence at relaxation. He was tense. Lightly tanned face. Patches of white faded the edges of his mouth. Evidence of more tension. The lack of a tie exposed his abnormally thick neck. Muscles bulged under his open shirt. His chest strained against the buttons of his jacket. His biceps swelled under his sleeves. He looked like he was about to explode out of his clothes.

Tina could do without having to clear up the mess. 'You can open your eyes,' she said. 'I'll be a good girl.'

Cooper raised his eyelids. 'I like you.' He offered her his hand. 'And I can tell you like me.'

She took it. 'Now fuck off,' she said.

FOURTEEN

Joe put his hands on the table. They hadn't cuffed him this time. He glanced around him. Yet another police interrogation room. Windowless, which was probably why it reeked of sweat. Bare walls. The table where the three of them were sitting, four plastic chairs, a tape deck. Same layout as the interrogation room in Kirkwall. The only difference was the colour of the walls. Grey, this time, instead of yellow.

Monkman obviously felt at home. Slumped in his chair, the detective's head hung to the side. Slobber trickled out the corner of his partly open mouth. His arm twitched and he moaned.

'You'd think he'd spent a night in the cells,' Joe said to the other detective. 'Want me to fetch his slippers?'

'He was up all night.' Detective Sergeant Grove's brown eyes were huge behind the thick lenses of his glasses. He was very much awake. 'Working on your wife's case.' He placed his hand on Monkman's shoulder and shook him gently. Monkman's eyes snapped open. He stared at Joe, bewildered, and no doubt a little disorientated.

'The plane crashed,' Joe said. 'You're dead. It's just you and me and some ugly bloke with horns goes by the name of Satan.'

Monkman turned to face Grove. 'Sorry. Don't know how—'

Grove cut him off. 'How do you take your coffee?'

'Huh?'

'Coffee, sergeant. I think you need it.'

Monkman yawned and cupped his hand over his mouth. He nodded.

'How do you take it?'

'White.' Monkman wiped his lips with the heel of his hand. 'No sugar.' He sniffed his wrist and pulled a face.

'Mr Hope?' Grove said.

'Very kind of you to offer.'

'How do you take it?'

'Same as Sleeping Beauty.'

Grove turned to the uniformed cop by the door. 'Would you be kind enough to fetch two coffees, constable? White. No sugar.'

'If you think you're up for the challenge,' Joe said.

The constable grunted and let himself out.

Monkman said, 'I'm sorry I—'

Again DS Grove stopped him. 'We're all tired. Mr Hope's been through a lot, too.' Grove peered at Joe over the top of his glasses. 'He must be exhausted.'

Joe said, 'Is this rehearsed?'

'I'm not with you.'

'You and him. Good cop, bad cop. You offer me coffee. What's he going to do? Spit in it?'

Grove sat back, removed his glasses and squeezed his nose. 'How are your ribs?' He put his glasses back on and looked at Joe. He pinched his nose again.

'What's it to you?'

'You feel well enough to proceed with the interview?'

Somehow, despite the heavy strapping, Joe felt able to move more freely. And he could breathe now without feeling that somebody was chiselling splinters off his ribs. 'I'm fine.'

Grove said, 'Unfortunate you fell over.'

'Unfortunate,' Joe said. 'Sure.'

'Unfortunate, also, that you refused medical attention.'

'Is this concern for my health leading somewhere? What's your point?'

DS Grove shook his head as if he was disappointed. 'I want to establish something, Mr Hope. Nobody's playing games here. No good cop, bad cop routine. We're not that inventive. I'll be honest. We like results. So we do what's most likely to obtain a conviction. And frequently, believe it or not, that means following protocol. Our insistence that you see a doctor and have your ribs looked at was entirely procedural.'

First thing last night after he was placed in the custody of Lothian and Borders police force, they drove him to the hospital, checked him for breakages, and, despite finding none, bandaged him up. Joe had to admit, the strapping helped. Even if he looked like a mummy under his shirt.

From the hospital, they escorted him to St Leonard's, Edinburgh's main custody centre. They booked him in and immediately led him to the cellblock. When the turnkey opened the iron door, he released a stench that made Joe gag. 'You'll get used to it,' the turnkey said. Joe's eyes watered. The air was rancid. Puked-up alcohol, laced with stale sweat and piss. The policeman holding his arm urged him forward.

Muffled shouts escaped from the cells lining the corridor. Outside each locked door was a pair of trainers.

They made him remove his shoes before shepherding him into one of the cells. Blue plastic mattress on the floor. Toilet bowl minus its seat in the corner. A combination of graffiti and smeared blood decorated the mustard-coloured walls. The turnkey dropped a grey blanket on the mattress and said, 'Try to get some sleep.'

The policeman removed Joe's handcuffs and left with the turnkey. Joe lay down on the mattress and buried his head under the blanket. He thought he'd never get to sleep. In fact, sleep came like a headlong fall into a pit.

When he awoke, his mouth tasted like a cat litter tray. Still did. He should ask if he could brush his teeth.

Grove was speaking again. He seemed to have a problem with his nose, the way he was squeezing and pulling it all the time. 'Sometimes brute force won't open a safe. The trick is to get hold of the combination. We get results here. If anybody steps out of line we send them home.'

Joe glanced at Monkman and grinned. Grove seemed okay. For a policeman. 'You know I'm not saying anything until my lawyer gets here,' Joe said.

Grove pulled back his cuff and looked at his watch. 'Our young, idealistic Mr Brewer appears to be late. It's practically lunchtime. You hungry?' When Joe shook his head, Grove took off his glasses and placed them on the table. He held the bridge of his nose between his forefinger and thumb and screwed his eyes shut as if he'd just experienced a stabbing pain. When he opened them, he said, 'Touch of indigestion, excuse me.' He gave his watch another glance. 'If Mr Brewer doesn't turn up within the next ten minutes, we'll give him a ring and find out what's happening. I apologise on his behalf for the delay.'

'Don't know about you,' Monkman said to Joe, 'but I've got nothing better to do today.'

'Now you mention it,' Joe said, 'I was going to visit a mate.'

'What's his name?'

'Like I'm going to tell you.'

'This mate piss you off, did he?'

'Why would you think that?'

'Just wondering whether it's only women you beat to death.'

'Sleeping Beauty's definitely woken up,' Joe said to Grove. To Monkman he said, 'My friend's an accomplished classical pianist. He accompanies me while I indulge in my favourite pastime of singing Schubert *Lieder.*'

Monkman said, 'Wanker.'

'Piss off,' Joe told him.

'Gentlemen,' Grove said. 'Please.' He said to Joe, 'You're an educated man.'

'He's a smart-mouthed little shit,' Monkman said.

'I pick things up,' Joe said, ignoring Monkman.

'Aye,' Monkman said. 'Busted ribs.' He grinned, delighted with himself.

'You went to university,' Grove said, also ignoring Monkman.

'Doesn't mean anything.'

'On the contrary. It means a great deal.'

'It does?'

'Means you're bright.'

'Your logic's debatable. But, suppose what you say is true. How does it help?'

'It means you can be reasoned with, Mr Hope.' Grove retrieved his glasses from the table, held them by the leg and swivelled them from side to side. 'You can't possibly appreciate how valuable that is. Intelligence is not something we see very often within these walls.' Slipping on his glasses, he turned to face DS Monkman. 'You know what I'm talking about?'

'Yeah,' Monkman said. 'Criminals are thick.'

'Quite a generalisation,' Grove said. 'But it's not far from the truth. In my experience.'

Joe said, 'You think I'm special, then? Well, gee boys, I'm flattered. I hope you don't mind, Sergeant Grove, if I point something out.'

'Be my guest.'

'The criminals you see are only the ones you catch. The intelligent ones elude what you call justice. Therefore, your statement is wildly inaccurate.'

'You think so?'

'Criminals that get caught are thick. That's all you can say. And I'd also like to point out that criminals are not the only people within these walls. If intelligence is a rarity in your everyday life, you need look no further than the redneck sitting next to you to see why.'

'Thank you,' Grove said, placing his hand flat against Monkman's chest to keep him from diving across the table, 'for your observations. They're most interesting.' He said to Monkman, 'Detective, would you like to leave the room or do you think you can restrain yourself?'

Monkman glared at Joe. 'I'm okay,' he said between clenched teeth. He pointed at Joe. 'Five minutes alone with you,' he said. 'I'll fuck you up.'

'Up what? Up the arse?' Joe said. 'Sorry, love. Don't fancy you.'

Just at that moment the door opened. A young man in a navy blue suit entered the room. His face was so smooth it looked like he hadn't started to shave yet. Monkman lowered himself back into his chair and grinned at Joe. 'That must be your lawyer,' he said.

Joe's lawyer clutched a briefcase to his chest as if it was a baby the social services had threatened to take into care. 'Which one of you is Joe Hope?'

'Christ Almighty,' Joe said.

DS Grove held out his hand to the baby-faced lawyer. 'Good to see you again, Mr Brewer,' he said. 'That's DS Monkman from the Orkney Command. The gentleman opposite is your client.'

The lawyer manipulated the briefcase so he could hold it to his chest with only one hand. With his free hand he grabbed Monkman's and shook it. 'Ronald Brewer,' he said. 'From MacDonald Galbraith.' Then he offered Joe his hand.

Joe turned his head away and muttered, 'The fucking best Cooper could come up with. How old are you?'

'Twenty-five.'

'You don't look it. You had much experience in this line of work?'

'Well, a couple of cases. At university we covered—'

'What's your plan?'

'Well, I'm not sure—'

'I thought so.'

Grove said, 'You've been briefed?'

He patted his case. 'It's all here.'

'You'll be wanting some time to talk things through with your client before we begin our interview, I expect.'

'If that's okay,' Ronald Brewer said.

'Certainly,' Grove said. 'Detective Monkman and I will excuse ourselves for, what, an hour?'

Joe said, 'What about my coffee?'

'We'll have it sent in,' Grove said. 'And you have my word DS Monkman won't spit in it.'

FIFTEEN

Ronald Brewer said, 'How are they treating you?'

'Amazing,' Joe said.

'That's good to hear.'

Joe spoke slowly. 'Amazing that you're the best lawyer Cooper could come up with. I'd love to have seen the worst.'

The best lawyer Cooper could come up with planted himself in the seat vacated by DS Grove, placed his briefcase on the table between them and said, 'I will defend you to the best of my ability, Mr Hope. If you think someone else can do a better job, you're at liberty to change your counsel at any point. Our law firm is highly respected, and, by the way, I graduated top of my year.'

Joe was slightly taken aback by the young man's attitude. 'Well, Mr Brewer, I don't know that I want your counsel, as you put it.'

'That's up to you.' Neither man spoke for a short while. The young lawyer opened his briefcase. 'Now, while you're thinking, can I ask you a question?' He didn't wait for a reply. 'Do you know why you're here?'

'Are you for real?'

Ronald Brewer removed a stack of documents from his case and started shuffling through them. 'You understand you've been arrested for the murder of your wife, em—'

'Ruth,' Joe told him.

Brewer looked at him. 'Her name temporarily slipped my mind.'

'Don't forget again. It's impolite.'

'Sorry,' Brewer said.

'No need to apologise. Just don't be a twat.'

'Sorry,' Brewer said.

Joe glared across the table. 'Answer this for me, Brewer.'

'Sure, Mr Hope.'

'How did my wife die?'

'Are you saying you don't know?'

'Two earholes not enough? If my hands were free I could help drill you another one. How did my wife die?'

'I have to know something,' Ronald Brewer said. 'Are you guilty, Mr Hope?'

'Is that what you think? You're doing a great job of selling yourself.' Joe paused for a moment. 'I shouldn't be here, Brewer. I'm not guilty.'

'The evidence is pretty convincing.'

'I wouldn't know.'

'I would've thought they'd have told you.'

'Well, they haven't.' Joe took a deep breath. 'They haven't told me shit. That's why I'm asking you.'

Ronald Brewer tightened the knot in his tie. Joe tapped his fingers on the table. Eyes clouding over as if he was hearing news of his own young spouse's death, the lawyer said, 'She was beaten repeatedly with a baseball bat.'

'My bat?'

'You own a baseball bat?'

'Jesus.' Joe ran his hand over his scalp, resisting the impulse to grab a handful of hair. After a moment, he lowered his hand and placed it between his knees. 'Any fingerprints?'

'On the bat?' Brewer shook his head. 'Wiped off. They showed me pictures.' He switched his gaze to his notes.

'Keep them to yourself. I don't want to see them.'

'Oh, I don't have them now. I wouldn't want them, anyway.' Brewer looked up. 'The bat's streaked with blood. Your wife's blood. Rubbed into the wood by whoever wiped the finger-prints off.'

Joe cupped his hands over his nose and mouth. Breathed

into his hands. His breath was warm and sticky and smelled of blood and coffee.

'Want me to stop?' his lawyer asked.

Joe closed his eyes and held his breath. He dropped his hands and breathed out. He opened his eyes. 'How come nobody heard her?'

'Heard her what?'

'Screaming.'

Brewer flicked over a couple of pages of his notes. 'Nobody knows exactly where the attack took place. Probably some isolated spot.'

Joe screwed his eyes shut. When he opened them, he said, 'But she was beaten with my baseball bat.' He paused. Then he said, 'To death, right?'

'There's a massive injury to the back of her head. It's possible that she fell, and that the fall killed her. But she was hit, uh, extensively.'

'Maybe she wasn't supposed to die.'

'Maybe. It hardly matters.'

'Doesn't it?'

'You're my client. You tell me you're not guilty. That's all that matters.'

'I *tell* you. Says it all, doesn't it? Why are you and everybody else so sure it was me? I mean, if there are no fingerprints.'

'You really want to know why, Mr Hope? First. Your neighbours heard you arguing. Shouts and yells. The sound of something being thrown and breaking. Second. You've just admitted to owning a baseball bat. Not a common sport in this country. Why would you own a baseball bat? I don't know why they're on sale, really. Everybody knows what they're used for. Anyway, your wife was beaten to death with a baseball bat. One that appears to belong to you. But, most damning of all, her body was found in the boot of your car.'

Joe pursed his lips. 'I left my car at the airport.'

'According to the experts, it seems that the body was in the boot before you left for the airport.'

'What?' Joe's jaw felt slack. His lips felt thick, pulpy. 'I drove there with Ruth . . .' His mouth hung open. He'd driven his dead wife to the airport. He couldn't get his head round that. Ruth stuck in the boot of the car, while he hurried to catch a plane to avenge his daughter's death. Of course, he'd fucked up with that little mission, too. He was fucking useless. The lawyer was staring at him. Joe said, 'How was she found?'

'A joyrider.'

'Explain.'

'A joyrider stole the car. Drove it for a bit. Parked it in the Muirhouse area. Got out to have a look in the boot. Found your wife and ran away.'

'Leaving the boot open?'

'Leaving the boot open.'

'That's unlucky.'

'The fact that you had decided to fly to Orkney was even more unlucky. It looks highly suspicious. It confirms what the police were already thinking. You were on the rampage after your daughter's death. Blaming it on everybody who knew her. First your wife, then, uh, her cousin, Adam Wright—'

Joe broke in. 'Somebody who had access to the car.'

'What?'

'It must have been somebody who had keys.'

'The joyrider didn't have keys,' Brewer pointed out. 'Didn't stop him.'

'The joyrider doesn't exist,' Joe said. 'Nobody goes to the airport to nick a car. Anyway, I'm thinking aloud.'

'Can I try?' Brewer said.

'That's what I'm paying you for.'

'Technically, that's incorrect.' When Joe tilted his head to the side, Brewer continued, 'Did your wife own a set of keys?'

'Yeah.'

'It could have been anybody, then. Could have used hers.'

'Ronald, were the keys in the car when it was found?'

'I don't know. I can find out. What are you thinking?'

'If somebody wanted to set me up, they could have followed me to the airport, waited till my flight had taken off, got into the car with Ruth's keys and left them in the ignition.'

'An open invitation, as it were.'

'Better still, better still. I've got it. Who discovered the body?'

'We don't know. The police received an anonymous phone call.'

'What a surprise. Okay. How about this?' Joe bit his bottom lip for a second or two. Then he said, 'Two people are in the car tailing me. One of them gets out at the airport. The other drives off. The first one gets in my car, using Ruth's keys, drives it to a rendezvous spot at Muirhouse, opens the boot and gets in his mate's car. Then they both drive off.'

'Having very nicely set you up.'

Joe nodded. 'Muirhouse. Major dump. You automatically think, joyrider. I'm amazed the car wasn't burnt out by the time the police arrived.'

'If the boot wasn't open, it may well have been.'

'Shit,' Joe said, imagining Ruth's charred remains. 'Thank God the police got there so quickly.' He paused for a minute, then said, 'One other thing bothers me. How did the police know I was in Orkney?'

'Your flight number.'

'And how did they know that?'

'It was scribbled on a piece of paper in your glove compartment.'

'Ah,' Joe said. 'Convenient. Ronald, at no point did I write down my flight number. Can't they check the handwriting?'

'I'm sure they will, but it won't prove anything. Somebody else may have written down the details, but you were undeniably on the plane.'

Neither man spoke for a while. Eventually the lawyer broke the silence. 'Can you tell me something?'

'What do you want to know?'

'Did you have an argument with your wife?'

'Do *you* argue with your wife?'

'I'm not married. Did you often argue?'

'Yeah.'

'Did you love your wife, Mr Hope?'

'I hated the bitch.' Joe twisted his wedding ring a fraction. He tugged it towards his knuckle. No way was it ever coming off. 'But last time I checked, that wasn't against the law.'

'You want to tell me why you hated her?'

'None of your business.'

'I'm not asking out of idle curiosity. I believe it might help your defence if you tell me.'

'Tough.' Joe crossed his arms.

Ronald Brewer shoved his bundle of papers back in the briefcase. He coughed. He removed a notebook from the briefcase and unclipped a biro from his breast pocket. 'I spoke to Mr Cooper earlier this morning. He said to tell you that Tina had agreed to back up your story.'

'What story?'

'What game are we playing here, Mr Hope?' Brewer leaned forward and whispered, 'Nobody's listening, you know.' He leaned back. 'This is between us. Is there something you want to tell me?'

'I asked you a question,' Joe said. 'What story?'

'That on the night of your wife's death, you were at your

prostitute friend's flat all night. She's prepared to state that you didn't leave her bed until the morning. After your wife was murdered.'

Joe's eyes widened. What the fuck was this? He was at Cooper's the night Ruth was killed. Okay, he was at Tina's earlier in the evening, but he left, went home for a while and had a cup thrown at him by a very much alive Ruth, then went on to Cooper's where he stayed the night. 'Yeah?'

'It's an alibi, Mr Hope.'

'I can see that.'

'Your alibi. Your beautiful, watertight alibi. The police are interviewing Tina as we speak.' Ronald Brewer made a few marks on his notepad. 'You know,' he said, 'I can't help wondering why an innocent man would need to fabricate an alibi.'

Joe wasn't sure either. Cooper had obviously arranged it with Tina. Maybe Cooper had thought, being Joe's best friend, he wouldn't make such a convincing witness. Tina, on the other hand, had no such emotional attachment. Why would she lie? But would a jury see it like that? 'What makes you so sure I wasn't there all night?'

'Like I said, your neighbours heard you arguing.'

'Couldn't have been me. Maybe it was the TV.'

Behind the lawyer, the door opened. The policeman who'd vanished what seemed like hours ago to fetch coffee reappeared with a single white plastic cup. Obviously, he'd delivered Monkman's first. Bastard.

Joe said, 'What took you?'

The policeman didn't reply. He set the cup down next to Joe's right hand, acknowledged Ronald Brewer with the tiniest elevation of his eyebrows, turned and left the room.

Joe picked up the cup. Instant crap. From a machine. Freckles of undissolved granules floated on the surface.

Despite Groves' assurances to the contrary, he wondered if Monkman had spat in it. 'Don't suppose you have a spoon on you?' he asked the lawyer.

'Are you going to talk to me or am I wasting my time?'

Joe took a sip. Scalding. He smacked his burned lips together. They tasted of chicory. Like his grandmother's *Mellow Birds*. 'I don't know what you mean.' Joe had to make a decision. It wasn't hard. He asked himself who he trusted and immediately put himself in Cooper's hands. 'I was at Tina's all night. That's all there is to it.'

'What about the neighbours who heard you having a row?'

'They're mistaken.' Maybe that's what Cooper was trying to cover up. 'If it wasn't the TV they overheard, then maybe Ruth was arguing with her killer. How should I know? I wasn't there.'

'Why did Mr Cooper insist I pass on the message?'

'About Tina? I suppose he just wanted me to know she had agreed to cooperate. It was likely she may not have wanted to get involved.' He took another sip. 'You're young, Ronald. It may surprise you to learn that some prostitutes are shy of our friendly police force.'

'Mr Hope,' Ronald Brewer said. 'If anybody saw you that night and can place you at a location other than Tina's residence, a guilty verdict is likely to be a formality.'

'And if not?' Joe asked.

SIXTEEN

Adam Wright stared out of his bedroom window. In the distance, sea tangled with sky in threads of grey. Rain fell like dust shaken from a sheet of dark cloud. To the west, an island (Shapinsay, maybe, the one with the castle – there were sixty-odd islands, none of which Adam had visited yet) poked through the stormy water like the head of a drowning giant. Inland, new houses – in various states of completion – lined the suburban end of Berstane Road. From there, a series of fields – a couple used for grazing, one recently ploughed – rolled towards Wrighters' Retreat, this monstrous but cheap edifice he'd bought after his parents' fatal accident five years ago. Below, at the edge of the nearest field, was an ever-expanding pile of rubbish the council wouldn't pick up for reasons almost entirely beyond Adam's comprehension. For once, he observed the disgusting mess without a flicker of anger.

He'd had the opportunity to tell Monkman everything. But he'd chosen not to. Far from certain he'd made the right decision, he pressed his forehead against the rain-spattered windowpane, wishing Gem was still here to ask. What did she expect from him? It was a big fucking secret. The glass was cool against his brow. His breath was shallow, hardly misting the glass. He stepped back from the window and stumbled towards his unmade bed. He unlaced his shoes and kicked them off. Snatching Gemma's diary from the bedside table, he lay down. Why the hell had she left it with him? He didn't want it. The damn thing dug into his chest like a sharp stone.

The last days of her life were recorded in the book he held in his hand. He had found it stuffed in the top drawer of his desk, resting on top of a pile of unpaid bills. Curious, he had opened the book. Stuck inside the front cover was a hand-written note. It read: *Please make sure Daddy gets this. Thank you for everything, Adam. I'm sorry. I don't know what else to say.*

Her name appeared in red ink in a floral bordered box in the centre of the diary's title page. He flicked over. The first entry was dated Sunday, 8th September. Seven weeks ago. *I'm in Orkney! I can't believe it! Daddy saw me off at the airport. The flight was all taking off and landing and not much flying in between. Adam was waiting for me.* He'd broken out in a sweat when he'd realised that this was her diary, that it might be the suicide note she had failed to leave. Instantly he had turned to the end of the book. Fingers shaking, he'd flipped back through several blank pages. And there it was. Monday, October 26th. The day she killed herself. *It will soon be over.*

She must have visited the office in the early evening. Slipped her diary in his desk. Returned to her room. Swallowed the pills. At that point the sequence of events reached an impasse in his head. He still couldn't believe she'd done it.

He opened the diary once again. He skimmed over several pages dealing with her arrival. The book was full of vivid, poetic descriptions of Orkney scenery. She expressed delight at her room, excitement at discovering new friends. A trip she made to Skara Brae and Yesnaby. Another to Maeshowe. All written in a neat, backwards sloping hand. No mention of home, of missing it, or her parents. Like her bedside table, her diary was absent of all reminders of her past. Adam carried on turning the pages, glancing over the words, pausing only to scrutinise the occasional sentence where he saw his own name. Vanity. Hey, nobody's exempt.

She described him on more than one occasion as being slightly overweight. Well, now. Adam occasionally stole a glance in the full-length mirror in his bedroom and agreed he could lose a few pounds. Five eight. Eleven and a half stone. Hardly obese. Fat or not, though, there was little doubt she liked him. Described him as 'paternal' on one occasion, 'wise' on another. Mentioned several times that he had a terrific sense of humour. Claimed he had cheered her up more than once. She was getting better, she thought.

Then, just over a week into her stay, she had written this:

I imagined I was getting over it. I was dead wrong. On my way back from the toilets, it crashed into me again. Knocked the wind out of me like a kick in the stomach. It really terrifies me, the way it makes me feel. Writing about it now, safely back in my room, my hand's shaking and my mouth's dry and, Christ, I'm scared. Now I've started crying again. God, I'm so fed up with crying. So fed up with my stupid self.

And a couple of days later:

I'm filthy. I want to pour bleach down my throat. I can't sleep. If I turn out the light I'll see his face. I'll smell the whisky on his breath. I'll hear his words. 'Be nice to Daddy, Gem. It won't hurt. Won't hurt at all.'

Adam stopped reading. No matter how many times he read it, it was equally incomprehensible. No wonder she'd left home in such a hurry.

Maybe Ruth had found out. Maybe that's why Joe had killed her.

Adam ought to go to the police. If it wasn't for the note, that's exactly what he'd do. But Gemma had trusted him. For reasons best known to herself, she wanted the diary delivered to her scumbag father.

If only there was someone he could confide in. He considered the possibilities. A sad reflection of the loneliness of his life was that he could only think of two candidates.

Dorothy Kelly was twenty-four, divorced, childless. She was his receptionist, cleaner, cook and accountant. To boost her otherwise paltry salary, Adam provided free accommodation. Since her marriage ended painfully a couple of years ago, she'd lived in the Orwell room. She liked her job. She loved talking to writers. You see, she wanted to write as well. So far, she'd written the opening chapter of a romance novel which she refused to show Adam no matter how much he begged. She was a little shy. She still got depressed from time to time.

Had he asked her, Adam was sure she'd be happy to talk about Gemma. And he was sure, if he mentioned it, she'd keep the diary's existence a secret. This was the problem: Adam suspected Dotty was a little bit in love with him. He had witnessed the way she smiled at him, the look in her eye a couple of times when he caught her watching him, her embarrassment when she realised her furtive glances had been observed.

No, that wasn't the problem. If he was truthful – and *this* was the problem – the feeling was mutual. When he talked to her, invisible fingers clawed under his skin and massaged his bones. Sometimes it felt as if a giant ladle had plunged down his throat and was stirring the contents of his stomach. She, well, she turned him on. It was impossible to deny it.

Unfortunately, a relationship with Dotty was something he was unable to foster. Nurturing a sexual relationship with his only member of staff was against the rules. His own rules, admittedly, but he wasn't about to change them just because it suited him. Adam held a position of trust. He had to rise above his baser desires. Difficult though it was when you lived in the same building, the only way he knew of achieving this was to keep contact with Dotty to a minimum. Which was hard when all he wanted to do was strip her naked every time he saw her.

Then, in the Stevenson room, there was Willie Lang. Adam's only current client. No such sexual designs on him, fortunately. Van driver, mobile phone salesman, interior decorator, museum caretaker, baker and, latterly, screenwriter. There wasn't much Willie hadn't turned his hand to. He claimed he'd held down two jobs most of his life (he was a security guard in the evenings and weekends) and after a protracted divorce, he'd given up both his current jobs and left home. He gave Adam most of his savings, which wasn't much. Enough to pay for his stay at Wrighters' Retreat for seven months. Long enough, Willie hoped, to produce a top quality screenplay. At the tail end of his forties, Willie's midlife crisis came a little late. Willie was friendly, intelligent, open, witty, knowledgeable and a superbly bad writer. Couldn't get beyond seeing dialogue as a series of questions and answers. As for confiding in him? On several occasions they'd spoken long into the night on various heartfelt topics. But for the conversation Adam had in mind, secrecy was vital, and Willie probably wasn't the right person. It wasn't that Adam didn't trust him. He just didn't trust him completely. Big difference.

Bottom line, Adam concluded, he'd have to face this alone. He wasn't going to get any help.

He turned his attention back to the diary. Monday 19th October. The week before she died. He read:

Feeling numb. Just a rape, I tell myself. Once again. I'm going to be okay. No more tears. I'm fine. I'm doing okay. I'm calm. Just a rape. Just a four-letter word.

Somebody knocked on the door and I jumped out of my skin. I told whoever it was to go away. I was shaking and cold. He'd tell me to deal with it. I'm trying, God help me. Nobody will ever know how hard I'm trying. But I can't deal with it. I don't see how I can ever deal with it. Sometimes I think I deserved it. Something I did must have triggered it. I must be sick. In my head. Another knock. Dotty's voice asking me if I'm all right. I told her to go away.

Sometimes I wake up and forget where I am. Sometimes I wake up and don't know I've been asleep. My dreams are as real as everything else in my life. Maybe I don't sleep. I only dream. Maybe none of it really happened.

Dotty said to focus on the good things.

When I was thirteen we stayed up late one night to see a meteor shower. Just me and Daddy. The sky was clear. Daddy drove. We left the car at the foot of Calton Hill. By the time we'd climbed to the top, we were out of breath and freezing cold. A few small groups of people were there already, huddled over bottles of whisky. I told Daddy I should have worn my mittens. He just looked at me like I was daft. He took off his coat and wrapped it round my shoulders.

About twenty feet away, a group of half-a-dozen kids, much younger than me, were crammed into a two-seater settee, necks craned towards the sky. Another couple of kids balanced on the arms of the settee. 'How did that get here?'

Daddy shook his head. 'Beyond me why anybody would carry a settee to the top of a hill. Handy, though.'

I dragged my eyes away from the settee. Edinburgh lay spread out beneath us. Even at this late hour, buses and cars scuttled about the gridlike streets of the New Town like desperate insects. Across the Forth a fringe of lights sparkled along the coastline. I pointed. 'Where's that?'

'Fife.'

'I know.' I kicked him. He pretended it hurt. 'The town, I meant. Which town?'

'Way in the distance,' he said, 'is Kirkcaldy. Towards us,' he indicated a closer cluster of shimmering lights, 'that's Burntisland.'

Focus on the good things.

I was seven, maybe eight. Market Day. Sometime in July, August maybe. I don't know. I remember it was warm. I wasn't wearing a coat. The Ferris wheel was scarily big. I closed my eyes and pictured the hill, the Binn, the backdrop to the town. And the island of scorched rocks in the harbour. Blackened. Burned. Burntisland. I didn't want to go on any of the rides. I was too scared. Daddy said there was nothing to be scared of. He would protect me. Did I trust him? Of course I did. Before long, I was at the top of the wheel screaming with delight.

He pointed in the direction of Edinburgh. 'Wave to Mummy.'

I waved. Mummy was sick. In hospital. Something wrong with her head. I didn't understand. I do now.

Back on Calton Hill, I stamped my cold feet. 'Yeah,' I said, grabbing Daddy's arm, leaning my head against his shoulder. 'Burntisland. I knew that.'

Falling stars arced through the night sky. We watched in silence. I hugged him. I couldn't hug him hard enough.

'I'm still cold,' I said.

After about ten minutes, he said, 'We better go before you turn into a pillar of ice.'

'You mean you're bored.'

He looked down at me and kissed me on the forehead.

Okay, so she was grasping for memories of happier times. Understandable. Nonetheless, Adam wondered how she was able to write so fondly of her father. It seemed inappropriate, incompatible. No, it was worse than that. It was wrong. Unless Adam had missed something.

Adam read on. The entry for the next day was blank. Wednesday simply stated:

I can't do this any more.

Thursday was more philosophical.

The hardest thing of all is living with this secret. No, that's not true. The hardest thing is knowing that I'll have to live with it for the rest of my life. I can never let anybody find out. I can't slip up. Not once. I have to live a lie. From now on my life has to be based around one big falsehood. Once or twice, I've come close to spilling it all out to Dotty. I can't let myself do that. It has to remain a secret. As long as I live. Oh, God.

I can't stay here forever. One day I'll have to go back home, speak to Daddy and Mummy. I can't do it. I know there are other people I can talk to. Professionals. I'm not stupid. I talked to one of them already. She was very nice and caring, but she was doing a job and at five o'clock she was going to go home to her family. She'd forget about me. I couldn't help but think that. All the time she was listening, I was thinking that she didn't give a shit. She told me there were cognitive methods of coping. I said thank-you and never turned up for the next session.

Coping. Do I want to spend my life coping?

I thought again about killing him. I thought how easy it would be. I just had to say the word. All I had to do was tell the truth. For the first time in ages I felt happy. So happy I cried. And then I felt sad.

I know I can never tell the truth. I couldn't cope with sending Daddy to prison. What would I have left? Cognitive therapy and Mummy?

Well, Adam thought, that was conclusive. If Gemma told the truth, she'd send her father to prison. That's what she'd said. He read the last couple of paragraphs again. There was something that didn't quite fit. To kill him, she need only say the word. Which made her happy. But sending him to prison was something she couldn't cope with. It didn't follow. Didn't make sense. Perhaps it was the illogic of emotion. Perhaps it was mere confusion. Throughout the diary she had repeatedly described her feelings as 'numb.' In other words, she didn't know how she felt. No doubt, she didn't trust her feelings. They had already betrayed her. It was safer to shut down, retreat inside herself, feel nothing.

Adam wished he could do the same. Reading Gem's last words was as hard as anything he'd ever done. Passing the diary on to her father – the man who'd raped her, for fuck's sake – was going to be even harder. Gem mentioned Dotty a few times. They'd grown close in the short time they'd had together. Maybe he should ask her advice. Could he risk talking to her? This was a big fucking responsibility. He just hoped that Ruth hadn't left him a little note as well.

SEVENTEEN

'If they can't place you anywhere outside of Tina's flat, and they can't persuade her to change her story, they'll have no alternative but to let you go.' The trace of a smile flickered over Ronald Brewer's lips.

Joe said, 'Thank Cooper for me.'

The young lawyer tried to hold Joe's gaze. After a while he looked away and said, 'Anything else you want me to do for you?'

'I was thinking.' Joe gulped down some coffee. God, it was awful. 'About Gemma's funeral.'

'What are the arrangements?' the lawyer asked. Joe said nothing. 'Is the body being flown here, or is she being buried in Orkney?'

Joe stared at the plastic cup. 'Ruth might have organised something. Maybe she had time. Before she . . . I don't know, she didn't tell me.'

Brewer waited a moment. Then he said, 'I'll find out.'

'Talk to Adam Wright at Wrighters' Retreat in Kirkwall. I want her home, Ronald.'

'I'll do what I can.'

Joe thanked the lawyer and meant it. His gaze shifted from his hands to the lawyer's baby face. 'Supposing I've not been released by then, will they let me go to the funeral?'

'No question. But it would smooth things along if the funeral was in Edinburgh.'

'That'll take time. I'll be out of here by then.'

'Let's hope so. Anything else?'

'You think I'd be allowed to brush my teeth?'

'I can arrange that. Anything else?'

'They likely to keep me in this shithole or send me to prison?'

Brewer looked at his watch. 'Even if they wanted to, they couldn't move you. Not today, anyway. Saughton Prison only accepts new arrivals in the morning. So, unless they release you, you'll be here overnight. There's a petitionary hearing scheduled for this afternoon.'

'Meaning?'

'You'll be remanded in custody until the trial.'

'What about bail?'

'Impossible.'

'I can get the money,' Joe said. 'Cooper'll help.'

'You've seen too many movies, Mr Hope. Money bail is so rare in

Scotland as to be practically non-existent. Basically, it doesn't happen.'

'Yeah? You sure?' The lawyer didn't reply. Joe said, 'I didn't know that.'

'Now you do. I'm not altogether useless, Mr Hope.'

'Isn't it worth trying anyway?'

Brewer sat back in his chair. After a moment he leaned forward and said, 'If you're arrested for murder you won't be released on bail. Period. Anything else?'

Joe shook his head.

'Okay, about your impending interview.' Brewer waited until Joe prompted him with a grunt. 'Stick to one-word answers.' He shook his index finger at Joe. 'Yes and no, where appropriate. Don't give them any more information than they need. If you think a question is inappropriate I'd advise you not to answer it. But it's up to you.'

'You think I shouldn't say anything?'

'I think you shouldn't say anything that might incriminate you.'

'And what's that?'

'Hard to tell, which is why it's better not to say anything at all.'

'That's not a lot of help.' Joe sighed. 'You think, if they believe Tina, that they'll release me?'

'They'll hold you for as long as they can. If they think there's insufficient evidence to prosecute, or if there's contra-dictory evidence, like Tina's, they'll eventually let you go. Just stick to your story and you'll be fine.' Brewer picked up his notepad and slapped it against his open palm. 'Assuming it's the truth.'

'What do you know about the truth?'

'In general, or are you talking about the specifics of your case?'

'In broad terms.'

'Is this some kind of test, Mr Hope?'

'I'm interested.'

'Well, in my opinion, lies make the innocent guilty.'

Joe fiddled with his cup, turning it round and round. He picked it up and took a long swallow. The coffee didn't taste so bad now he'd grown used to it. 'In my world,' he said, 'everybody's guilty.'

'I'm in your world now, Mr Hope. And, I can assure you, I'm not guilty of anything.'

Joe nodded. 'Hate to disillusion you.' He drank the rest of the coffee. 'But you're just as guilty as the rest of us.'

'Oh, yeah?' Brewer said. 'What's my crime?'

Joe crushed the plastic cup and tossed it onto the floor. 'How the fuck should I know? You haven't been caught yet.'

EIGHTEEN

Tina left the police station, swinging her handbag angrily by her side. The bastards could have spoken to her at home, but, no, they wanted her to accompany them to the station and give her statement there. Jesus. She hoped Joe (she still thought of him as Bob and had to be corrected a couple of times during the interview when she referred to him by the wrong name) appreciated what she was doing for him. Okay, there was ten grand in it for her. But, still. There was a limit to what she was prepared to do for money. And, of course, she didn't have it yet.

She stopped abruptly on the pavement. A tall woman wearing too much eye shadow bumped into her and apologised. Tina let her, even though it wasn't the daft cow's fault. Tina rummaged in her handbag for her cigarettes. Normally she didn't smoke until she started work. But after that stuff in the police station she needed a fag and she doubted she'd be in the mood for going to work. If you could call it work. For that matter, when was she ever in the mood? The best you could hope for was numb acceptance. The rest was just acting.

She lit her fag. She needed to give up. She was coughing up a pile of crap in the mornings. It was disgusting. She inhaled deeply, comforting herself with the thought that at least she wasn't a junkie.

Jesus. As if she didn't already have enough reasons to hate herself. She'd just given a murder suspect an alibi. For money. What next? She'd be giving freebies to policemen.

Well, maybe not the pair that had interviewed her. They were both young. One was skinny. Looked like he was flapping around inside his uniform. The other was okay. Nice hands. Soft face. Put him in a fireman's outfit and, well, that freebie might just be a possibility. Ah, frigging mother of

Christ. She couldn't remember when she last had sex for fun. Had she ever?

Her car was at home. That was nice, that was. Take her to the nick, grill her for an hour, then dump her outside without any transport. Buggers.

She glanced down at her feet. Mules. Pretty damn sexy, even if she did say so herself. But could she walk home in them? More to the point, did she want to? The sky was clear. She could walk a bit and if she spotted a taxi, fine. She didn't take buses. Not without a baseball bat. Some things you never got over.

It had been raining hard that day and her hair was plastered to her forehead. She must have looked a right state, but, then, obviously not, or what happened wouldn't have happened. Sitting upstairs, scuffed schoolbag resting on her dirty grey skirt. She was twelve years old.

A man sat down next to her, smiled. She noticed a mole in the centre of his left cheek. He was slim, good-looking, nice hazel eyes. And tanned. Like he'd just returned from a beach holiday.

'Finished school?' he said.

'Looks like a chocolate chip.'

'What does, sweetheart?'

She pointed at his face. 'That. Like a chocolate chip in a chocolate chip cookie.'

His hand went up to his cheek, fingers covering the offending mole.

'It's cute,' she said. 'Looks good enough to eat.'

'My, you're precocious.'

She frowned. 'I don't like words I don't understand.'

'I'm sorry.' He lowered his hand. 'A little bit cheeky, is what I meant. In a good way. An amusing way.'

'Mum says I'm cheeky.'

'She does?'

She gazed into the man's dark brown eyes. 'Not in a good way.' She pulled the strap of her schoolbag. Tightening it.

The man ran the heel of his hand over his short, brown hair. His hair, she noticed, was dry. Hers was still wet. How come? Rain pelted the window on her right, great gobs slithering down the glass. The window was starting to steam up. She was going to ask him how he'd managed to dodge the rain when she spotted the peak of a cap sticking out of his jacket pocket. A baseball cap. Naff. Instantly, she stopped liking him.

When he leaned over to point at something, she caught a whiff of his breath. It smelled like the rubbish bin at home on Thursday night. By the time she took it downstairs for collection on Friday morning, it was really honking. The man's hand was resting on her shoulder. She didn't like it there. She squirmed. Wriggled towards the window. What was he doing? He'd angled his body towards her. The hand that had been pointing out the window dropped onto her knee.

'I've got a knife,' he whispered. 'You scream, you little bitch, I'll cut your throat. All the way from one pretty ear to the other.' His hand slid up her skirt. 'Move your schoolbag.'

She moved it and his hand slid up her thigh. 'Put the bag down again.' She put the bag down. He touched her where he definitely shouldn't. Nobody had touched her there. Not even her mum's old boyfriend, Davie.

The sides of the bus seemed to close in on her. The ceiling pressed down on her head. Something inside her expanded. She filled with it, whatever it was, until she thought she'd burst. It pressed behind her eyeballs, against her chest.

'That's it,' he said. 'Keep quiet.'

She didn't want to keep quiet. 'Get off me,' she said. 'I don't like it.'

His fingers stopped moving, but his hand remained in place. 'Shhh,' he said. 'You want to see the knife?'

Her shoulders turned to lead. Her thighs turned to lead. She felt cold. No, she felt hot. Her head floated miles above her neck. He whispered in her ear, but the buzzing in her ears prevented her from hearing him. His breath stank. She felt dizzy. She was going to be sick. For a minute she thought he'd stabbed her. But his hand was under the schoolbag, under her skirt, inside her knickers. The pain was just the tightening of her stomach muscles. She was twelve, she wanted to tell him. She was only twelve. It wasn't right.

His finger started probing. It hurt. He whispered again. This time she made out his words. 'Stop wriggling,' he said.

'Sore,' she whispered back.

'Oh,' he said. 'I'm sorry.' He removed his hand and, without a word or another glance, got off the bus at the next stop.

Tina never saw him again. She could picture his face, though. The chocolate chip embedded in his cheek. And she could still smell him. Every time she put the rubbish out.

NINETEEN

DS Grove asked the first question. 'Mr Hope, we'd like you to reveal your whereabouts on the evening of Tuesday, October 27th.'

'You know where I was.'

'I'd like you to tell me.'

Joe told him.

'Would you like to refer to the young woman as Tina?'

'That's how I know her.'

'For the record, Mr Hope requests that we refer to Miss Ruth Shaw by her . . . by her working name. At what time did you arrive at Tina's flat?'

'It was early.'

'How early?'

'Between eight thirty and nine.'

'And what did you do at Tina's flat?'

'We drank camomile tea and ate cucumber sandwiches. We listened to Beethoven's late string quartets while discussing the relative merits of various Jacobean dramatists. You think we did? We fucked.'

'And when did you leave?'

'Mid-morning.'

'Can you be more precise?'

'About eleven.'

'So you, em, performed sex acts for about fourteen hours?'

Joe remembered the lawyer's advice. He wondered if answering this question might incriminate him. He didn't see how. He smiled at Monkman. The twat had obviously been instructed to keep his mouth shut. His lips were twitching, though. 'We fucked till about four in the morning,' Joe said. 'Until Tina got tired.'

'Very impressive, Mr Hope. Did you leave the flat at any time during the evening?'

'No.'

'Can anyone other than Tina corroborate your presence there?'

'No visitors, if that's what you're asking.'

'What did you have for breakfast, Mr Hope?'

'I don't eat breakfast.'

'Did anyone see you leave?'

'I didn't notice.'

'You didn't pass anyone on the stairs?'

'I didn't notice.'

'What time did you arrive home?'

'About half eleven, I suppose.'

'Facts please, Mr. Hope. Not supposition.'

'You think I spend all day looking at my watch? I don't fucking know. If I left Tina's at eleven I was home by half eleven. Twenty past, probably, depending on the traffic.'

'When you arrived home, at twenty past eleven' – DS Grove raised his eyebrows – 'didn't you worry that your wife wasn't there?'

'Why would I?'

'How would you describe your relationship with your wife?'

'Personal.'

'Mr Hope, I'm trying to establish whether there was any ill-feeling between yourself and Mrs Hope.'

'Motive, in other words.'

'Possibly. Part of the process involved here is one of elimination. Believe it or not, I would just as soon find a reason to eliminate you from our enquiries.' Grove pushed his glasses back into place. 'Would you answer the question?'

'My relationship with Ruth is none of your business. Next question.'

'You can understand why I ask, can't you? Most successful marriages don't involve extra-marital sex.'

'It's a bit late for marriage guidance.'

'How did Ruth feel about you using prostitutes?'

'The truth?' Joe paused. Then he said, 'She found it convenient.'

'Convenient?' Grove took off his glasses. 'Would you like to explain what you mean by that?'

'She didn't like sex.' He lowered his voice. 'I think maybe because of what happened to her a couple of years ago.'

'And what was that?' Grove put his glasses back on.

'It's a tragic story.' Joe shook his head. 'She was at the zoo. An ape broke out of its cage and, well, you know, it did its business with her.'

'All right,' Grove said.

'It was in all the papers.'

'All right,' Grove said. 'I'll ask again. How did your wife respond to the idea of you sleeping with prostitutes?'

'It's really none of your business.'

'You may be right, Mr Hope,' Grove said. 'May I ask, did Ruth enjoy having sex with anyone else?'

Yes, you fucking bastard. Joe stood up. Grove grabbed his arm and said, 'Hey.' Joe shrugged him off, thoughts like shrapnel in his head. *I heard her. Yes, she fucking did enjoy having sex with someone else. She doesn't know I heard her. Didn't know. Past tense. Fuck. She's dead and you're slagging her. Fuck. I hate remembering this. I hate . . . Wouldn't I love to know who she was shagging? No, that's the amusing bit. Tickles me bright fucking pink. You'd like that. Don't want to know, do you, Joe? I heard their voices. Well, to be precise, I heard her voice. I heard him groan. Before we were married. I heard them. Stood outside the door. Listening to them. Shocked. Couldn't believe it. Her and some twat of a student. Fucking. She was telling him it was good. His grunts, muffled. She was wailing the word, 'Goooood,' like she'd never done with me. Howling. Like a fucking wolf. Howling. 'Goooood.'*

Joe said nothing.

'Touched a nerve, there,' Monkman said

'You shut the fuck up,' Joe told him.

TWENTY

Adam placed Gemma's diary on the bedside table, swung his feet off the bed and padded to the door. 'Yes?'

'I have to talk to you.' Dotty's voice.

'Just a minute.' Adam leaned back towards the bed and smoothed the cover. After straightening the pillows, he opened the door for Dotty. She looked at her feet. Could be looking at his feet, come to think of it. Which were bare. Where were his slippers? He really should trim his toenails. A hot flush crept up the back of his neck. God, he was embarrassed. Like a schoolboy. 'What is it?' he said, curling his toes, praying that now she didn't look up. He'd rather she carried on looking at his feet than see him blush.

She looked up. 'It's warm in here.'

'I like it – warm's how I – it is.'

'You're letting the heat out.'

'What am I thinking?' He gave her a tight-lipped smile, which no doubt looked like the crack in a smacked arse. This was all going wrong. 'Come in.'

She walked past him, head bowed.

'Have a seat.' Instantly he realised there wasn't one. 'On the bed,' he added. 'I'll stand.' The shake of her head was almost imperceptible. Had he not been watching her so closely he might have missed it. 'No? Maybe we should go to the office. Maybe, yes, what do you think?'

'You sit down. I don't want to make you stand.'

'I couldn't.' For a moment, his breath wouldn't come. 'The bed's yours. Please.'

'Not if you're standing. It's your room.'

'But you're the guest in my room.' He paused to scratch an imaginary itch above his right eyebrow. The heat was finally leaving his face. 'If we go to the office we can both have a seat. Would that be more appropriate?'

Her voice was so quiet he had to make sense of her next sentence after she'd spoken it. From the fragments he heard, he was pretty sure she'd said, 'We could both sit on the bed.'

His stomach knotted. 'Oh,' he said. 'That makes sense.' Neither of them moved. 'Yes.' Dotty stared at the floor. Adam stared at Dotty staring at the floor. She was standing directly under the overhead light, the sleeve of her cardigan rolled up slightly, exposing a slender forearm jewelled with tiny blonde hairs.

Adam crept towards the bed. Lead by example, he was thinking. And for fuck's sake don't reach out and stroke her arm. The moment he sat down Dotty sprang towards him, eyes wide.

'You found it,' she said. Adam followed her gaze. She picked the diary up off the bedside table. 'I'm glad. It's what I wanted to talk to you about.'

'You know about the diary?' Adam asked.

'Gemma gave it to me.' Dotty looked at the floor. 'She wanted me to read it.' She looked up, eyes shiny. 'I tried. I tried hard. I couldn't.' She was silent for a while. Adam resisted the temptation to reach out and put his hand on her bare arm. He stared at his feet. After a while she continued, 'I didn't want the burden of her secrets.' Her eyes sought Adam's. 'It's hard enough living with your own.'

'I think she just wanted to share her feelings with some-body.'

She shook her head. 'She gave this to me the day she died. In the morning. She didn't need to share anything. She must have decided already she was going to . . .' Dotty took a step towards the bed, turned and sat down. Her thigh brushed against Adam's. Both her hands gripped the diary. 'She gave it to me because she didn't want the police to find it. I didn't know that then, but it's obvious now. I gave it back to her. Told her to give it to you.'

'I found it in my desk. With a note asking me to give it to her father.'

She nodded. 'I have to tell you something, Adam. Some-thing I haven't told the police.'

Adam turned his body towards her and tried to smile encouragingly.

'I went to Gemma's room that evening. When I got there, the door was closed and . . .' She swallowed. 'I knocked. She didn't answer. Other times when she hasn't wanted to talk, she's told me to go away. This time there was only silence. I thought about trying the door.'

'Was it locked?' Adam said.

Dotty glanced sideways at him. She turned her head. Her left hand plucked at the corner of the pillowcase.

'You didn't try it?'

She faced him. 'You don't get it.' Her face had hardened. 'It wasn't a cry for help,' she said. 'Gemma wanted to die. She took paracetamol, not aspirin.' Adam shook his head. She explained, 'Anybody who's seriously considered swallowing a lethal dose of pills knows that paracetamol is the most efficient. I never touch the stuff. Not since I discovered how dangerous it was.' She paused. 'Your body goes into systematic shutdown. If you're discovered in time, a liver transplant might save you.' She looked at him. 'But there aren't too many spare livers around and very few hospitals are equipped to perform the operation.'

Adam shivered. He felt as if he'd been throwing up for the past couple of hours. 'Maybe Gemma didn't know. Maybe—'

'She knew all right. We talked about it. More than once.'

Adam tried to make sense of what she was telling him. 'I'm not sure,' he said, stopping, uncertain of what he was saying. 'Are you suggesting—'

'I advised her,' she said, 'on how to commit suicide.'

'Of course you didn't, Dotty.'

Dotty's fingers tightened around the diary. 'I told her what happened to me. I thought I was putting a positive slant on it. Trying to explain that there is a way out of depression, however unlikely it seems at the time.'

'So how can you possibly—'

'I lied.'

'About what?'

'Some things you never recover from.'

'I don't believe that.'

'I wouldn't expect you to.' She took a deep breath, then blew the air out noisily. 'I knew with Gem, though. I've seen it before. That look she had in her eyes.'

Adam said, 'What are you talking about?' Dotty sprang to her feet, dropping the diary onto the pillow. He grabbed her hand. 'I'm sorry,' he said. 'I don't understand. I shouldn't have – I'm sorry. Please sit down.' His fingers circled her wrist. Her blood pulsed against his thumb. 'I want to know what happened.'

She drew her hand away from his grasp and he let his arm fall. She stared at her freed wrist, then stroked it with her little finger.

'I didn't mean to hurt you,' Adam said. She closed her eyes. 'Please sit down. Speak to me.'

'She wanted to die, Adam.'

'I can accept that. But I can't accept that it was your fault. If that's what you're telling me.'

'I made the wrong choice.' Dotty turned and faced the door. She spoke quietly, her back to Adam. 'I went to her room. Knocked. She didn't answer. I tried her door. It was open.' She rubbed her wrist with her thumb. 'I poked my head into the room. She was on the bed. I thought she was sleeping. I didn't want to wake her.' She turned her head slightly. 'Maybe she could have been saved. If I'd seen the bottle of pills . . . She looked peaceful. Asleep. I didn't want to disturb her.'

'Don't blame yourself, Dotty. How were you to know?'

Dotty yelled at him. 'I was there.' She clenched her jaw and squeezed the words out for a second time. 'I was there. I should have realised what she'd done. Instead, I walked away.'

'It's not your fault.'

'It feels like it is. I couldn't even read her diary, Adam. I couldn't even do that!'

Adam picked the book off his pillowcase. 'You know what's in here?'

'Gemma wanted her father to know something.' Dotty lowered her head. 'But she couldn't tell him. That's why she wrote it down.' She looked up at him. 'I told her to give it to you. You'd do the right thing.' She took a step towards the door. 'I'll pack now. I can't stay here any longer. I'll leave in the morning.' Another step. And another. Her fingers closed on the handle.

Adam said, 'Did you know about her father?'

'That he was the one human being she truly loved?'

'She loved him? But she couldn't have done. The diary . . .'

'That's what she told me. Not only did she love him, but she liked him too. She loved her mother, she said. Sort of. But she didn't *like* her. Not in the slightest. That was the difference.' Dotty's eyes were wet with tears.

Adam looked away. He opened the diary.

'You know I could have saved her,' she said.

'And what about me?' He didn't look up. 'I promised her father I'd take care of her.' He flicked through the pages, searching for those passages about Joe.

'We both screwed up, then,' Dotty said. 'I'll go pack.'

Gemma's words swam on the page. 'Will you have dinner with me tomorrow night?' he asked Dotty. 'Just the two of us?' His heart was hammering against his ribcage.

'I don't know, Adam.'

'In Edinburgh?' he said.

TWENTY-ONE

'It's good to be out,' Joe said, looking out the car window. Approaching the Odeon cinema, traffic was dense. Getting home was taking forever, but he didn't care. Life was sweet. The petitionary hearing had been cancelled. His ribs hadn't hurt when he'd climbed into Ronald Brewer's car. He had his shoes back. He'd even had the bag he'd taken with him to Orkney returned. It was two o'clock in the afternoon and he was out of jail. The world was getting better all the time.

The lawyer said, 'Let's hope we can keep you out.'

Nothing like a bit of realism to keep you grounded. Joe turned and stared at the young man. He didn't look old enough to drive. 'You think the police don't believe Tina?'

Brewer's face scrunched up and he tilted his head. 'It's not just that.'

'Mr and Mrs Harvey?' Joe's neighbours, an elderly couple, hadn't been prepared to swear it was his voice they'd heard arguing with Ruth. A man's voice, they'd claimed. Of that there was not doubt. And it wasn't the TV. They were sure, absolutely, you see, because the sound had come from the kitchen and, unless she'd installed one recently, Mrs Hope didn't have a TV in the kitchen. They thought it was Mr Hope's voice they'd heard, but when asked if there was any possible doubt (all this Brewer had narrated to Joe less than twenty minutes ago) they'd conceded that it might have been another man they'd heard. Unlikely. But possible. Their uncertainty, together with Joe's alibi, had been sufficient to substantially reduce the weight of circumstantial evidence otherwise incriminating him.

Ronald Brewer shook his head as he drove slowly along the Bridges. He bit his bottom lip as a maroon and white Lothian bus pulled into a stop just ahead. 'Despite Tina's statement and the equivocal testimony of the old folks, you're still the prime suspect.' The street was too narrow to overtake the bus. He put on the handbrake. 'There's still a lot of evidence against you. Look at it.' Enumerating each item by tapping the successive fingers of his left hand with the index finger of his right, he said, 'Your baseball bat. Your car. Your rapid escape to Orkney.' The bus indicated and pulled out. He released the handbrake. 'The police still think it was you. They just can't prove it.' He tucked in behind the bus. 'Yet.'

'After all this,' Joe said, 'you still have doubts about my innocence.'

'Your alibi is false.' The lawyer took his eyes off the road and glanced at Joe. 'I know that. The police know that.' His hand beat against the steering wheel. 'They'll keep questioning Tina until she cracks and then you'll be, excuse my language, fucked.'

Joe ran his hand slowly over his face. When he spoke, his voice was unusually quiet. 'It buys me time.'

'To do what?'

'Whatever I can't do locked in a jail cell.'

Brewer said, 'So you weren't at Tina's when your wife was getting killed?'

Joe leaned his head against the windowpane and said nothing.

'Off the record, Mr Hope. You're still my client. Everything you say to me is confidential. Where were you?'

'Maybe I was sleeping off a hangover in a friend's spare room.'

'Why invent this elaborate cock and bull story, then? What's wrong with the truth?'

Joe took a deep breath. Faced the lawyer. 'The police might not believe my friend.'

'And what, they're more likely to believe a prostitute?'

'Tina has no reason to lie.'

'And your friend does?' A smile spread across Ronald Brewer's mouth. 'You were at Cooper's.' He nodded when Joe didn't reply. 'And Cooper's your best friend. A man who'd lie for you without thinking twice about it. A man with a well-documented disrespect for the law. You might have a point. Maybe the police wouldn't believe him.' He tapped the steering wheel with alternate hands. 'Nobody else see you there?'

'Sally. His girlfriend.'

'And she'd lie too, would she?'

'If Cooper asked her to.'

'You fabricated an alibi because your real alibi sounds fabricated?' 'That's about the height of it. At least, I think so. I won't know until I talk to Cooper. It was his idea. I knew nothing about it till you passed on the message from him.'

'Maybe he just doesn't want to get involved.'

Joe leaned his head back. 'That's a shocking thing to say, Ronald. I should smack you quite hard for saying that.'

'I don't hear you denying it.'

'Off the record,' Joe said. He shook his head. 'Never mind.' What he didn't say was that the same thing had occurred to him. The lights turned red as they approached the High Street and the car trundled to a stop. 'People have a habit of dying around me, Ronald.' Joe placed his hand on the lawyer's leg. Gave it a gentle squeeze. 'Breathe a word of this – to anyone – and you'll be joining them.'

The lawyer surprised Joe by placing his left hand on Joe's leg and gently tightening his grip. 'You don't have to be so melodramatic, Joe.'

'You calling me Joe for?'

'You called me Ronald, Joe.'

'You really think I'm being melodramatic?' Joe removed his

hand from the lawyer's leg and noticed the cut he'd sustained from Cooper's whisky glass. Seemed like it happened weeks ago. The cut had almost healed. When he pressed his thumb against it, it didn't hurt. He pressed harder. Nothing much. If he wanted pain he could always pay Tina to take a baseball bat to his ribs.

The lights changed and Ronald Brewer started to drive off. 'I'll forgive you,' he said. 'You have a lot to be melodramatic about.'

'Let me out,' Joe said.

'Here? If that's what you want.'

'It is what I want.'

'Okay. Sorry if I offended you.'

'Nothing to do with you.'

'You don't want to go home?'

'Not such an attractive proposition.'

'Must be difficult, Joe.'

'Save the sympathy. I don't need it. What I need is to see Cooper and find out what was so important he couldn't come pick me up at the station. I want to know why he paid Tina to fabricate an alibi. I want to know why he doesn't want to admit I was at his house that night. And I don't think I can wait to find out. The more I think about it, the more I want answers right now.'

'You want to phone him, see if he's in?'

'Don't have a phone.'

'Use mine.' Ronald wriggled in his seat. After a series of painful-looking contortions, he handed his phone to Joe.

Joe dialled Cooper's number. After a couple of rings Sally answered, sounding pleased to hear Joe's voice. Joe asked after the baby. Hairy ears, poor little bastard. She started to chuckle when he referred to it as Cheetah. He let her laugh for a while, then asked to speak to Cooper.

She told him to hang on a minute.

Joe hung up. 'He's home,' he said to the lawyer.

'Tell me where he lives. I'll take you there.'

'Don't you have anything better to do?'

'Better than this?' Ronald said. 'You must be joking.'

TWENTY-TWO

Joe had never mentioned her infidelity. Or should that be infidelities? He suspected she'd been unfaithful more than once, but he had no proof. He'd caught her only on that one occasion at university. Standing outside the door, listening, as an ache spread through his bones. He could knock on the door. It probably wasn't locked. He could walk right in and say, 'Hello, baby, who's this you're fucking?' But he couldn't do it. The thought of a confrontation made him feel old and tired.

Shortly afterwards he sought out Cooper. Asked him if he had any jobs going.

Cooper had just quit his half-arsed attempt at studying law and was making enough on the side now to have decided he didn't want to be a lawyer, anyway. Too easy to get disbarred, he said. 'You any good with a baseball bat?' he asked Joe.

Joe thought, well there's an easy way to handle confrontation.

Part of the reason Ruth's infidelity had hurt so much was that she'd persevered with him. At the outset it took a couple of weeks of her coaxing him before he managed to keep it up long enough to do anything with it. It wasn't physical. Fair enough, the problem manifested itself as a limp dick. And, sure, it helped that she kept her hand cupped round his balls and, with the other hand, shoved a finger up his arse. But his problem was centred in the notion that the sex act itself was going to be painful for her. He was convinced of that. Not that she was special. He imagined it would be painful for any woman. What she coaxed out of him was the idea that he was going to hurt her. The thought had been with him for a couple of years. Having a stiff cock inside you has got be painful. He didn't know where the notion came from. He didn't like to think about it. When they finally fucked, when he finally came, it was a relief. And maybe that was the greatest pleasure of all. He tried to be caring, considerate, always asking her if she was comfortable, if she was wet enough, if he was too heavy, if he was going too fast, too slow, too deep, not deep enough. Surprising, retrospectively, that his regard for her comfort hadn't annoyed the tits off her. Maybe it did, eventually. Something did. Maybe that's why she fucked somebody else.

Pity she wasn't around to ask. Now that it was too late, he wanted to find out. He was ready to cope with her reply, whatever it was.

'Why did you have to fuck somebody else?'

'He was better than you.'

'In bed?'

'And out.'

Or:

'Why did you have to fuck somebody else?'

'I never liked you. You were a project.'

Or, most likely:

'Why did you have to fuck somebody else?'

'I always wanted to fuck somebody else. You were my second choice.'

Well, fuck that. It was over. He had to stop thinking about it.

The car was turning into Cooper's street. 'Black door two along,' Joe said to Ronald Brewer.

The lawyer pulled into the kerb.

'Thanks for the lift,' Joe said.

Ronald turned off the engine.

'You waiting?'

'I'll come in with you if you want.'

'Don't know if that's a good idea.'

'Make sure you don't do something you'll regret, Joe. You're in enough trouble.'

'Jesus Christ,' Joe said. 'I never really knew my mum. But if she was anything like you, I'm fucking glad.'

'I'll wait here for you.'

Joe opened the door and stepped onto the pavement. All this shit bubbling up from the past. Fuck. He didn't need it. He walked along the path towards the block of flats where Cooper lived. Not now. Fuck. Once it started, it didn't bloody stop. His hand was shaking. You turned on the tap and it stuck and the fucking tank emptied. He tried to hold his finger steady on the buzzer.

After a moment, Cooper said, 'That you, Joe?'

Joe felt like he'd spent a week at the bookie's, filling his lungs with second-hand smoke, shouting encouragement for horse after horse, yelling, yelling above the rage of other voices. Calm down. He closed his eyes, rubbed his forehead. Calm. 'No sir, it's your pussy snorkel delivery man.' Not a trace of humour.

After Cooper finished laughing, he buzzed Joe into the building.

It was dark, the air colder than outside. The soles of Joe's shoes scraped against the stone floor. In one of the flats, someone was preparing dinner and the smell of frying sausages mixed with the antiseptic odour of stair cleaner. Maybe with a hint of lemon.

The silver nameplate on Cooper's door was the size of a laptop computer. Joe made a fist, ready to knock. He brought his arm back just as the door opened.

Cooper's head poked through the opening. Stubble peppered his chin. 'The fuck you so miserable about?' he said. 'You're out of jail, eh? Should be dancing like a dog on a hot floor. Look at you. Miserable git.' The door swung open. Unlike the last time Joe had seen him, Cooper was wearing more than just his pants. A lot more, in fact. He rested his baseball bat against the doorframe and zipped up his padded coat.

'Cut the crap, Cooper. I'm not in the mood.'

'If you hadn't hung up I'd have told you not to bother coming round. Good to see you and all that, but I don't have time to chat.' He rubbed his hand over his chin. 'What did they do to you in there? You don't look too great.'

'I'd feel better if I knew what was going on.'

'I don't follow.' Cooper pulled his gloves out of his coat pocket.

'Don't lie to me. Something's going on.'

'You've been caged up, Joe. I don't know what fantasies have been running riot in your brain, but I'll tell you, I'm trying to help. That's all I've been doing. I've only done what's best for you, eh? There's no secret. No fucking conspiracy. You think I'm in direct contact with the CIA or something? Just say the word into my little wrist mike and a black helicopter'll land in the street outside.' He chuckled. 'You been doing drugs in there, Joe?'

'You got Tina to alibi me.'

'Exactly. Cost a lot of money, that did. I don't say you're not worth it, but she isn't cheap.' He slid his fingers into one of the gloves. 'I don't expect any gratitude, you know, but I don't like what I'm hearing.'

'What was wrong with my real alibi?'

'Full of holes, Joe. Hardly an alibi at all. Thought you'd prefer something more substantial, given the evidence stacked against you.' His eyes probed Joe's. 'Want me to explain, you ungrateful bastard?'

'Maybe you better.'

Cooper put on his other glove. 'You're forgetting something about your *real* alibi.' He paused. 'I never saw you leave my flat. I was up early, visiting someone in hospital. I was seen there. I can't lie about it. You could have left any time. What kind of an alibi is that?'

'Sally saw me. Her word's good enough.'

'Better than Tina's?'

'Just as good.'

'You think so?' Cooper nodded. 'Let's say the police believed she was telling the truth. Let's say, for the sake of argument, they believe that the teenage girlfriend of an infamous crook who just happens to be your best friend saw you leave her flat the morning after the killing. Let's take a giant leap and suppose they buy that pile of crap. Okay. Now, this is a big flat. Costs enough to heat, I should know. Anyway, we're in the bedroom at the end. You're in the spare room near the front door.' He stuck his hands in his coat pockets. 'What's to stop you getting up in the middle of the night, leaving the door on the latch, killing Ruth, coming back, getting into bed and getting up after I've left, claiming to Sally that you slept like a log?'

'You'd have heard me.'

'Positive?'

Joe thought about it. He shrugged. It was possible he could have done what Cooper suggested. 'How is Tina's alibi any different?'

'Ah,' Cooper said. 'At Tina's you were in her bed. Very difficult for you to sneak out and beat somebody to death without Tina knowing about it.'

'Not impossible, though.'

'The law's based on the opinions of the reasonable man. Did you know that?' Occasionally, as a result of spending less than a year studying law, Cooper would produce a nugget of legal information and throw it at Joe. Cooper clasped his gloved hands together.

Joe said, 'You want a wig or a round of applause?'

Cooper's hands parted. 'What's your problem, Joe? I'm trying to help you here.'

'I've got a real lawyer waiting outside.'

'A real alibi, now a real lawyer. You prefer his company? Fuck off, then.'

'More friendly advice?'

Cooper pulled back his coat sleeve and showed Joe his watch. He tapped it three times. 'I'm late.' He barged past Joe.

Joe pointed his foot at the baseball bat, still propped against the doorframe. 'Don't you want your bat?'

'Won't need it. Client's a woman. Put it in the bedroom for me, would you?'

Joe nodded. 'What is it you were going to tell me about that reasonable man?'

'Don't know why I'm bothering,' Cooper said, turning. 'It's like this. A reasonable man would think it unlikely you'd have been able to commit a murder without Tina knowing about it. That's all.' He paused. 'I mean, what you going to say when she asks where you've been?'

'Taking a long dump?' Joe said.

Cooper flung his hands in the air. 'You're out of prison and you have a credible alibi. Thanks to me. If you don't appreciate what I've done for you, Joe, then just get out of my face.' He strode down the corridor. 'And shut the fucking door when you leave.'

TWENTY-THREE

This time Joe invited Ronald Brewer to join him. The lawyer was proving to be an excellent chauffeur. Which was convenient, since Joe wasn't going to see his own car for a long time. He'd been told he'd get it back as soon as the scene of crime officers were finished with it. When's that? he'd asked. When they're finished with it, he was told. In case you've forgotten, the twat had added, a dead woman was stuffed in the boot. Not something Joe was likely to forget in a hurry. In fact, every time he looked at the car it was going to trigger that memory. Joe told the dickhead he could keep the fucking car for as long as he liked.

'You want to call her?' Ronald asked.

What kind of question's that, Joe thought.

He must have looked confused. Ronald said, 'You want to call Tina?'

Ah, yes. 'I'd rather surprise her.'

'What if she's, you know, with somebody.'

'Unlikely. She doesn't work from home.'

'Except with you?'

Joe didn't respond.

When they arrived, the main door was open. They climbed the stairs and rang Tina's bell. No answer. Joe tried again. Still no answer. They were on the point of leaving when they heard her voice.

'Who is it?'

'Bob,' Joe said.

'As in Joe?'

Of course, Joe thought. She knew his real name now. 'Yeah,' he said. 'Joe Hope.'

The chain rattled and the door clunked open. Tina's face was extremely pale. Her eyes were heavy-lidded, vulnerable without their usual protective layer of blue mascara. Her lips were thin, the colour of starved earthworms. Without makeup, there was nothing to draw attention from her nose. It was bigger than he remembered. You could poke your thumbs up her nostrils without touching the sides.

'They let you out,' she said.

'Bunch of fools,' he said. 'You okay? You don't look well.'

'It's how I look,' she said. 'Who's your friend?'

'My lawyer, Ronald Brewer.'

Tina opened the door wider. 'What happened to the last one?'

'I'm not with you. Ronald's the only lawyer I've had.'

'We playing games here?' she said. 'You coming in? Draught's blowing right up my crotch.'

She led them into the sitting room and invited them to take a seat.

Joe said, 'Good to see you again.' The room was unnaturally tidy, just as it was last time Joe had visited. Tina's face was slowly gaining a little colour. 'You sure you're okay?' he asked again.

She stared at him. 'What do you want?'

'Tell me about the other lawyer.'

She glanced at Ronald. 'Is it safe?'

'Ronald knows what I know. You can trust him.'

Ronald said, 'Even if I am a lawyer.'

'The other one,' Tina said, 'came here with that wanker, Cooper.'

'Can you describe him?'

'Tall. Slightly shorter than you. Slim. Dark hair. Wearing a dark suit. Polite. Cooper gave me a pile of abuse. Mr Park, on the other hand, was a gentleman.'

'Did you say Park?'

'That was his name.'

'Fuck,' Joe said. What was Cooper doing with Park? It didn't add up. Park was a killer, not a negotiator. Clammy fingers circled the base of Joe's spine. 'How much did he pay you?'

'I haven't been paid yet.'

'You did it for free?'

'We agreed a sum. Cooper's bringing it over later this afternoon.'

'I don't like this.' Ronald Brewer locked his fingers together, pulled them apart. 'Another lawyer?'

'Nothing to worry about,' Joe said. 'The other lawyer's bogus.'

'You sure?'

'I know Mr Park. He's as bogus as you can get.'

Tina said, 'Why did Cooper introduce him as your lawyer?'

'Trying to figure that out myself.'

After a moment, Tina asked, 'How about you, Joe? Are you okay?'

'Fine,' he said, instinctively. He followed Tina's gaze and realised he was hugging his side. 'Habit I picked up in Orkney,' he said, removing his hand and resting it on his knee. 'How much you getting paid?'

'Why should I tell you?'

'Cooper's putting up the money.' Joe looked sideways at Ronald, then back at Tina. 'He's a loan shark. I'll have to pay him back. Just want to make sure I'm not getting ripped off.'

'He's your friend,' Tina pointed out.

'You heard the expression "There's no sentiment in business"? Cooper invented it.'

She said, 'Hope you don't mind me saying so, him being your friend and all, but he's a real piece of scum.'

'Got his good points.'

'Name one.'

Joe puffed his cheeks. He hugged his side again, realised what he was doing and clamped his hand on his knee.

'Never mind.' Tina lowered her head. 'Look, I'm sorry about your wife, Bob. Joe, I mean. I know you couldn't have done it.'

Joe shifted in his seat. 'How's that runaway from Dundee I saw when I was looking for you. She still working?'

'Kylie?' Tina said. 'Up and left one night. Had enough.'

'She go home?'

'Glasgow.'

'Lure of the big city, huh?' Time dragged. Joe clenched his fist. The silence pressed in on him. 'Cooper bringing the money here?'

'That was the plan.'

'When?'

'He's going to phone.'

'How much?'

Tina stepped into the kitchen and picked a packet of cigarettes off the work surface. 'He offered me five grand.' She tapped out a smoke and stuck it between her lips. 'I asked for ten.'

'And he agreed?'

'Didn't take any persuading.' She lit her cigarette.

'Doesn't sound like Cooper.'

'If you're paying him back, maybe it doesn't matter too much. What's the point of haggling when it isn't his money?'

'Matter of principle,' Joe said.

Tina sucked on her cigarette. 'What are you trying to say? You're getting me worried.'

'What would you do,' Joe said, 'if Cooper didn't pay up?'

Tina thought for a moment. 'What could I do? Go to the police. Tell them I lied.'

'And that would just about seal my conviction,' Joe said.

Tina said, 'There's no sentiment in business.'

'Follow that through,' Ronald Brewer said. 'If you went to

the police, you'd get charged with making a false statement. You'd get fined. You'd lose money.'

'Cooper's not fucking me over,' Tina said. 'I'm not a charity.'

'What about Joe?' Ronald asked.

Joe said, 'Hey, leave it.'

Tina took an angry drag of her fag and said, 'Until recently, I didn't even know Joe's name.' She faced Joe, left hand supporting her right elbow. 'No offence, but you're a punter, not my boyfriend.' She glanced at Ronald, back at Joe. 'I don't like lying to the police. Makes me nervous. I don't like Cooper. Your friend makes me nervous, too.' She examined the floor. She dragged the ball of her foot in an arc towards Joe. When she looked up, she couldn't hold his gaze. She smoked, staring at the ceiling, nostrils flaring.

'You regret having made this deal with him?' Joe asked her.

'The bastard had better show up. That's all I care about.'

'I'm not asking you to lie for me,' Joe said. 'Do what you think's right. Anyway,' he said, standing, 'I'm sure Cooper will pay up.'

Ronald followed Joe's lead and got to his feet. The lawyer offered his hand to Tina. 'Nice meeting you. Good luck.'

'You think I'll need it?'

TWENTY-FOUR

When Ronald dropped Joe off at his flat, Joe paused before getting out of the car to tell him he really appreciated his help. Joe invited him in for a cup of coffee, but Ronald declined. Something stronger? Ronald checked his watch and told Joe he was already late.

Joe closed the car door. 'Something I need to know,' he said through the lowered window, jerking his head towards the tenement on the left. 'Did Ruth die in the flat? Not that I'm squeamish or anything.' Home had never looked so unappealing. 'But . . .' No Gem, no Ruth. Nobody to blame but himself. 'I mean, when I was last home, it didn't look like anything had happened. No sign of a struggle or anything. No blood-drenched walls or bits of teeth on the floor. But, for all I know, the murderer might be extremely house-proud. Might have cleaned up afterwards.'

'There's no evidence to suggest it happened in your flat,' Ronald said. 'In fact, the police are pretty sure she was murdered elsewhere. That much blood, it would be pretty obvious, no matter how much the killer tried to cover it up.'

'Good,' Joe said. 'I feel better already.'

As he was about to go, Ronald leaned across and said, 'They searched your stuff while you were inside. They're supposed to make an effort to tidy it up again, but you might find the place a bit of a mess.'

Joe nodded, not caring. A shower, a change of clothes, brush his teeth. He'd feel like a new man. 'Hang on,' he said, opening the back door and retrieving the bag he'd taken to Orkney. It was nice to have it back. It had his toothbrush inside and he never did get to use it.

He climbed the stairs slowly. As he passed the Harveys' flat he thought how, in an ideal world, he would stop for a minute to tell the old couple they were right. Yes, it was him they'd heard arguing with Ruth that night. But, honestly, it wasn't him who'd killed her. They had to believe him. He was telling the truth. And they'd take one look at his eyes and shake his hand and say, yes, they believed him and if he ran out of milk or sugar not to hesitate to pop downstairs and borrow theirs.

Of course, Joe didn't live in an ideal world. In an ideal world his mother would be more than a solitary black and white photograph he kept in a shoebox in the cupboard. Fuck her. She'd pissed off when he was three. Left him to be brought up by his dad. That was hardly a success. Before long Joe was living with his grandmother. Thinking about it, Joe let out an angry yell. The sound echoed in the stairwell. He could spend his life resenting his mother – and his father, come to that – but, the truth was, he was glad his grandmother had brought him up. She encouraged him to read. Took him to the theatre. Dad had done his best. Visited, when he could. Once a fortnight, then once a month, then, after he remarried, only on little Joey's birthday and maybe Christmas if his new family let him. Joe only saw Mum once after she left. She took him to Musselburgh for the day and stuffed him with ice cream. When she brought him home, she pecked him on the forehead and told him she'd see him next week. She didn't. He hated her for it for a long time. She'd promised.

Dad told him she'd gone to Canada to live and she'd write soon. She never wrote. He kept asking when the letter would arrive.

Years later, when he was ten, his grandmother told him the truth. His mother had suffered from aplastic anaemia, a rare blood condition. A couple of days after he last saw her, she'd gone into hospital, knowing she wasn't coming back out. She'd made the family promise not to tell Joe the truth.

See, the women in his life started dying a long time ago.

Shame Dad wasn't still alive. Joe could phone him. Tell him Gem had gone to Canada.

As Joe put his key in the lock, the door opened of its own accord and Joe found himself staring at the familiar face of his uninvited guest. 'The fuck are you doing in my house?'

Detective Sergeant Monkman of the Orkney CID took a step forward. 'Full of the joys of freedom, huh?'

'I asked you a question.'

'Enjoy it while you can.'

'Well?'

'I was tidying up.' Monkman raised his hand, palm towards Joe. 'No, no. I don't expect any gratitude.'

'Go home.'

'I'm going to find something that'll put you away for life. Mark my words.'

'Get out of my house.'

'I'm going to keep looking. You can't kill somebody without leaving traces. Somewhere along the line, you fucked up. I may not know where or how, but you can bet your fucking baseball bat I'm going to find out.'

'Piss off,' Joe told him. 'Now.'

'Think I'll take another quick look round first.'

Joe shoved the policeman. He reeled backwards. Joe followed him through the doorway and, without turning, pushed the door shut with the sole of his shoe. He dropped his bag on the floor. 'Looking for traces of blood?' he said. 'I'm sure I can help you with that.' He smacked his knuckles against his palm.

Monkman said, 'You wouldn't dare.'

'Just you and me.'

'I'm a policeman.'

'I'm a prime murder suspect,' Joe said. 'Pleased to meet you. What's the matter? Don't fancy the odds?'

Monkman tried to smile, lips quivering. 'You won't get away with it.'

'Why not? You did.'

Fists balled, Joe rushed forward. Monkman dropped to his knees, arms thrust protectively in front of him. Joe grabbed the policeman's wrists and yanked his arms to the side. 'If I wanted to,' Joe said, 'I could kick your head into touch.'

Monkman struggled to free his hands. 'Fuck you,' he said, shaking his exposed head, eyes darting from side to side through narrowed lids. His mouth twitched in a series of grotesque grins.

'Scared?' Joe asked him. Fear sends massive quantities of adrenalin surging through your body. A primitive biological response to confrontation. To which even Joe wasn't immune. 'A big bad cop like you?' Joe felt it now. He felt it every time he visited one of Cooper's clients. The trick was to hide it. As Cooper knew only too well. He'd mastered the art and built his reputation on it. The trick was to know that your body, realising you only had two choices, was preparing itself. Run, or fight. Come on, it was saying. Choose. Work with me.

Monkman lowered his head. Hunched his shoulders. He started to shake. Joe observed the tiny nods of the policeman's head. Nowhere to run, and he couldn't fight. Joe dug his fingers deeper into the poor twat's trembling wrists.

'Nothing but a coward.' Joe released his grip and loomed over Monkman for a moment, before stamping his foot on the floor next to the policeman's fingers. Monkman's hand darted to his side. 'Different story when it's a fair fight,' Joe said.

Monkman wrapped his arms around himself. 'I won't fight you.'

Joe laughed. Monkman glared at the floor, still shaking. Joe said, 'I asked you nicely. I'll ask you one more time. Will you get the fuck out of my house?'

In a small voice, Monkman said, 'You'll pay for this, you little wanker.' He started to get to his feet. He lunged forward. His fist shot out.

Joe blocked the punch with his left hand. The knuckles of his right slammed into the point of Monkman's chin. The policeman's head snapped back, striking the wall with a crack that sounded like a small bone snapping. Monkman sagged. His head rolled to the side.

What have I done? Joe thought. What have I fucking done? Expecting to see blood trickling out of the back of Monkman's head if he took a closer look, Joe stayed where he was. He didn't want to know. Didn't want to see the evidence. What with everything else that had happened, murdering a policeman wasn't going to look too fucking good. He stared at Monkman, willing him to wake up. There. He saw the stupid fucker's chest rise. He was breathing. Or was he? Joe kept looking. Nothing. Maybe he had imagined it. Oh, shit. He cupped his hands over his nose. He wanted to hide his eyes, but he carried on watching, hoping he'd see the bastard breathe. Look at the situation rationally, he told himself. Monkman had taken a blow to the back of the head. Nothing to worry about. Happens to dozens of people every day and they don't die.

That's right. Fine.

But some do, don't they?

If he was dead, what was Joe going to do? Get in touch with Cooper. He'd know what to do. And if he didn't, he'd ask Park. Hitmen knew how to handle corpses. Knew how to dispose of dead bodies.

Fuck. Images bubbled and burst in Joe's head. Cooper. A baseball bat. Park. A baseball bat. Ruth's face. Tear-streaked. Hair wild. A baseball bat. Cooper standing perfectly still. Cooper slamming the bat into Ruth's face. Park saying, 'Won't be long.' Politely saying, 'If you could try not to struggle it would be easier.' Cooper and Park lifting her body into the boot of a car. Joe's car. Cooper's voice, explaining how easy it was to sneak out of his flat without waking anyone up. Especially someone as drunk as Joe. Cooper saying he'd walked right past the snoring cunt.

Joe collapsed on the floor beside Monkman. Fuck. Oh, fuck. Cooper went to Tina's with Park. Why involve Park? That had been bothering Joe since the minute Tina mentioned the hitman's name. Moral support? Hardly. Cooper had sufficient confidence in his own ability. He didn't need to drag a mate along. No, the reason he involved Park was that Park was already involved. Had to be. It was the only thing that made sense.

No, none of it made sense. How could it? Cooper was his best mate. He wouldn't kill Ruth. He wouldn't frame Joe. He wouldn't. Would he?

Joe forgot about Monkman and ran into the sitting room. For a moment he thought he'd been burgled. The furniture was all in the wrong place. The settee was a foot out from the wall, chairs at the wrong angle. A couple of cushions lay on the floor. The top of the ugly chest of drawers Ruth was fond of had been swept clean of photographs and ornaments. The mantelpiece was likewise bare.

Then he remembered the police had been here. Fucking thieves.

He picked up the phone and dialled Cooper's flat. He pressed the wrong key. Swore. Hung up. Dialled again. He kept swearing until Sally answered.

'Hang on a minute,' she said. Joe could hear the baby screaming in the background. While she was settling him down, Joe wondered if he should ask her straight out if she remembered Cooper leaving his flat in the middle of the night. The night Ruth died. When Sally came back on, he decided against it. He didn't see how he could phrase the question without arousing her suspicion and then she'd tell Cooper and Joe didn't want Cooper forewarned.

'The man in?' Joe asked, knowing he was out.

'Left soon after you phoned. Thought you were coming round, Joe. I was looking forward to seeing you. How're things?'

'I need a phone number.'

'Can't you give Cooper a bell on his mobile?'

'No good. Doesn't have the number on him.'

'So what can I do?'

'Check his address book for me.'

'He doesn't have an address book. Just a desk drawer full of scribbled bits of paper.'

'Can you have a look?'

'Drawer's locked.'

'Oh, shit.'

'Is it really important?'

'Might make the difference between me going to jail or not.'

'Can you keep a secret?' she said. Before he could reply, she said, 'Of course you can. Well, I know where the key is.'

Joe's ears filled with a buzzing sound. 'Can you have a look?'

'What name?'

'Park.'

'First name?'

'Don't know. Just Park.'

'You at home? I'll phone you back in five or ten minutes.'

Back in the hallway, Monkman hadn't moved. Joe lifted the policeman's head. No sign of a wound. Joe let Monkman's head roll to the side. His mouth had started to bleed. Bright blood slipped through his slightly parted lips. Not enough to suggest the twat had bitten his tongue in half. Still. If he was bleeding, he wasn't dead. Wasn't that right? Shit, Joe wasn't sure.

Jesus, he thought, exploring Monkman's neck for a pulse. Why would Cooper want to kill Ruth? Why? He had no idea. There. He felt it. A gentle throbbing beneath his fingers. He breathed a tiny sigh of relief. The policeman was alive. Maybe Joe could slap him awake and ask his opinion. Maybe not. What he could do, though, was fetch a bucket of water from the kitchen.

All the knives were gone. Not much else had been taken, though. At least, not that he could see. He turned the tap on full. Water battered the stainless steel sink, splashing over the side. Made a hell of a racket. He dug a plastic bucket out from under the sink. As the bucket slowly filled, he tried hard to block out the images of Ruth that kept flashing into his head. He last spoke to her in this room. He saw her face, grey and hard, telling him there was a lot he didn't know. Her face, tight with rage as she launched her mug of tea at him. The cooker was marked still, scuffed white where the mug had hit it. Her face changed to Gemma's. He thumped his fist against the tap. Gemma's face. He hammered the tap again. His dead daughter's face. His hand reached towards his scalp. He grabbed a fistful of hair and pulled, his mouth open wide in a silent scream. After a while, only after his eyes had started to water, he stopped. Scalp burning, he turned off the tap. He walked back to the hallway, his knees balls of string that were slowly unwinding.

He was about to throw the bucket of water over Monkman when the telephone rang. He left the bucket on the floor and returned to the sitting room.

It was Sally. She had the number.

'Hang on,' Joe said. The penholder normally sat next to the phone. He had a look in the chest of drawers. Each drawer was empty. The bastards had completely cleaned him out.

In the hallway, Monkman groaned. His eyes were open. He looked like a baby that had just woken up. With a bemused expression, he watched as Joe stuck a hand in the inside pocket of his jacket and withdrew a ballpoint pen. 'Back in a minute,' Joe said.

Sally read out the number. Joe ransacked his wallet for a scrap of paper. All he had was a couple of photos. One of Ruth, the other of Gemma. He removed the picture of Ruth and wrote the number on the reverse. He read it back. Sally confirmed he'd taken it down correctly and made him promise not to tell Cooper how he'd got it.

'I understand,' Joe said. 'I wouldn't want him knowing I'd been rummaging about in his drawers.' He could hear Sally chuckling as he hung up.

Joe returned to the hallway. Monkman's eyes looked slightly less glazed. Joe picked up the bucket of water and poured it over the policeman's head.

Monkman performed a series of whoops, took a few rapid breaths and said, 'Aaagh.' He shook his head and moaned. Licked his lips. Frowning, he spat blood on the floor.

Joe said, 'Use the bucket,' and propped it on Monkman's lap.

Monkman spat into the bucket. Half a dozen times.

'Thought I might bring some mates round,' Joe said. Monkman glared at him. 'See if anybody else wants a shot.'

'You could charge an entrance fee.' Monkman pulled a face. 'My fucking tongue hurts.'

Joe touched his side. 'Makes us about even, then.'

'You got a towel?'

'If your colleagues haven't nicked them.' Joe went to the bathroom and returned with a clean powder blue hand towel.

'You going to charge me?'

'With what?' Monkman rubbed his scalp with the towel.

'Assaulting a police officer.'

'No point.' Monkman grimaced as he touched a tender spot. 'No witnesses.'

'That's what I thought.'

'Fuck, my head hurts,' Monkman said, wiping his, mouth. 'Fucking tongue hurts.' He spat into the bucket. Joe turned his head in disgust. 'Fucking chin hurts.' Monkman spat again. 'Hope,' he said. 'Can I ask you a question?'

Joe faced him. 'I want you out of here.'

'I don't feel too good.' He placed the bucket on the floor beside him. 'Seriously.' He stared at his shirtfront. 'Bloody soaking,' he muttered. In a louder voice, he said, 'Soon as I can move. That okay with you?'

Joe made a small gesture with his hand. 'Ask your question,' he said.

The policeman hesitated, then said, 'We both know your alibi's fake.' He plucked his wet shirt away from his chest. 'So, since there are no witnesses, why don't you tell me why you killed your wife?'

'Off the record?'

'What, you think I'm wired?' The policeman spread his arms. 'Search me.'

Joe looked at the ceiling. He looked back down again. Monkman's hair was sticking up in the middle. Joe spoke quietly. 'I didn't kill her.' He folded his arms. 'I was framed.'

'Why?' Monkman loosened his tie. 'I don't understand.' He whipped his tie out of his collar. 'Who framed you?'

'Promise I'll tell you as soon as I find out. You feeling better?'

'Getting there.' Monkman stuffed his tie in his pocket. He opened the top button of his shirt. And the next one. 'Get me a glass of water, would you?'

'You know where the kitchen is,' Joe said. 'Get it yourself.'

TWENTY-FIVE

The phone was ringing. Might be important. Joe straightened up and reached over the side of the bath to pick his towel off the floor. Which would have been fine, if he'd remembered not to lean against the side of the bath. It was as if Monkman's boot had driven into his ribcage once again. The blood drained from his face. He held on to his side, taking a series of shallow breaths, sweat making his forehead prickle. After a moment, he braced himself and sucked in a lungful of air. Okay. He exhaled. Another breath. Okay.

The phone was still ringing.

Monkman, the little arsehole, had left after half-an-hour or so, still unsteady on his feet. Joe had called him a taxi. Joe hoped it crashed. He hoped Monkman was an unidentifiable mess in the mangled wreckage.

Slowly, taking care to avoid the side of the bath, Joe reached over and once again tried to pick up his towel. This time he succeeded. He wiped his face. The phone stopped ringing. Joe sighed, wondering whether to drop the towel on the floor and sink back into the water. Close his eyes. Relax. Think nice thoughts. Mind you, he'd already tried that and hadn't been able to think of anything remotely pleasant.

It wasn't that he never had nice thoughts. He wasn't such a bad guy. He was no saint, either, admittedly. Like most people, he was somewhere in the middle. If anybody asked him what he did for a living, he'd tell them. It didn't bother him. If he didn't do it, somebody else would. And if somebody else did it, they'd enjoy it a lot more. It was a job. It paid well. It wasn't hard work. So piss off, you judgemental fuckers. He wasn't a bad guy.

When he tried to think of something pleasant, his thoughts kept returning to Gemma. Gemma as a young kid. Gemma as a toddler. Gemma as a baby. He remembered how he felt when Ruth got pregnant. Christ, was he angry. Like he'd told Tina, he was too young. Too irresponsible. He didn't want a baby, didn't want a job. Didn't want, didn't want. Listen to it. Negative rhythm pounding away in his skull. His hand struck the bath water. Didn't want. Incessant. Well, he fucking had, whether he wanted or not. A baby. A girl. A gem. He had a baby daughter.

At the time Ruth announced her pregnancy, Joe had been thinking of becoming a teacher. Another couple of years, he'd graduate. Then a year of teacher training. Three years more study. No money. A baby to support.

Cooper had given up his law studies to devote himself full time to his lending business. He invited Joe to work for him. Joe accepted. Until he graduated, Joe worked part time for Cooper.

Ruth said, 'I'm going to be so proud of you when you become a teacher. I can't wait.'

Cooper said, 'This teaching shit, how much you going to earn?'

Joe told him.

Cooper laughed. He said, 'You carry on working for me, I'll double that.'

No contest.

The phone rang again. So much for lying down and thinking nice thoughts. Carefully, Joe clambered out of the bath and stood for a minute, dripping. Dabbing himself with the towel, he strode through to the sitting room. He draped the towel over his shoulder and picked up the phone. 'Speak.'

'Joe?' Ronald Brewer's voice said. 'It's not looking good.'

Another problem. Just what Joe needed. 'What's happened?'

'Witnesses. They can place you outside Cooper's flat the night Ruth was murdered. Prove you weren't cosily tucked up in Tina's bed.'

'They reliable?'

'As reliable as Tina. Listen, I'm in the car. On my way over.'

'Who are they?'

'A bunch of football fans were making a racket. Sound familiar? The din caused some irate neighbours to look out their windows. One of them phoned the police.'

'It was dark. No way anybody could identify me.'

'What about the football fans? They get close enough for a good look?'

'You're right,' Joe said. 'If the police trace them—'

'That's the point. Two of them were arrested for urinating in the doorway of Gayfield police station not long after you bumped into them. They admitted to causing a breach of the peace earlier in the evening. The police are on their way to ask them if they remember seeing a man in Cooper's doorway. The police will show them pictures. They're the witnesses, Joe. Think they'll identify you?'

'Doesn't matter. They were drunk.'

'That's your defence?'

'Tina—'

'Tina's a prostitute. It's her word against theirs. And they had four other mates with them. If they all identify you, you're fucked. I told you—'

'What should I do?'

'Get out of the house. Now.'

Joe glanced down at his bare legs. 'Don't think that's a good idea.'

'In a very short while you're going to get arrested.'

'And I'll avoid that by running outside stark naked?'

After a moment, Ronald said, 'Well, get dressed and get fucking serious. Meet me outside in five minutes.'

'What's the point? If I run, it'll just look worse.'

'Can't believe I'm hearing this.' The line crackled. The lawyer's words faded in and out. Something about a frame-up. Something about taking it lying down. Joe chuckled. The lawyer said, 'Well?'

'What am I going to do, Ronald? Fuck off to France?'

'Good idea. You'll need a false passport.'

'I'm not serious. You think I'm going to hide for the rest of my life?'

'Did you kill Ruth, Joe?'

'Piss off.'

'Well it looks like you did. If you want, you can get

GUILTY tattooed on your forehead. Then in prison you can have TWAT tattooed on your buttocks.'

The line went dead.

Joe stared at the phone, wondering how his life had reduced to a single decision: stand and fight like a man, or run. Not much choice, was there? He glanced around him, examining his home. Well, what was left of it. When he'd gone into the bedroom, he'd discovered the police had taken all his clothes. He felt dirty. Even after his bath, he felt dirty. Putting on his old clothes wasn't going to help. The air was stale. He ought to open a window. He couldn't blame the police for messing up his life, though. Assuming his suspicions were correct, the person he really had to blame wouldn't be seen dead in a policeman's uniform. And if he was right? Jesus. He didn't want to think about it. The sensation of a spider crawling across his skin was so vivid he slapped the back of his neck. He looked at his palm. There was nothing there.

Granted, Cooper wasn't the most warm-hearted man in Edinburgh. But Joe had always considered loyalty to be one of his best friend's redeeming features. Loyalty to his family. Loyalty to his friends. Loyalty to Joe. The idea that Cooper was a traitorous bastard was almost as incomprehensible as the news of Gemma's death.

Joe had to run. No matter what it looked like. He had to meet Ronald, maybe even tell him what was going on. What *might* be going on. Joe still had no proof. But he was going to see about getting some.

He dried himself hurriedly and draped the towel over the side of the bath. He pulled on his old clothes, grabbed his coat and ran outside.

The wind chilled the back of his neck where his hair was still damp, but at least the sensation of insects crawling over him had vanished. For a minute back there he'd thought he was wimping out. He jogged to the corner of the street.

Almost immediately the lawyer's car pulled up alongside him.

Joe opened the door and jumped in. 'Where we going?'

'Somewhere nobody'll think to look for you,' Ronald said.

TWENTY-SIX

Ronald Brewer's sitting-room window looked out over the Meadows. Groups of book-laden university students returning from classes intersected a jackets-for-goalposts football match. Kids. Joe couldn't bear to look at them. 'You got a spare set of keys?' he said, stepping away from the window.

'Stay here,' the lawyer said. 'Sit down. Have something to eat.'

'Got to go out sometime. No point postponing the inevitable.'

'I don't think it's wise to go out, Joe. Not at the moment. The police are looking for you.'

'You going to hold me prisoner here, Ronald? You know that's against the law.'

The lawyer approached the fireplace. 'The police will be watching your house. And stay away from your friends. Especially Cooper. The police will have his house under surveillance, too.'

'They don't have the manpower.'

'You're wanted for murder, Joe. Not shoplifting. They'll find the necessary resources.' He dug a bunch of keys out of a plastic jar. 'One with the red cap opens the outside door.'

'Think I'll figure it out,' Joe said. 'You got an alarm?'

'Waste of money. Nothing worth stealing.'

Joe took a quick glance round the room. No TV, no DVD

player, no CD player, no video, no Playstation, no computer. The lawyer was right. Joe nodded at the floor to ceiling bookcase. 'Those must have cost a lot.'

'I can just see your average hood from Craigmillar going out of his way to rip off a pile of legal textbooks.' Ronald strolled over to the settee and sat down.

Joe said, 'You got some Chomsky and Pilger there. Probably get a few bob for them.'

'Not highly coveted, Joe, by the criminal fraternity. Not even signed first editions.'

'Not much in the way of fiction.'

'Some Zola on the bottom shelf. He's about the only novelist I have time for.'

'I read *The Earth* once. Good socialist stuff, if you like that sort of thing.'

'I'd recommend *Nana*,' the lawyer said. 'More your cup of tea, I'd have thought. It's about a prostitute.'

Joe laughed and felt himself relax. 'What do you do in the evenings apart from read?'

'Answer my emails.'

'So you do have something worth stealing. Where do you hide the computer?'

'I don't. I normally work at the office. Get home pretty late. I don't need much here.'

'Answering emails keeps you busy all night?'

'I do a spot of *pro bono* – voluntary work.'

'Who for?'

'A handful of human rights groups. And, more recently, a non-aligned left-wing coalition group. They contact me mainly by email. Sorting out their legal problems keeps me pretty busy.'

'Your firm's happy to let you do that?'

'Yeah. Makes it look as if they care.'

'Well, Ronald. It's good to know somebody gives a shit.'

The lawyer shrugged. 'I have to leave in a minute. Meet a friend of yours. I can't help you if I stay here chatting.'

'Off you go. I'm long past needing a babysitter.'

'Help yourself to tea, coffee, whatever.'

'Don't need a waiter either. Just fuck off, Ronald. I'll put my feet up and watch some TV.'

'I don't have—'

'I know. I noticed.'

'I'm slow. Sorry. I better get going.'

'What friend?' Joe said. ' I didn't know I had any.'

'Adam Wright.'

'What's he doing in Edinburgh?'

'That's what I'm about to find out.'

After Ronald left, Joe waited a few minutes, then located the lawyer's phone (at least he fucking had one) on a table in the hallway. Joe dug out the photo of Ruth and dialled the number he'd written on the back.

A young male voice answered. 'Florida Al's Tanning Studio.'

'Who am I speaking to?'

A slight pause, then the voice said, 'This is Dom.'

'Pleased to meet you, Dom. I'd like to speak to Mr Park.'

Another slight pause, a little longer than the previous one. 'Don't know anyone by that name.'

'I don't believe you, Dom. I'd like to speak to Mr Park.'

The line went dead.

Joe redialled. After half-a-dozen rings Dom answered. This time he just said, 'Hello?'

'Me again.'

'Look,' Dom said, 'I told you. I don't know anybody named Park. Nobody works here with that name.'

'Can I speak to Florida Al?'

Dom laughed.

'I say something funny?'

'There's no Florida Al. It's a made-up name.'

'Hilarious,' Joe said. 'So let me speak to Sunshine Jim, then, or whatever the owner wants to call himself.'

The silence lasted a long time. At last Dom said, 'He's out.'

'Does he have a mobile number?'

'Can't let you have it.'

'When will he be back?'

'Back where?'

'In the studio, Dom. You told me he was out. That suggests that he's been in and will be returning later. I'd like to know when.'

'Not today.'

'Then why don't you give me his number?'

'Can't do that.'

'His name, then. Can you give me that?'

The line went dead again.

Joe tried ringing the number a few more times. Each time it rang out. He yanked the yellow pages from underneath the table the phone sat on. The list of tanning studios was longer than he imagined. He found the address of Florida Al's. It was in Bruntsfield. Ten minutes walk round the corner.

Joe had to get to the tanning studio before it closed for the day. He was hoping he hadn't spooked Dom. Probably shouldn't have called. No, he should have pretended to be a customer and asked for the address. Or just hung up once Dom had answered and done what he ended up doing anyway and getting the address from the Yellow Pages. If only he hadn't smashed his mobile in that fit of rage with Adam, he could have tried phoning again. Maybe Dom would have answered, assuming the anonymous caller would be fed up of pestering him by now.

A pleasant afternoon was turning into a pleasant evening. Low in the sky, the sun burned brightly. Much more of this kind of nonsense and Florida Al's would be out of business. Classes over for the day, the Meadows teemed with students. Hanging around in groups, walking in pairs, in threes, on their own. For a moment, he thought he'd spotted Gemma. But it was just a girl, laughing with her friend, who wore her hair the same way. Same colour, too. They could have passed for sisters. There she was, this student, strolling in the park with not a care in the world while Gemma was dead. Didn't seem right. Joe knew it wasn't the girl's fault, but he still wanted to run across the road and wipe the grin off her face. It seemed disrespectful.

A police car passed, siren screaming. Joe turned his head to follow the sound and bumped into a fat guy carrying a couple of shopping bags. Joe apologised. The fat guy was sweating and said, breathlessly, 'My fault.' The police car disappeared, heading towards town.

Joe followed a footpath that cut through Bruntsfield Links, breathing in the smell of freshly cut grass. Within a few minutes he was standing outside Florida Al's Tanning Studio.

A hand-written sign on the window said, 'New – nipple piercing.' A sign on the door said, 'Open.'

Joe walked in. Behind a bright red reception desk, a couple of tanned young men looked at him, their eyes widening as they watched him flip over the card on the back of the door. One of the men had jet-black hair. The other's was straight and shoulder-length and pink where it wasn't blue. Neither of them looked a day over twenty.

'Closing early today,' Joe said. 'Now which one of you twats is Dom?'

'You're the guy on the phone,' the one with the colourful hair said.

'So you must be Dom.' Joe strode towards the desk.

Dom backed against the wall, bunching a fistful of his garish shirt like a woman whose blouse buttons have all popped. He glanced at his colleague. Dom was the less tanned of the two.

Joe ignored Dom. He said to the other one, 'And you are?'

'Carlos Garcia Gonzalez. And you, senor?'

'You think I could speak to Mr Park, Carlos?'

Carlos started speaking in Spanish. Joe didn't understand a word of it. The closest he'd come to Spain was reading Thomas Kyd's play 'The Spanish Tragedy' at university. Carlos clasped his hands in front of him.

Joe said, 'I don't understand, Carlos.'

'Please, senor, I do not know this man of whom you speak.'

Joe ran his tongue over his teeth. He placed his hand on his forehead and closed his eyes for a second. He breathed deeply and exhaled. 'Okay,' he said. He leaped forward and smacked Dom as hard as he could on the cheek.

Dom's face blanched.

'Mr Park,' Joe said.

Dom shook his head.

'Carlos?' Joe said.

'You want me scared, yes?' Carlos held his hands in front of his face as if he was ready to catch a football. 'Like this?' His voice quaked. 'Please, no. I don't know no Mr Park. Please, senor.' He lowered his hands and smiled. His voice returned to normal. 'Is that what you want?'

'Disappointing,' Joe said. 'I was hoping you'd cooperate. I don't want to hurt Dom for nothing.'

A little colour had returned to Dom's face. At Joe's words he dived round the side of the reception desk and bolted towards the back of the shop. Joe cut him off. Dom kept running. Joe stuck out a foot and tripped him. Don flew for a couple of feet and cried out when he hit the floor. When he pushed himself onto his hands and knees, Joe could see blood dripping from his mouth. Dom turned. The colour had drained from his face again. Any paler and he'd have been dead.

'I really want to get in touch with Mr Park,' Joe said, hovering over Dom. Dom flinched. Joe pulled the young man's hand away from his face and examined the cut. Upper lip. Nasty. Probably put a tooth through it. 'You'll need that stitched,' he said. 'Why don't you just tell me the number? You do phone him, right? Or is it Carlos who gets in touch?'

Dom said nothing. He dabbed his mouth with the back of his hand and stared at the floor.

'Well?' Joe looked up. 'Carlos, are you going to tell me?'

'I don't know no Mr Park, senor.'

Joe cuffed Dom, aiming for the boy's cut lip. Judging from Dom's cry, his aim was perfect. Joe said, 'However scared you are of Mr Park, you really ought to be more scared of me. I'm a complete psychopath. Know what that is, Carlos? Maybe Dom can translate for you. No, tell you what. I'll demonstrate. I'll take Dom through the back and shove him under a sunbed for a while. Got all the time in the world, you know. Couple of hours in there might refresh his memory.'

'No good,' Carlos said. 'He will pass out from the heat and tell you *nada*.'

'Thank you for the advice, Carlos.'

'Is my pleasure. I know, also, the word psychopath. In Spanish we say, *psicópata*. What is your name, senor?'

'Joe Hope.'

'Joe Hope,' Carlos said, watching Dom shake. 'Joe Hope?' He faced Joe, grinning. 'My father was a *psicópata*. One day he tried to run my mother over in his car. She went to the police but they didn't give no shit. She went to a lawyer and he told her it was very bad if she moved out of our home. She moved into the spare room. She kept *tijeras* – scissors – under her pillow.' Carlos lowered his head. 'It didn't help.'

'I'm very sorry about your domestic problems,' Joe said. 'But right now I have other things on my mind. I need to speak to Mr Park about certain domestic issues of my own.'

'My father killed my mother. Then he killed himself. I was lucky he didn't try to kill me.'

'You've had a rough time, Carlos. I know how you feel. I'm very sorry for you.'

'He did this to her.' Carlos positioned his hands as if he held an invisible ball between them. His fingers curled. 'To my mother.'

'He strangled her,' Joe said.

'Strangled. Yes.' Carlos relaxed his fingers and his arms dropped to his sides. 'I was in my bedroom listening to music. I heard nothing. There is a very high bridge in the town where I come from. My father drove to this bridge and stopped in the middle. He climbed onto the wall and jumped into the *precipicio.*' Carlos made a whistling sound as he described his father's descent by drawing a line in the air with his index finger. '*Muerto.*' He tapped his chest twice. '*Huérfano.*'

Dom tried to get to his feet. Joe looked at him and he stayed where he was.

Joe said, 'How did you end up in Edinburgh, Carlos?'

'My girlfriend was a student here. She is no longer my girlfriend. I have a new girlfriend.' Carlos smiled.

'Good for you, son,' Joe said. 'And you've got a job, too.'

'More than a job. Florida Al's is my business.'

'You own this place? Then you know Mr Park.'

'You want to speak to him? I might be able to help.'

Joe looked at Dom and said, 'Get up.'

Dom got to his feet. 'Carlos,' he said. 'You can't let this fucking ape get away with beating me up. Look at my lip.'

'Go to hospital,' Carlos said. 'I will pay you three times.'

'Treble time? For the whole day?'

Carlos nodded. Joe said, 'Want me to come back tomorrow, Dom?'

Dom ignored him. 'I'll get my things and go out the back.'

Carlos waited until they heard the door close. He picked up the phone. 'You are staring at me. It is not polite.'

'Just wondering,' Joe said. 'Why are you helping me? I could be anybody.'

'But you are not anybody. I have heard the name of Joe Hope,' Carlos said. 'You are the man who murdered his wife.'

'I didn't—'

'No matter,' Carlos said. 'You remind me of my father.'

'Your father killed your mother.'

'Aye. *La hija de puta*. I hated the bitch.' Carlos dialled. After a few seconds he raised his thumb and said, 'Mr Park, I am phoning about your appointment at Florida Al's.'

TWENTY-SEVEN

Adam sipped mineral water from his brandy glass and waited for Joe's lawyer to arrive, trying his hardest not to look at the girl in the black mini-skirt. He wondered what Dotty would look like in the same outfit. Pretty damn stunning, he thought.

He picked up his copy of the *Evening News* and read the headline on the front page. A prostitute had been found dead in an industrial estate in the Seafield area of the city. She was fifteen years old. The police had no clues as to her killer.

Adam placed the newspaper on the table and leaned back in his seat. He didn't want to read about death. Especially so young a death. Fifteen. That was nothing. Still a baby, really. He wondered how her parents must be feeling. Like Joe, perhaps. Or maybe not. They didn't have quite as many worries.

Ronald Brewer had contacted Adam about Gemma's funeral arrangements, and they'd got talking. He'd updated Adam on Joe's current situation. Joe was on the run. However, the lawyer believed he was innocent. Brewer was insistent that Joe had been set up. The lawyer seemed a nice young man. Keen. Dedicated. Adam wondered if he could trust him, though. Whose side was he on? Did he want to get Joe back in custody at the expense of justice? Or was it justice? Did Joe kill Ruth?

Adam didn't know the answer to that. Recent events had shown him just how wrong he could be. Maybe Joe did kill his wife, maybe he didn't. But he didn't appear to be guilty of raping Gemma. And if Joe hadn't been responsible for that, then he didn't have the motivation to kill Ruth that Adam had previously attributed to him. But somebody else did. Adam wanted to give Joe the benefit of the doubt. Gemma had loved her father. That ought to count for something.

His eyes wandered to the corner table where the girl with the mini-skirt was drinking with some friends. Her head rolled back as she laughed. It felt as if a small stone was lodged in his throat. Quickly, he averted his gaze. He wondered what Dotty was doing. Pity she'd decided not to join him. She'd stood there in his bedroom staring at her chest, twiddling a button on her cardigan. 'It's not a good idea,' she said without looking up.

Her quietly spoken words were a slap in the face. For a moment, he felt dazed.

Her head bobbed up and down. Her mouth turned down at the sides.

He wanted to stride forward and envelop her in his arms. Instead he said, 'A wise decision.' Pursing his lips, he nodded.

She nodded back at him.

He held out his hand and she took it. They shook. Then he spoiled what could have been a dignified rejection by saying, 'Sure you don't fancy the wee drive to the airport?'

Her eyes turned towards the floor. He felt her gaze on his feet and felt uncomfortable. 'Of course, no, of course you don't. Dotty,' he said, holding Gemma's diary aloft, as eager to change the topic of conversation as he was to get at the truth of Gemma's assault, 'there's a passage in here I'd like you to look at. I need your opinion, if you can bear to read it. It's about Gemma's father. Perhaps. I'm not sure.'

She looked at him with liquid-filled puppy eyes. 'Okay.'

'Might take me a moment to find it. Would you tell me what you think it means?'

Her words were a whisper. 'Thank you.'

He didn't understand why she was thanking him. What did she have to be grateful for? He sighed and began turning the pages. 'There,' he said, after a while. 'There it is.' He held the diary towards her.

She took the book from him. 'Here?' She pointed to the passage.

He was silent while she read. When she finished, she said, 'What do you want to know?'

Adam blinked. He swallowed. He cleared his throat. 'Who she's talking about.'

'Well,' she said, 'Gemma was . . .' She closed her mouth and her chin dimpled. After a moment she said, 'The man refers to himself as Daddy.' She was quiet again. Her hand went to her mouth and she spoke through slightly parted fingers. 'But that doesn't necessarily make him her father. He might be role playing. Getting his kicks from pretending he's her father.'

Adam prised the diary from Dotty's fingers and flicked forward through the book. 'Here,' he said. 'I'll read this to you. Only a couple of sentences, but they don't make sense. She says: *I know I can never tell the truth. I couldn't cope with sending Daddy to prison.*' He pointed to the page he'd just read.

'You're like a child sometimes,' Dotty said.

'For Christ's sake!' Instantly, he wished he hadn't spoken. He'd sounded hostile.

'I meant that in a nice way.' She looked at the floor. 'I like children.'

'Don't know that many,' Adam said. After a second he added, 'But those I've met have been nice enough.'

Dotty shuffled her feet. She raised her head slightly. 'That passage in the diary,' she said. 'Gemma didn't want her father to know what happened because she was scared he'd kill the man who raped her. That's what she means about sending him to prison.'

Adam slowly closed the diary. 'Perfectly obvious.' He nodded his head. 'Now that you've pointed it out.'

Dotty said, 'Can I go now?'

He glanced at her. She was evidently upset. He wished he hadn't reacted badly to being called a child. She hadn't intended any criticism. 'I'm sorry about this, about putting you through all this.' She shook her head and turned her cheek towards him. It took him a moment to accept her unspoken invitation. He placed his hand on her shoulder and she leaned towards him. He held her. She started to shake. He dropped the diary on the floor and wrapped his other arm around her. His neck was wet with her tears.

'I'm sorry if I behaved like a child,' he said.

Dotty didn't reply. They stood like that for a long time. Adam would have stayed like that for a lot longer. But she left. Hurriedly. Darting across the room and out the door.

His flight had left early the next morning. He saw her for five minutes at breakfast and before he knew it he was in Edinburgh and Dotty was hundreds of miles away.

His phone was lying on the table next to his glass of water. He thought about calling her. His eyes swept the bar. The girl in the black mini-skirt was struggling back to her table with a couple of pint glasses, a clear drink in a shot glass and a small bottle of orange. The high heels didn't help. She had good legs. Her calf muscles bunched nicely with each step. Just imagine those tanned thighs are Dotty's. Just imagine them gripping your waist. All of a sudden she stopped. He looked up and realised she was staring at him. He wanted to look away but his eyes were glued to hers. 'You want to get down on your knees and take a closer look?' she said.

'No,' he said, knowing the question was rhetorical but feeling compelled to answer it all the same. 'No,' he repeated.

When she moved away, he realised he should have denied that he was staring at her. He no longer felt like phoning Dotty. He had the sensation that all the eyes in the bar were focussed on him. His face was hot. He gulped down his drink and then dared look up. No one was interested in him. Apart from the boy in the suit gazing at him from the doorway. Looked too young to get served. He started heading this way.

Adam buried his head in his newspaper.

Seconds later he heard a voice say, '*Evening News*. Drinking mineral water out of a brandy glass. You must be Adam Wright.'

Adam lowered his newspaper. Surely not. He was far too young. 'Mr Brewer?'

PART THREE

TWENTY-EIGHT

'Thank you for agreeing to see me, Mr Park.'

The hitman's handshake was firm. 'If you'll excuse me for a second,' he said. 'You'll need some privacy.' He walked over to the window and pulled the curtains. The room darkened. He switched on the table lamp. 'I must ask you to remove your clothes.'

'Mr Park,' Joe said. 'I didn't think I was your type.'

'If you don't remove your clothes, Mr Hope, we have nothing to discuss.'

'Can I ask why you want me to undress?' Was this an exercise in humiliation? Carlos had managed to persuade Park to agree to the meeting and Joe knew he ought to be grateful. But now that he was closeted in a hotel room with the hitman, Joe didn't feel an ounce of gratitude. The weird fucker wanted him to remove his clothes.

'I'd like to know you're not wearing a wire. Or hiding a weapon.'

'You don't trust me?'

'Not in the least.'

'I really don't want to take—'

'Good day, Mr Hope. Don't forget to pay the room bill at reception on your way out.'

Joe shook his head and filled his cheeks with air. He let the air out with an exaggerated puff. He smacked his lips together. They felt crusty. 'Why don't you just search me, Mr Park?'

'Good day.'

A fucking striptease, then, if that's what he wanted. Park sat on the bed, eyeing Joe's every move. Painfully, Joe slipped his jumper over his head. Folded it. Placed it on the room's solitary chair. He did the same with his t-shirt. Then he bent down, ribs protesting, untied his shoelaces, kicked off one shoe, then the other. His socks smelled pretty bad. He hoped Park got a whiff. He removed them and tucked them in his shoes. He undid his trouser belt, the button, then pulled down the zip. He slid his trousers down and stepped out of them. Slowly, he folded his trousers and added them to the pile of clothes in the chair. Wearing only his boxer shorts, he looked at Park.

Park gesticulated with his fingers.

'Come on,' Joe said. 'You seriously think I have a wire down my pants? Maybe you should check up my arse.'

Park looked thoughtful. Then he said, 'I don't think that'll be necessary.'

Joe turned his back and tugged his boxers off. 'Okay?' He heard Park get to his feet. He could sense the bastard behind him. For a second, he imagined Park really was going to bend him over so he could inspect his backside. But he didn't. Park disappeared into the adjoining bathroom with Joe's clothes and re-emerged, minus the clothes but with a hotel bathrobe, which he handed to Joe. Joe offered Park his boxers in return. Park shook his head. Joe looked around and dropped his underwear on the chair. He shrugged into the robe and turned to face the hitman.

'I can't tell you anything, Mr Hope,' Park said. 'You do know that, don't you? I know you're aware of the nature of my professional activities as an expurgator through our mutual acquaintance Mr Cooper. I'm sure you understand that I can't discuss that. If you came here for information, you're wasting your time.'

'Why did you agree to see me?'

'You know the score. And your, what shall we call it, *situation* intrigues me.'

'I don't want information.' Joe toyed with the belt on his robe. Park wasn't as clever as he thought he was. Joe could yank the belt out of the robe and strangle him with it. Easy.

Park said, 'What, then?'

Joe sighed and tied the belt on his robe. The robe smelled fresh.

'I'll give it to you straight, Mr Park. Maybe you should sit down.'

Park sat on the bed. 'Ah,' he said, as if in sudden pain. He opened his jacket and Joe saw a gun tucked down the front of his trousers. Park eased it out and laid it on the bed beside him. Just as well Joe hadn't decided to strangle him.

There was nowhere for Joe to sit but he felt awkward standing. After a moment's hesitation he sat on top of his boxers. He crossed his legs at the ankles. 'I want to offer you a job.' Park said nothing. Joe waited a while and then said, 'I want you to kill the person who murdered my wife.'

Park started to laugh.

Joe let him carry on, for a while. 'Well?'

'You get a blow on the head as well as in the ribs?'

'I'm serious.'

Park tapped his fingers against his forehead. 'So, perhaps you should tell me who that is.'

'You know.'

'I'm afraid you're mistaken, Mr Hope. Perhaps you should leave.'

'You were there.'

Park picked up the gun. 'Grief does strange things to a person. You're not thinking clearly.'

'You don't want the money? I thought you were a professional.'

Park made a clicking noise with his tongue. 'As you say, Mr Hope. I am a professional.' He lowered the gun. Kept his hand on it.

'So? Will you do it?'

'Explain something to me, Mr Hope. If you believe I was in some way involved in your wife's demise, why don't you want to kill me?'

'Did I give that impression?'

Joe's heart was beating furiously beneath his bathrobe.

'So what's this charade about?' Park said.

'You're a pawn. You're insignificant.'

'I am? Tell me who I have to kill.'

'Why?'

'Fundamental part of the operation, knowing who the target is.'

'You already know.'

Park laughed again. 'Mr Hope, why don't you get in touch with me again when you are aware of the facts? It'll make the job a lot easier when I know who you want me to kill.'

'If I do,' Joe said, 'will you do it?'

'Can you pay?'

'I just inherited a bundle.'

'Which you won't get if you're found guilty of your wife's murder.'

'True. If I can't prove I'm innocent I won't get the money and I won't be able to hire you so you won't get any money either. What are we talking here, Mr Park? Fifty grand? A hundred?'

'The second figure's closer.'

'Think about it,' Joe said. 'Can I get dressed now?'

Park stood and stuffed the gun back in his waistband. He went into the bathroom and returned with Joe's clothes. 'If you discover the killer's identity, be sure to let me know.'

Joe put on his boxers. He took off the robe and let it fall on the floor. 'What about you? The prospect of a hundred grand might jog your memory.'

'There's nothing to jog.'

'Just in case, I'll give you my lawyer's phone number. You got a pen? I might be hard to get hold of for the next little while.'

'No need for a pen,' Park said. 'Just tell me the number. My memory's flawless.'

TWENTY-NINE

The girl in the black mini-skirt gave Adam a hard stare as she left the pub. He breathed a sigh of relief.

'Give the diary to me.' The lawyer drank a mouthful of coffee. 'I'll make sure he gets it.' His coffee had arrived in a glass with a handle, looking like vanilla and chocolate ice cream. Even had a long spoon like the Knickerbocker Glories Adam used to love as a kid.

Adam said, 'It's for Joe's eyes only.'

'What's so special about it?'

Adam swilled what remained of the water in his brandy glass. The fizz had all but disappeared. 'That's personal.'

'Mr Wright, I'm aware of the incident at your establishment in Orkney. Are you still angry at Mr Hope? Is this about revenge? You still think he killed Ruth? Is that the real reason you want to see him?'

'Here.' Adam pulled Gemma's diary out of his coat pocket and opened the book at the first page. 'I'm not making this up.'

He showed the lawyer her name. Then he flicked through the rest of the book. 'These are Gemma Hope's last words.'

The lawyer was quiet for a moment, stirring his coffee. The spoon clicked against the sides of the glass. 'Do the police know about this diary?'

Adam shook his head very slightly.

The lawyer tapped the spoon once on the lip of his glass and laid the spoon on the table. 'Why not?'

'Perhaps I should leave.'

Brewer grabbed his wrist. The boy's slender fingers had a tight grip. 'Just a question, Mr Wright. Nothing more. Your information is confidential, I promise you.'

'You know where Joe is?'

'I already told you. He's on the run.' The lawyer's hand slid off Adam's wrist and attached itself once more to his coffee glass. He played with the glass, turning it to the left, and back again. He picked up the spoon. Turned it over. A drop of clay-coloured coffee landed on the table. He smeared it across the surface with his finger.

Adam said, 'Can I meet him?'

'Why ask me?'

'Why are you protecting him, Brewer?'

'Why do you say that?' The lawyer twirled the spoon, then passed it from his right hand to his left.

'Because you're lying. Your eyes are darting all over the place. And look at your hand, fidgeting with your cup, your glass I mean, playing with that spoon as if it was some fancy new toy. And now you're licking your lips as if they were covered in cream. How on earth have you managed to fool the police?'

Brewer's gaze fell. He placed the spoon back on the table. 'I haven't spoken to them.'

'When you do,' Adam said, 'you'll need to give a much better performance.'

'Give me the diary,' Brewer said. 'I promise Joe will get it.'

'Either I deliver it in person,' Adam said, 'or I keep it and Joe never gets to see it.'

'Why are you so protective of it, Mr Wright?'

'Gemma's final words.'

'That's it? Nothing else?'

'Are you thirsty, Mr Brewer? Another coffee? A latte, is it? I'm parched. The heat in here is oppressive. I live in an old building, you know, and it doesn't get hot too often in Orkney.'

'It's not hot.'

'Close. Sticky.'

Brewer's eyes scanned the room. He looked into the distance for a second, then switched his gaze back to Adam. 'I take it the diary contains something you don't want the police to see. I'm not the police, Mr Wright. Tell me what it is.'

'Gemma entrusted the diary to me before she died. I intend giving it to her father as she instructed and I'd appreciate your help in that matter.'

'Give me the diary and I'll deliver it.'

'I told you, no.'

'Something happened to her that her father doesn't know about?'

'Stop fishing, Mr Brewer.'

The lawyer started fiddling with his glass again. 'I can't help you, then.'

Adam laughed. 'Of course you can.' He lowered his voice and leaned forward. 'You're harbouring a criminal. Why are you doing that?'

Brewer's young face suddenly looked ten years older. 'If you don't mind me speaking frankly, you're talking shit,' he said. 'You have no justification for that statement. None at all.'

'Okay,' Adam said. 'But let's suppose I'm right.'

'You're not.'

'Hypothetically speaking. Just pretend for a minute. Humour me.'

The lawyer moved his glass to the side and clasped his hands on the table.

'I'm interested,' Adam continued, 'in what would make a lawyer such as yourself protect a fugitive like Joe. Did he offer you a large sum of money to keep him out of jail?' Adam paused, then answered his own question. 'I don't think so. You couldn't be bought, could you, Mr Brewer? You're young. Idealistic. Aren't you? But what about justice, I wonder? You must respect the judicial system. You're a lawyer, after all.'

The pub was rapidly filling up with after-work drinkers. Above the rising drone of their voices, the lawyer said, 'At university we had to study jurisprudence. One of the essays I had to write was on whether an unjust law was law. What do you think of that, Mr Wright? How would you answer?'

Adam thought for a moment. 'Literally,' he said, 'it is. It's a law. It may be one that's unjust, but it's nevertheless a law.'

'Indeed. And you know what that taught me? The law has nothing whatsoever to do with justice. You're right. I am an idealist. I do believe in justice. But that doesn't make me believe necessarily in the judicial system.'

'Is Joe innocent of the murder of his wife?'

'I believe so.'

'He was framed, then?'

'That would appear to be the logical assumption.'

'Who framed him?'

'I wish I knew.' Brewer got to his feet.

'I'm coming with you.'

'You can't.'

'You think Joe will understand that you were only protecting his best interests when he finds out about the diary?'

'You're an unacceptable risk.'

'Is that what I am?' Adam chuckled. 'Look at me. I'm overweight and unhealthy. Joe could snap me in half with a flick of his wrist. Jesus, Mr Brewer, *you* could snap me in half with a flick of your wrist.'

The lawyer sat down again. 'What happened in Orkney, is that forgotten? How do I know you don't have a gun tucked in your trousers or a knife up your sleeve?'

Adam tossed the diary onto the table. 'A token of my trust,' he said. 'Read it. Take as long as you like. Decide for yourself if it's genuine, Mr Brewer.'

Brewer reached out a hand.

'But you can't deliver it,' Adam said.

'Why?'

'You don't trust me. Why on earth would I trust you?'

Brewer started to read. Before long, Adam found himself thinking about the girl in the mini-skirt and his face flushed until sweat bubbled on his forehead. He picked up his newspaper and pretended to read, watching Brewer out of the corner of his eye. Gradually, Adam's face cooled and he relaxed a little. He wiped his brow with the index finger of his left hand. Ran his wrist from eyebrow to eyebrow. When he glanced at the lawyer once again, he learned nothing. Brewer's face was expressionless. He was flicking the pages over quickly, faster than he could possibly read them.

Adam said, 'You believe me?'

The lawyer looked up, tongue poking through his teeth. After a while, his tongue retreated into his mouth and he said, 'I wouldn't know.' He closed the diary and handed it to Adam. 'But you've told me a good story. And you have some kind of evidence to back it up. I don't think you're a threat.' He stood. 'So let's go.'

They left the pub, walking some distance before they reached Brewer's car. Brewer unlocked it and Adam climbed in. Brewer was quiet and Adam didn't want to disturb him. Adam thought about Dotty, kept seeing that girl in the mini-skirt. In a couple of minutes, Brewer pulled up outside a tenement block and told him to wait.

Adam watched the lawyer cross the road and disappear into the nearest building. Adam gazed ahead. A couple of fields. In Orkney that's all they'd be. Just a couple of fields. Mind you, somebody'd probably plough them before too long. Here, they masqueraded as a park. Traffic trundled along the main road bordering the near side. A couple of youths crossed the road, zigzagging through the traffic, holding beer cans aloft like stop signs.

The car door opened and Brewer got back in. 'Joe's not here.'

'You expect me to believe that?'

The lawyer faced him, eyes narrowed. 'Believe what you like.'

'That's it, then, is it? Shall I just get out? Catch a bus to the airport?'

'I don't know where he is.'

'We can wait, if you think he might come back.'

'I couldn't say.'

Adam placed his hands on the dashboard. 'Don't you have any idea? Who does he know? Who would he go to see?'

Brewer's forehead creased. He turned on the engine. 'Why doesn't he have a mobile like any normal person?'

Adam didn't say anything.

Joe's friend, Cooper, wasn't at home. Brewer said, 'There's only one other possibility I can think of.'

They drove in silence. After a while, Brewer said, 'How did you know I was helping Joe?'

'I couldn't think of any other reason you'd be so nervous.

You're his lawyer. You believe he's been framed. It made sense.'

The lawyer bit his lip.

He was biting his lip twenty minutes later when Adam noticed the traffic had thinned. 'Where are we?'

'Leith.'

The sun had disappeared behind a bank of clouds. The Firth of Forth was grey and flat and dotted with dark islands. When they turned left, a wall obscured their view. A couple of seagulls scrapped loudly on the pavement, wings flapping as they danced around a few chips a young lad in a Hibs jersey had just spilled. The car turned left again and Brewer pulled in to the kerb. Hardly anyone about. Just a couple walking past holding hands and a short, burly man, wrapped in a fawn-coloured padded jacket with a red design on the front, crossing the road.

Adam swivelled in his seat and reached for the door handle.

'Hang on.' Brewer's face was frozen.

'What?'

'Guy getting into that car over there.' The lawyer said no more, eyes staring straight ahead.

'What, for goodness sake?'

'It's Cooper.'

Adam studied the squat figure he'd observed crossing the road. 'What's he doing here?'

'Shit,' the lawyer said. 'You see that?'

'See what?' Cooper drove off. Adam turned, watched the tail-lights disappear. Brewer was out of his seat in a flash.

'What's the hurry?' Adam shouted through the open door, feeling his bulk as he raised himself out of his seat. 'What did I miss?'

'His coat,' Brewer said. 'There was a stain down the front.'

'So he's a scruff. What's the big deal?'

'Looked like he spilled a carton of cranberry juice.'

Adam slammed the car door shut. 'Right behind you.'

THIRTY

Joe was thinking about Monkman. No doubt the bastard would be delighted with the recent turn of events. Probably reinstalled himself in Joe's house by now. At this moment, he'd have his feet up watching Joe's TV, drinking a glass of Joe's whisky. Well, he was welcome to the damn house. He could squat there as long as he wanted, because Joe couldn't go home. Even if Monkman wasn't there, the police would be watching the flat.

Things didn't look too good for Joe. A policeman was living in his home. He had no car. His daughter was dead. And he was wanted for his wife's murder. He'd love to go round to Cooper's and joke about it with him. But (and this was something Joe still couldn't get his head round), it looked increasingly likely that Cooper was the person who had set him up.

Joe kept looking for flaws in his logic. Well, it wasn't logic. It was guesswork. Conjecture, supported by circumstantial evidence. Park hadn't given anything away. Joe still had no real proof. He ought to go to Cooper's and batter the truth out of him. Problem was, if Ronald was right about the surveillance, the police would nab him as soon as he poked his head down Cooper's street. Then he'd be screwed.

But what if he was wrong? What if Cooper hadn't set him up? What if his friend had acted for the reasons he'd stated and somebody else had killed Ruth with Joe's bat and stuffed her in the boot of his car? Guilt gnawed at Joe's stomach. It was good to have something else now the pain that had been nagging away at his side had dulled. Who else could it have been, though? That image flashed back into Joe's mind. A snapshot of Cooper whacking Ruth with the baseball bat. So easily envisaged. Jesus, there weren't too many people who could have beaten a woman to death. Cooper was more likely and more capable than most. Joe wanted it not to be true, but, deny it all he wanted, Cooper looked guilty as hell.

When Joe was talking to Park, he'd wanted to come right out and ask him. But questioning a hitman was a sensitive matter and, ultimately, Joe knew it would do no good. Park wouldn't answer. And if Joe pushed it, Park would invite him to leave. Maybe even try to kill him. Joe had done what he could. He was almost certain Cooper was guilty. About ninety percent certain. Which wasn't certain at all. But it was enough to make the odds sufficiently small not to bother betting on. Cooper couldn't have done it. Could he? However convoluted, there had to be another explanation. There had to be.

Joe looked up, realising he'd walked all the way back to Ronald's flat. He fumbled in his pocket for the keys the lawyer had given him. Instinct had roped him back in to safety. It was good to know that his sense of self-preservation was still intact. Ronald was right. He'd never make it to Cooper's. But damn it, he thought, how was he ever going to find out the truth?

Joe shoved the keys back in his pocket and turned around. He sat on the doorstep. After a while he got up again. He unlocked the door and climbed the stairs. He headed straight for the phone.

Sally answered. 'Cooper's still out.'

Joe hung up and dialled Cooper's mobile. He didn't answer and Joe didn't bother leaving a message.

THIRTY-ONE

The girl answered the door with a cloth held over her face. The cloth looked like it had been used to mop up a spillage of red wine. Only the edges of the cloth retained the white of its original colour.

Her eyes latched onto Adam's. His mouth twitched in the beginnings of a smile, but when her gaze switched to the lawyer, Adam let his smile collapse. Her voice was nasal. 'What do you want?'

'You okay, Tina?' the lawyer asked.

'What does it look like?' She turned, leaving the door open. Brewer waited a moment, then followed her into the flat. Adam stepped inside, turned to glance down the empty corridor and closed the door after him.

In the sitting room the lawyer said, 'Did Cooper do that?'

'How do you know?'

'Saw him getting into his car.'

'Was he walking funny? I got him a pretty good kick in the balls.' She moved the cloth away from her face. Dried blood clung to the rim of one puffed nostril. 'I was about to give him another when he nutted me. Can't believe I walked right into it. You ever been headbutted?'

Brewer shook his head. She looked at Adam. He also shook his head.

'I don't believe we've met.' She held out the hand that wasn't holding the cloth. Her fingers were cold and trembled in his grasp. For all her bravado, he suspected she was badly shaken up.

'You sure you're okay?' he asked her.

'I'm used to getting knocked about. This' – she touched her nose, tenderly – 'is nothing.'

'I wouldn't say that. Could be broken.'

'Wouldn't be the first time.'

'You should get it looked at.' He was still holding her hand.

'What happened?' Brewer said.

'Still don't know your friend's name,' Tina said to the lawyer while continuing to stare at Adam.

Adam told her his name. 'I'm Joe's wife's cousin,' he added. Her fingers dragged away and his hand hung in mid-air for a second before he let it fall to his side.

'What happened?' Brewer repeated.

'Sit down,' she said. 'Got to wring this cloth out again.' She marched into the adjoining kitchen and turned on the tap.

Adam followed the lawyer. Brewer sat down on the settee and Adam sat next to him. Tina's flat was as pristine as a showroom. Maybe she was selling it. Keeping it tidy for prospective buyers. Adam scanned the carpet. Not a trace of blood. How the hell had she managed that? Bust nose, Cooper's shirt apparently covered in gore, but no sign of any here. 'Nice flat,' he said. 'Very tidy.'

'I don't really live here,' Tina said. 'I mean, I do – what I mean is I spend most of the time in my bedroom. You should see the state of that!'

Adam perched on the edge of his seat. Leaning back, he felt, might damage the cushions. He was about to ask Tina if she would explain why there wasn't any blood on the floor when Brewer said, 'You sure you don't want to go to the hospital? Got the car outside. No problem giving you a lift.'

Tina stepped back into the sitting room, holding the newly rinsed cloth in her hand. 'I'm okay,' she said. 'Really. Where's Joe?'

Brewer looked at Adam. Adam stared back at him. 'We don't know,' the lawyer said. 'We hoped he'd be here.' An awkward silence descended, during which Tina dabbed her nose with the cloth and Brewer flicked imaginary fluff off his trousers. 'Thing is, Joe's sort of disappeared,' he said at last. 'The police are looking for him. We need to find him. He's in a lot of trouble.'

'So I hear.' Tina opened the cloth, inspected it, folded it again. 'I don't understand, though. I thought he was off the hook.'

Brewer explained about the football fans who'd seen Joe at Cooper's flat. 'When he was supposed to be with you,' he told her.

'I hoped it wasn't true,' she said. 'Bugger. The police must know I lied. So now I'm in the shit along with Joe.'

'I imagine they had their suspicions anyway,' the lawyer said.

'No wonder Cooper refused to pay me.'

'Cooper doesn't know about any of this.'

Her eyes bored into Brewer's. 'He does.'

Brewer held her gaze. 'If he refused to pay you, it must be for some other reason.'

'He told me he wasn't going to part with any cash on account of the new witnesses. He told me what you just told me. I said I'd retract my statement. He told me to go ahead. See if he cared. He said Joe was well fucked. Past our help. I got the impression Cooper had come here to gloat. I offered him a cup of coffee. I was going to throw it at him. I think he knew, but he played along for a while. Came into the kitchen. I felt him creeping up behind me. I didn't wait for the water to boil. Just turned on my heel and kicked him in the balls.' She demonstrated, swivelling, her right foot shooting out in front of her with sufficient speed to make Adam flinch in his seat. 'Wiped that smug grin off his face.'

'But how would Cooper know about the witnesses?' the lawyer said.

Tina said, 'I couldn't say.'

'I don't know Mr Cooper,' Adam said. 'But I get the distinct impression that he's no friend of Joe's.'

Brewer said, 'No question, somebody set Joe up. It would have to be somebody close, somebody who knew Joe pretty well. Could be Cooper. I mean, there aren't too many candidates.'

And it was somebody close to the family who'd raped Gemma.

'I could have done it,' Tina said. 'Jealous prostitute thing, you know? Sick of hearing Joe prattle on about his wife.'

'Does that really happen?' Adam said.

She ignored him. 'And I'm pretty mean with a baseball bat.'

'Are you?' the lawyer said. 'Look what Cooper just did to you.'

'Get me a baseball bat. I'll show you.'

Adam looked at her.

'You fancy some?' she asked him. 'Want to try me?'

Adam grinned. 'I'm sure you'd win.'

'Cooper caught me unawares,' Tina said. 'You'd think I'd know better. Anyway, I doubt Joe's wife would have been as tough a proposition as Cooper.'

'Let's say you're right.' Brewer stood up and faced Tina. 'You're now a murder suspect. Would you consider going to the police? Voluntarily?'

'I've had more than enough contact with them.'

'One way or another you're about to have more.'

'I'll wait, thanks.'

'Even if going to see them got you off the hook for your false statement? And cleared you as a suspect?' He paused. 'And if it helped put away the man who did that to your nose?'

Tina threw the cloth into the kitchen. It landed with a smack in the centre of the sink. 'What did you have in mind?'

THIRTY-TWO

It occurred to Joe that although he might not be able to reach Cooper, his lawyer wouldn't have the same problem. Ronald wasn't on the run and the police weren't going to arrest him if he appeared at Cooper's flat. And if Cooper wasn't at home, Ronald could wait at his flat until he turned up and nobody would bat an eyelid. Getting his lawyer to beat the truth out of Cooper might be a shade more difficult, but at least Ronald would be able to arrange a safe meeting place with Cooper where Joe could do the physical work himself.

Joe picked up the phone and called Ronald. He sounded flustered when he answered. 'Problem?' Joe said.

'We were just talking about you. Where are you?'

'In your flat. Taking it easy. Just like you suggested.'

'I called earlier. Where were you?'

'Popped out for a chat with my new best friend, DS Monkman.'

'I hope you're taking the piss, Joe. Look, we need to see you. We have things to discuss. Stay there, please. We'll be right over.'

'We?' Joe said, but Ronald had hung up. Joe considered calling him back, but decided not to bother. He'd see him soon enough. Along with whoever he was bringing along. Cooper, maybe? Joe felt a nervousness flutter in his stomach and spread towards his groin. Not knowing the truth was eating him up. He hoped the lawyer was bringing Cooper. He formed a fist with his right hand and smacked it into the open palm of his left. After a while he became aware of a low, rumbling sound. His eyes were wet at the corners. He let out a long breath. The rumbling sound stopped and he realised it had been coming from his chest.

A cigarette. What he'd give for a cigarette right now. Not to smoke it. Just to light it and hold it between his fingers and watch it burn down.

Some comfort.

That sound again. He gasped.

What he really wanted was to talk to Gemma. Find out how she was doing up in Orkney. Maybe he could ask her why she'd left. Something happened that had forced her to leave. Or so Ruth had said. Something Gem hadn't been able to talk about. And Joe had no reason to suppose Ruth was wrong. Why hadn't Gem said anything? He hated the idea of his daughter suffering. More than anything in the world. Well, one thing was certain. She would never suffer again.

He should ring Adam. Joe had the number somewhere. Shit, it was at home. Not a problem, though. He could get it from directory enquiries. Then he remembered that Adam was in Edinburgh and his landline number wouldn't be of much use. Ronald had left for a meeting with him, though. If anyone knew how to get in touch with him, it was Ronald.

Joe called his lawyer again, but Ronald's mobile was switched off. Joe would just have to wait.

They arrived fifteen minutes later. The lawyer and Tina and Adam. Tina had taken a thump on the nose. The swelling made her nostrils even larger. It was strange seeing her in company. Joe couldn't remember that ever happening before. He nodded to her and she nodded back. Adam looked troubled, clutching a book to his chest.

'Adam,' Joe said, 'I didn't kill Ruth,' hoping those few words would help put him at ease.

'Mr Brewer explained,' Adam said. 'I'd like to believe you.'

Ronald said, 'Mr Wright has something of Gemma's he wants you to have, Joe.'

Joe put his hand to his mouth. His fingers pressed against his lips. Adam stepped forward and detached the book from his chest.

'This will tell you what you want to know.' Adam held the bottom edge of the book with both hands. 'Gem entrusted it to me,' he said. 'She didn't want it to fall into the hands of the police. It's her diary. What's in here is very private. Something happened to her, Joe—'

'You know about that?'

'I took the liberty of turning down the corners of the relevant pages.'

'It's in there? What happened to her? Why she left?'

'Read it,' Adam said.

Joe reached out, accepting the diary. He opened the book and saw her name written in red ink. He rubbed his thumb over it.

Adam said, 'Maybe we should leave you alone.'

'Let's go through to the kitchen,' Ronald said. 'I'll make coffee.'

'Adam,' Joe said to the retreating figure of his wife's cousin. 'What I said about Ruth. It's true. Whatever you might think.'

Tina placed her hand on Joe's shoulder as she passed.

THIRTY-THREE

The sitting room door was slightly ajar. The rise and fall of animated voices carried from the kitchen, although Joe couldn't make out any of the words. He looked at the passage he'd just read, and read it again. When he finished, he read it again. He placed the book on the cushion next to him and closed his eyes. When he opened his eyes, he picked up the diary and read the passage once more. It still made no sense, so he read it again.

He read it until he knew it by heart.

He flicked forward to the second passage Adam had marked. He read each sentence a dozen times before advancing to the next. The words made no sense. What they said, what he read into them, was overwhelming. He started with the first sentence again. Moved on to the next. *Just a rape, I tell myself.*

His brain rejected the concept. He couldn't imagine Gemma being hurt like that. He moved further down the page, across to the next page. Gemma was reminiscing about that time he took her up Calton Hill to see a meteor shower. An insignificant event in his own life. Who'd have expected she'd . . . Joe's shoulders started to shake.

He moved on to the next passage. After a while he closed the diary. He was still shaking.

Maybe the whole thing was an elaborate hoax. Someone else had written the diary. Maybe Gemma had made it all up. It was a bad joke.

He knew it wasn't. No matter how hard he tried to deny it, he knew this had to be dealt with. He swallowed, picked up the diary and opened it again. His mouth was dry as paper. He forced himself to read through the marked passages once more. He tried to understand it. Gemma's words did not state that Cooper had raped her. No, not exactly. More of an indication. Someone had raped her, of that there was no doubt. Someone close to her. Someone who referred to himself as Daddy. Someone who called her Gem. Someone she suspected Joe would kill if she told him who it was. Someone in a position of trust. A man who was capable of doing a thing like that was certainly capable of murdering Ruth. But Cooper wasn't mentioned by name. Still, Joe knew it was him. No more proof than he had before, but the weight of circumstantial evidence was crushing. Only a fool would doubt Cooper's guilt now. And Joe was nobody's fool.

He closed the diary and pressed it to his chest.

Joe didn't know where to take this. Killing Cooper with his bare hands might have been satisfactory if Cooper's only involvement had been to kill Ruth and frame Joe for the murder. But if Cooper had forced himself on Gemma, Joe couldn't begin to imagine the pain he'd have to inflict on the scumbag for justice to be done. Death was far too lenient.

Joe couldn't understand why he wasn't angrier.

Bile rose in his throat. He stood up and spewed all over the carpet. He doubled up. Folded to his knees. Puked once more. His guts hurt. His damaged ribs were throbbing again. He stayed on his knees, resting his head on the arm of the settee. His head was hot. Thumbs pressed into his eyes. His stomach lurched again. He made a retching sound. He shuddered. His nose was running. His stomach cramped. Nothing left. He wanted to throw up. His pores had opened and sweat coated his skin. His stomach was empty. He retched, croaking like a frog. A moment later, he croaked again.

When he raised his head, Adam was looking down at him. He offered Joe a glass of water.

The diary was still clutched to Joe's chest. He gripped it so hard his fingers hurt. Then he laid it on the settee and accepted the glass from Adam. Joe poured the water down his throat. The cold water salved the tenderness in his gut and diluted the rancid taste in his mouth.

'More?' Adam asked.

Joe wiped his brow. He cradled his head in his hands. When he looked up again, Adam had gone. Joe breathed jerkily. He'd made a mess of the lawyer's carpet. Ronald wasn't going to be too happy.

Adam returned with another glass of water. Ronald and Tina came with him.

'Sorry about that,' Joe said, indicating the puke on the carpet.

Ronald disappeared into the kitchen, saying nothing. After a moment, Joe heard the sound of running water.

Adam said, 'Was it Cooper?'

'Why do you say that? You don't even know him.'

Tina said, 'You want to talk about it, Joe?'

Joe looked at her and shook his head. He couldn't hold her gaze. Her nose was puffy and shiny and comical and yet not at all funny. He wiped his mouth. 'What's it to you?'

Adam said, 'We're all concerned.'

Joe told him to piss off.

'If that's what you want.' Adam walked towards the door. 'Good luck,' he said. 'See you at the funeral.'

Joe looked across the room at him.

'Day after tomorrow,' Adam said. 'Brewer has the details.'

Joe wasn't sure which funeral Adam was referring to. He said, 'Gemma's?'

Adam said, 'Your lawyer has the details.'

'I asked you if you're talking about my daughter's funeral.'

Adam nodded.

'Here? In Edinburgh?'

Adam nodded again.

'And Ruth?'

Ronald returned from the kitchen, wearing a pair of rubber gloves and carrying an orange basin. 'That's been delayed,' he said. 'They still need the body.'

Adam stood in the doorway, hand on the doorknob, shoulders hunched. His eyes were focussed on Ronald's attempts to mop up Joe's sick. 'You didn't do it, did you, Joe? You didn't kill Ruth?'

Joe knew he should be grateful to Adam for bringing Gem's diary. The guy had travelled several hundred miles to hand deliver it to someone who'd not so long ago been intent on killing him, someone who was also wanted for the murder of his cousin. Someone who – shit! Joe suddenly realised why Adam's behaviour had been so strange. Jesus fucking Christ! How could he have believed that for a minute? Joe waited until Adam's fascination with the lawyer's cleaning activities finally wore off. 'You thought I had sex with my own daughter,' he said, calmly.

Adam opened the door. 'I should never have doubted you, Joe. I'm sorry.' He hung his head for a moment, then said, 'Who was it? Do you have any idea?'

Joe spoke in a monotone. 'A friend of mine. Cooper.'

Adam looked at him. 'What about Ruth? Do you think he was . . . responsible?'

Joe nodded.

'Can you handle it from here?' Adam asked.

'Go.'

Adam apologised again.

Joe watched the door swing shut. 'Didn't think you'd have the stomach for it,' he muttered to himself.

Tina said, 'What did Cooper do?'

'In a minute,' Joe said. He tapped Ronald on the shoulder. 'Give me the gloves. I can clean up my own puke.'

THIRTY-FOUR

Despite an apparently thorough cleaning, the carpet still stank of vomit. Joe had sluiced disinfectant straight onto it and the smell of antiseptic-masked sick had driven the three of them into the kitchen where they now sat round Ronald's kitchen table. Joe and the lawyer faced each other. Tina sat between them.

'Thanks for telling us,' she said to Joe.

Joe stared at his hands. He'd washed them, but they still felt sticky from wearing the gloves. 'My trusting friend Adam knows about it,' he said. 'Why shouldn't you two?' He flexed his fingers. He could still make out the faint scar where he'd broken the whisky glass that night at Cooper's.

'Nothing we can do about your daughter,' Ronald said. 'She's dead. Any evidence of a rape has died with her.'

Joe said, 'Is that right?'

'We have to concentrate on Ruth's murder.' The lawyer paused, making eye contact with Joe, then switching his gaze to Tina.

Joe felt Tina's hand on his arm. This time she said, 'Is that right?'

'Forget Gemma. This is the question we need to address,' Ronald continued. 'Do we have enough evidence to persuade the police to take Cooper into custody?'

Tina leaned back and studied the young man, her forehead creasing. Joe noticed a tiny shake of her head before she leaned across and slapped Ronald hard on the cheek. The sound made Joe wince.

Ronald reeled back in his chair, eyes wide. After a minute he put his hand to his face. 'What the fuck was that for?' He rubbed his cheek, his mouth hanging open.

'You want to tell him, Joe?'

'Next time you dismiss my daughter like that,' Joe said, 'it'll be me who hits you.' He paused. 'I might even use my fist.'

'I'm fucking breaking the law here.' Ronald closed his mouth. He kept rubbing his cheek.

'Your choice.'

'I'm doing it for you.'

'Crap.'

'Tina?' Ronald held his hands out, palms upwards. 'You know this man better than I do.' His face creased in a grimace, lips pulled back from his teeth. Momentarily he looked his age. 'What's his problem?' Fingers rigid, his hands balanced invisible weights.

Tina didn't say anything for a moment. Then she reached for Joe's hand and squeezed it. 'He told you, Ronald.'

'This has nothing to do with Gemma,' the lawyer said, sinking back in his chair. He touched his cheek again. 'Whatever Cooper may or may not have done to her is entirely speculative.'

Joe's fist lashed out, narrowly missing the lawyer's chin.

'Okay, okay,' Ronald said, leaning back, breathing fast. 'I won't mention it again.' He looked at Joe, eyes dropping to Joe's fist, still balled and ready to strike once more. 'Okay?' Joe rubbed his thumb over his knuckles. 'Okay,' the lawyer continued, 'but can we concentrate on procuring evidence that'll put Cooper away for the eminently more provable crime of murdering your wife? Face facts. We won't be able to prove that he raped your daughter, Joe. She's' – he spread his hands – 'gone. She can't testify. Not to mention the fact there'd be absolutely no way of obtaining physical evidence after this length of time.'

Joe wondered. He'd pulled his punch. He didn't really want to hurt the boy. Ronald was genuinely trying to help and he'd put himself out for Joe, no question. Put his neck on the line. Not just breaking the law, but offering Joe, a stranger, a possible criminal, a possible murderer, the sanctuary and hospitality of his home. Dubious hospitality, mind you, given the lack of available entertainment. Tina's slap ought to have been sufficient warning, but some people just didn't know when to stop. If Joe hit him properly and knocked his lights out, he'd probably wake up mumbling something about Gem. He was that kind of persistent little bastard. It was built into him.

At least he was honest.

Joe uncurled his fingers. 'What makes you think I want Cooper put away?'

Tina said, 'You live in a very simple world, Ronald.'

The lawyer stared at them both for a minute. 'What are you saying?' A slow smile spread across his lips. 'Ah, revenge. You want to exact revenge on Cooper, is that it? Christ, help me get him locked up, then. What better form of revenge do you want? Look, if you kill him, Joe, you'll find it damned difficult to prove you weren't responsible for killing your wife.'

'Did I say I wanted to kill him?'

After a moment, Ronald said, 'I assumed that's what you were getting at.'

Joe didn't reply.

Ronald tapped his fingers on the table. 'Why don't you tell me what's on your mind?'

'I don't think you should be part of it,' Joe said.

'I'm already in this up to my eyeballs.'

'Good reason not to get in any deeper. Another few inches and you'll be in over your head.'

'Look,' Ronald said, 'you can't do anything without me. I'm your go-between. I can talk to the police. I can talk to Cooper. Whatever you want.' His voice lowered. 'Don't shut me out, Joe.' He stood up and walked towards the window. He looked out.

Joe glanced at Tina. Her nose looked to have swollen some more. He grinned at her, sensing he might burst into hysterical laughter at any moment. She sucked her teeth, forcing her lips into a pout.

The lawyer continued to stare out the window.

Joe ran his hand through his hair. He didn't know what to do about Cooper. Death was too good for him. Joe wanted to make him suffer and he couldn't suffer unless he was alive. Cooper had murdered Ruth. Then he'd tried to frame Joe. Unknown to Joe, by that point Cooper had . . . Joe felt sick again. He swallowed and breathed out. Cooper had raped Gemma. That's how it was. He'd raped her. And as if that wasn't bad enough, in doing so he was responsible for her subsequent suicide. Indirectly, Cooper had killed her. Indirectly, yeah, but he might as well have shoved a knife into her heart. Might as well have shot her in the head. Might as well have beaten her to death with a baseball bat like he did Ruth.

Joe wanted Cooper to suffer all right. The question was how best to achieve it.

If Joe wanted him dead all he had to do was call Park and agree on a fee.

The outrage of Cooper's betrayal gripped Joe by the balls. A pain struck low in his belly, just as if somebody was squeezing his nuts in their fist. One of the first times he'd slept with Ruth, she'd ran her fingers across his stomach and he'd tensed up like this, muscles knotting. His dick slumped and he hated it and her and himself. He'd cried out and she'd wondered what the fuck was wrong with him.

Joe felt Tina's hand on his arm. 'Don't,' she said.

The warmth of her fingers soaked through his shirt. He let go of the fistful of hair he was trying to rip out of his scalp. Odd sensation, her warm fingers.

He'd never slept with Tina. She kept offering him her body, or her services. He was paying for it, she said. But he'd always refused. The one occasion they went to bed, they just slept. Well, she slept and Joe listened to her breathing, listened to raindrops kissing the window. He was drunk, but his brain was buzzing. After a while, only the occasional swish of night-time traffic punctuated the damp silence. He thought about Ruth, wondering who she was sleeping with, wondering why he'd grown to hate her, wondering why he didn't want to find out who she was sleeping with, wondering why he didn't give a fuck, wondering why he couldn't fuck even if he wanted, wondering if lying here with Tina counted as infidelity, wondering how Ruth justified her extra-marital sex to herself, wondering if he should leave her now that Gemma had left home, wondering if he'd ever fuck Tina, wondering what it would be like if he really didn't give a fuck.

The reason he couldn't fuck Tina was because he was married. And he couldn't fuck his wife because she was fucking somebody else and he couldn't get the thought out of his head.

He couldn't blame everybody else, though. He had to take responsibility for himself. He turned on his side and took his cock in his hand. It was daylight before he got to sleep.

'Stop it,' Tina said.

Joe let her steer his arm towards the table. She placed her hand on his. Her fingers were warm. He slid his trembling hand out of her grasp.

His thoughts shifted back to Cooper. Joe considered the tantalising option Park had dangled before him. If Joe wanted Cooper dead, all he had to do was phone Park and convince him he was good for the money. Ruth's life insurance, the house. More than enough. He'd never get close enough to do it himself. But did he want Cooper dead? Maybe, like Ronald said, prison was a better punishment. It wasn't so personal, though.

Ronald turned and walked away from the window. 'What's on your mind, Joe? What's your great plan?' When Joe said nothing, Ronald continued, 'You won't get near Cooper. The police will arrest you on sight.'

Joe pressed the palms of his hands together. 'What do you propose?'

Ronald brushed his fingers over his cheek, as if still feeling the sting of Tina's slap. 'We don't have enough evidence to take this to court. We have to get him to confess.'

'That's going to be easy.' Joe steepled his fingers.

'Without using baseball bats.'

'Even easier,' Joe said. 'Anyway, where am I going to get a baseball bat at this time of night?'

'I have to speak to the police. I'll speak to Grove.'

'They're not taking me in,' Joe said.

'You might not have a choice.'

Joe thought of Park again, of giving him the go-ahead. How would he do it? Gun, knife, bare hands? Joe shuddered. Park still scared him. Joe recalled how he felt stripping off in front of him at the hotel room this afternoon. 'Shit,' he said. 'What a twat I am.' He stood, staring at Ronald. 'One thing you can rely on with Cooper, he likes to brag.' He looked down at Tina. 'How would you feel about wearing a wire?' She looked puzzled. 'To trap Cooper,' he said.

'You really think he'll blurt it all out to me?'

'You don't know unless you give it a shot.'

She closed her eyes. 'How's the nose, Tina?' she said, voice lowered. 'By the way, I killed Joe's wife, eh?' Her eyes opened and she spoke in her normal voice. 'I don't think so.'

'Not at first, maybe. But after a bit of persuasion?'

'I told you,' Ronald said. 'No coercion.'

'And I told you,' Joe said. 'You shouldn't be involved in this.'

'So who the fuck do you think should be? I mean, say you've got Cooper in some secluded spot. Soundproofed for the benefit of the neighbours. You beat the shit out of him and he spills the truth about Ruth. Meanwhile, you've got Tina wearing a wire, transmitting all this information. But who's she transmitting it to, huh? Who's listening on the other end? Who's prepared to authorise this sort of thing?'

Joe started to laugh.

'What's so funny?'

Joe carried on laughing, wondering if Monkman's head felt any better.

THIRTY-FIVE

The light was beginning to fade. Adam checked the grass for dog crap and sat down beneath a clump of scrawny trees as still as statues in the stagnant air. He took out his phone. Dialled.

'How's it going?'

Adam told Dotty what had happened so far.

Her voice didn't register surprise. 'Her dad's best friend?' It was almost as if Adam's words were no more than confirmation of her suspicions. 'Family member. Family friend. It's usually someone close.' She said, 'What's her father planning?'

'Some kind of payback.'

'How do you feel about that?'

He wasn't sure how he felt. 'I don't want any part of it, obviously.'

'That's it?'

'I don't follow.'

'What did you expect?'

'I didn't think about it. The important thing was to get the diary to Joe and I've done that—'

'There was always going to be hell to pay. Can you sit back and watch it happen? However much this Cooper character deserves it?'

'It's out of my hands.'

'You let Gemma down.'

'Listen, I don't think—'

'No, don't argue, Adam. You have to be honest about this.'

Adam ripped a few blades of grass out of the soil while he waited for Dotty to continue.

'She died under your roof. She was your responsibility.'

'It's my fault. Is that what you're telling me?'

'Do you know what's right, Adam? Do you think Joe might kill him?'

'He might do something worse.'

'What could be worse?'

'I don't know. I don't have his imagination.' Adam plucked a few more blades of grass.

Dotty said, 'Come on. What could be worse?'

'I don't like to think about that.'

That's how their conversation might have been. He re-dialled and this time he didn't hang up before Dotty answered.

When she came to the phone, his throat tightened. His voice sounded squeaky. He asked how things were back home. She told him that Willy had been rushed to the dental clinic for an emergency extraction. He was okay. One tooth fewer and still couldn't chew properly, but his life wasn't in danger. She said she was handing in her notice. Adam asked if the council had picked up the mound of rubbish bags in the field at the back of Wrighters' Retreat. They hadn't. He asked Dotty if she'd do him a favour and give them a ring. She said she didn't like to hassle people about stuff like that. She said she was leaving, she couldn't stay any longer at Wrighters' Retreat. She was sorry, but she'd made her decision and nothing he could say would make her change her mind. He told her not to worry about the bins, he'd take care of them when he returned. He asked if she'd arranged her flight for the funeral. She told him she was booked on the first flight out in the morning. She'd have to stay in Edinburgh overnight. He asked if there was anything he could do to help. She asked him if he was listening.

'Any calls for me?' he said.

She sighed audibly. 'A policeman. Wanted to speak to you about Gemma.'

Immediately, he thought of Monkman. He recalled watching him kick Joe's defenceless body. And all of a sudden he was telling her what had happened that night. He told her about Monkman beating up Joe. About how he wanted to join in, yet was revolted by his feelings. How he felt sick with guilt now, knowing Joe had been innocent. About how pathetic he felt that he couldn't help.

She didn't comment. He waited. Still she said nothing.

'Dotty?'

'What do you want to happen between Joe and Cooper?' she asked him.

'I want to see justice being done.'

'What does that mean?'

After she hung up, he sat for a while. Then he got up, hailed a passing taxi and gave the driver the name of his hotel.

He thought about what Dotty had said. He wasn't sure he was doing the right thing. There was something tempting in the idea of running over to Brewer's flat and asking if he could help. Offering to hold that bastard fucker Cooper down while Joe bashed his brains in. The very idea that Cooper could have done these things made his stomach churn. To Gemma. To Ruth. Hell, to Joe. To Tina. The man was no better than a beast. Dotty had said she was resigning. He felt as chilled as if he was suddenly naked. Cooper deserved whatever punishment Joe had in mind for him.

The taxi dropped Adam off at his hotel. He got his key from the reception desk and walked along the narrow corridor to his room.

Why was Dotty leaving? Was it something he'd said?

When he opened the door he thought at first he'd entered the wrong room. A middle-aged man in a smart suit was facing him. 'Mr Wright?' The man raised a hand in greeting, then took a pair of glasses out of his pocket and put them on. The tip of his nose was red, like he had a cold.

'Who are you?' Adam said. 'What are you doing in my room?'

'Come in,' the man said. 'I won't bite.' He strode over to the table against the far wall and picked up the kettle. He disappeared into the bathroom with it. Adam heard the sound of running water. He considered leaving while he still could, but the stranger had looked harmless enough. A bit mad, perhaps. He reappeared, placed the kettle back on the table and pressed the switch. 'Tea?' he said. 'Coffee? Hot chocolate?'

'Are you going to answer my question?' Adam asked him.

'If you'll answer mine.' He indicated the pair of cups he'd set next to the kettle. One of the cups had a teabag in it.

'Nothing for me, thanks. But why don't you just go right ahead and make yourself at home?'

The man poured an individual portion of milk over the teabag. Once the kettle switched off, he added water. He stirred the brew while he introduced himself. 'Grove,' he said. 'Detective Sergeant.'

It fitted. Only a policeman would be this rude. 'What do you want?'

'Just a moment or two of your time.' He sipped his tea. 'You're not busy, are you? I'd like to ask you a few questions.'

'I have a few questions of my own.'

'Be my guest.'

'How did you find me?'

'I called you. A young lady answered the phone. She told me you were in Edinburgh.'

'Why did you call?'

'There were some matters I wanted to discuss with reference to the death of Mrs Ruth Hope. I'm involved in the investigation.'

'How did you find out I was staying here?'

'I asked the young lady. She told me.'

'How did you get into my room?'

'I showed my badge to the receptionist. He let me in.'

'I don't like it,' Adam said. 'I don't like you invading my privacy. I want to make that clear before I answer any of your questions.' He blinked. His eyelids were wet with sweat.

'I appreciate you may not take kindly to the intrusion and I apologise.' The detective placed his cup in its saucer. It rattled and the noise set Adam's teeth on edge. 'How about it? Will you please accept my apology, Mr Wright?'

What could he say? He chose to ignore the question and ask one of his own. 'What do you want to know?'

'I'd like you to tell me where I can find Joe Hope.'

'How would I—'

'Let's not pretend, Mr Wright. Where is he?'

'What do you—'

'Take a seat, Mr Wright.' The policeman pulled out a chair and Adam slumped into it. 'Your voice sounds dry. Are you sure you won't join me in a beverage?'

'Coffee,' Adam said. 'Black.' Grove ripped open a coffee sachet. Adam hurriedly tried to piece together this latest development. He thought he was out of the picture. He'd left Tina and Brewer and Joe to their own devices. Left them to carve out Cooper's future. And here stood this policeman asking if he knew where Joe was. Well, Adam wasn't going to tell him. Thank God he didn't know what they were planning. No amount of interrogation could reveal what he honestly didn't know. He breathed out, glad that he'd left the lawyer's flat before he became privy to any more details.

He accepted the coffee the policeman offered him and said, 'There's really nothing I can do to help you.'

'Tell me why you're here in Edinburgh.'

'For the funeral of Joe Hope's daughter, Gemma.'

Grove burped. 'Pardon me,' he said. 'Touch of indigestion.' He patted his chest. 'You're very punctual, Mr Wright. Are you sure there isn't another reason?'

THIRTY-SIX

'You think you can get hold of one?' Ronald was in the hallway, using his landline. The kitchen door was ajar and

Joe listened intently, trying to gauge the success of the lawyer's mission from the tone of his voice. Right now, he sounded excited.

Joe's stomach was still tender from throwing up. Thinking of Cooper was bad enough, but when he thought of Monkman, bile started to rise in his gullet. Blood thumped like heavy drumbeats in his temples.

As Ronald spoke, he paced in a tight circle, got tangled in the phone lead, then changed direction. He said, 'As soon as possible. Right.'

'He's agreed,' Joe said to Tina. Turning in her seat, she gave Joe a slight nod. He leaned towards her, his side hurting a little as he did so. He touched the back of her hand lightly and spoke into her ear: 'We need to talk.' He pulled away from her.

Her eyebrows bunched. 'What's stopping us?'

Joe glanced through the open doorway into the hall. Ronald was still pacing, phone plugged to his ear. Joe faced Tina and pointed over his shoulder. He leaned towards her again. 'Can't risk our friend overhearing.'

'He won't,' she said. 'Not if we whisper.'

Joe leaned towards her again. She tilted her head to the side. Her hair smelled of smoke. He inched forward until his lips were almost touching her ear. He could smell the faint trace of cheap perfume and feel the warmth of her neck. 'I don't want him to suspect anything. If he sees us whispering, he'll know we're keeping something from him.'

Her head bobbed up and down. Then she pulled back and glanced over Joe's shoulder. Her gaze switched to Joe, then her eyes focussed on the spot behind him and she smiled.

Joe turned.

Ronald was swaggering into the kitchen, grinning like a schoolboy. 'I told him the plan.'

The plan was as follows.

Tina would get fixed up with a wire (that's why they had phoned Monkman – he was the only one who had access to the equipment). She'd arrange to meet Cooper under the pretext of Joe joining them later. Over the course of the evening, Tina would use all her considerable experience in the art of seduction to persuade Cooper to forget about Joe. She'd let Cooper know that she responded to a man who roughed her up a bit. She'd flatter him. Stroke his ego. Maybe even stroke something else. If events turned out as Ronald imagined, Cooper would admit to Ruth's murder. Joe told the lawyer that Cooper was so full of himself that a confession was a real possibility. And that's where the wire came in. Record his confession and he'd have a hard time explaining himself to the police. He would have incriminated himself and Joe would be free. Everybody would be happy. Justice would be served.

The plan was Joe's and had he known no better, he might have thought it had some potential. And, certainly, it had to appear so. It was vital that the plan convinced Ronald and Monkman.

The plan, however, was a crock of shit.

'I know I shouldn't be surprised,' Ronald said. 'But I didn't think he'd go for it that easily. As soon as I said you'd be at the pub, his attitude completely changed.'

'I told you he would,' Joe said. 'Monkman's one of the more predictable individuals I've come across. He doesn't like me very much.'

'It's definitely on, then?' Tina said.

'He said he'd see what he could do.'

'That means yes,' Joe said.

'What's going to happen when you don't turn up?' Tina asked him. 'Monkman might barge into the pub and ruin everything.'

'There's no reason for him to do that.' Joe looked at Ronald.

He was still smiling. Joe continued, 'To begin with, he'll just think I'm late. He'll wait. He'll expect me to turn up. By the time he's figured out that I've stood you up, he'll be riveted to your conversation with Cooper and won't consider interrupting it. Breaking up your date won't serve any purpose.'

'You seem pretty sure that Cooper will agree to meet us.'

Despite the fact that Cooper had killed his wife and raped his daughter, Joe couldn't help but believe that he still knew what made Cooper tick. 'He wouldn't miss it for the world.'

What Joe didn't say was that although Ronald had been led to believe that Cooper might boast about what he'd done, Joe knew that Cooper wasn't that stupid. He was, however, driven by his hormones and there was little chance he'd say no to a free fuck.

'We're going to get you off the hook,' Ronald said to Joe. 'Anybody want a drink?'

Joe desperately wanted a drink, but it was the last thing he needed. What he needed was to get the lawyer out of the way. How did you get rid of somebody you didn't want hanging around? Hard enough when you weren't a guest in his house. One look at Tina was enough to inspire him.

Joe said, 'I can think of a better way to celebrate.' He leaned towards Tina. She turned her cheek towards him. He kissed her once. Reached for her hand. She let him hold it.

'I'll give the drink a miss,' she said. 'But I could really do with something to eat. I'm starving.'

Joe's stomach lurched at the thought of food.

Ronald looked at his watch. 'That time already? What do you fancy? I don't have much food in. Tend to live on takeaways. Fancy Indian?'

Joe felt his oesophagus burn, but he saw the intent of Tina's comment. 'You know,' he said, 'I have a real craving for fish and chips.'

'Yeah?' Ronald said. 'How about you, Tina?'

'Sausage supper. And none of that disgusting brown sauce.'

'Salt?'

'Just vinegar.'

'Joe?'

'Salt and sauce.' He dug in his pocket. 'Get you some money.'

'On the house,' Ronald said. 'Be back in a few minutes.'

As soon as he left, Tina said, 'Two things. You didn't pay me. And, even if you had, I don't kiss.'

Joe folded his arms. 'You want me to pay you for your time with Cooper tonight?'

'That's not business,' Tina said. 'That's strictly pleasure.' She rummaged in the shiny white handbag that dangled over the back of the chair and fished out a packet of cigarettes. 'Do you mind?'

'I think Ronald might.'

'Shame he's not here to ask.' She lit up. 'Are you going to tell me what you really want me to do? Or am I supposed to guess?'

Joe wanted to kiss her again. He didn't fancy her. Just a peck on the cheek. But he stayed planted in his chair, elbows firmly on the table. 'When you get there,' he said, 'start off playing it as we planned. Get Cooper as hot and excited as you can.'

'You still want me to get him to talk?'

'He won't.'

'You know him that well?'

'I think I do,' Joe said. 'In certain areas, at least.'

'Fair enough. I get him steamed up. But I don't try to make him talk.'

'No, no. By all means make the effort. I'm just saying it won't work. But to fool Monkman, you're going to have to pretend. Can you do that?'

She exploded in a great belly laugh. Smoke caught in her lungs and she started to cough. When she stopped, tears in her eyes, she said, 'You're seriously asking me if I can pretend? What do you think I spend my evenings doing?'

'What if Cooper wants to kiss you?'

The buzzer rang.

Tina's eyes darted from side to side. She whispered, 'Should we answer that?'

Joe shook his head.

The buzzer rang again.

'Might be Ronald.' She was still whispering. 'Forgotten his keys.'

'Whoever it is, they'll leave in a minute.'

The buzzer rang again. It rang in three long bursts. As if it was a pre-arranged signal.

Tina said, 'Whoever's out there knows somebody's home.'

Seconds later the phone rang.

Joe said, 'Leave it.' He walked into the hallway and Tina followed him. They watched the phone as if it was a dangerous animal.

The door buzzer sounded again. Three long bursts. Three short bursts. Three long bursts. The phone kept ringing.

When silence eventually returned, Joe heard a phantom ringing for a few seconds. Then a crash.

Tina grabbed his arm. 'What was that?'

The noise had come from the sitting room. Joe looked around. Couldn't see anything at first. Then he noticed a small stone surrounded by glistening glass fragments nestling in the carpet. A small shard of glass lay near the damp patch where he'd spewed. He looked towards the window. Several hairline cracks spread from a small hole right of centre in the bottom left hand pane. He edged his way towards the window.

THIRTY-SEVEN

Adam looked over his shoulder. Walking out of his hotel room in the middle of a conversation with a police detective probably wasn't the smartest move he'd ever made. But the policeman's charm and good manners were proving a lethal combination and he could feel himself allowing the policeman to gain his trust. Adam was starting to like him and it felt horribly wrong.

'If I don't agree?' he'd asked the detective.

Grove placed his cup on its saucer. He pinched his nose between finger and thumb and said nothing.

Adam watched him for a moment, then asked, 'Are you going to arrest me?'

'My boss would be very impressed if I catch your cousin's killer. I think you can help me.'

A shiver wriggled down Adam's back. 'If you're not going to arrest me then please leave my room.'

'I don't like fancy coffees, you know,' Grove said. 'Lattes and mochas and frappawhatevers. I was brought up on tea. A family of tea drinkers, my lot. Mainly Assam and Darjeeling. Indian teas. Ceylon. My mother went through a Kenyan phase. Never liked green tea much. Can't stand coffee. Even instant gives me a headache. I can't imagine what an espresso would do. I like my tea weak. And not too hot. Don't like it too milky either. You mind if I help myself to another cup?' 'If you won't leave, then I will.' Adam turned towards the door.

'One moment,' Grove said. 'Work with me to catch this man.'

'Goodbye,' Adam said.

'Wait.' Grove marched towards him, reaching into his jacket pocket. For a moment Adam thought he was going to slap handcuffs on him and drag him off to the nearest police station.

Instead, he handed Adam his card. It read: Detective Sergeant Arnold Grove, Lothian and Borders CID. His mobile phone number was written along the bottom. 'If you find out where Joe is, call me.'

'You really think I'm likely to bump into Joe?' Adam said. 'Anyway, Joe isn't guilty.'

'And how would you know, Mr Wright?'

'I just – I just have an instinct.'

'Fortunately, we don't rely on instinct in the police force.'

'Can I go now?'

'One more question, Mr Wright, if you can spare the time. If I were Mr Cooper I'd be very nervous. Have you seen him recently?'

'I don't know anybody of that name.'

Outside the hotel Adam stared straight ahead, scarcely registering that a taxi had just rushed past. His fingers gripped the card in his pocket as he crossed the road. He walked past a couple of newsagents and an African restaurant and a pub blasting some kind of thudding music with what sounded like a cement mixer for a vocalist, and stopped in front of a rubbish bin. He took the card out of his pocket. Then put it back again.

He stood by the side of the road. When another taxi approached, 'for hire' lights on, he flagged it down.

In the back seat, he closed his eyes and tried to see the pond at the foot of his parents' garden. No joy. It was as if his imagination had closed down. He concentrated on the garden, trying to picture the row of gooseberry bushes. 'Take one,' he'd say to his new friend. And his new friend would take one of the swollen fine-haired berries, and bite into it. His friend would cry out in disgust and grimace and spit out the berry. Few passed the test. None came back. His mother advised him to stop it or he'd never have any friends. Once, when he was eleven, he yelled at her: 'Why can't I go to school like other children?'

He pictured the vegetable patch bordering the left side of the lawn, the greenhouse on the right, and at the foot, under the shade of the sycamore tree, at last he made out the pond. He closed in on the image. Fingers of sunlight caressed the surface of the water. A breeze rustled the sycamore's leaves. The splash took him by surprise. He saw it, but heard nothing. It was like watching a video in slow motion. Silently, twists and ribbons of water rippled towards the edge of the pond. Exposed, on the grass, the sole of a naked foot. Slender ankle. Thin calf. Thigh descending into the water. The torso was submerged. Beneath the water, tiny nipples thrust out of pubescent breasts. Dotty's eyes were open, her hair fanned out like a shell. The water lapped over her.

He looked up. The taxi was cruising towards the Meadows. 'Let me out,' he said.

'You what, pal?' the taxi driver said.

Adam tried the door handle, pulling it hard.

'Hold on to your fucking pyjamas.' The taxi pulled into a bus stop, braking fiercely.

Adam tried the door again. It was still locked. 'Let me out.'

'Six pounds thirty.'

Adam's wallet was empty. He found some change in his pocket, but it wasn't enough to pay the full fare. He dropped a pound coin and it rolled across the floor. He stooped to pick it up. 'You take credit cards?'

'What do you think this is? Edinburgh's smallest supermarket? You see any tins of soup in the back there?'

'Well, where's the nearest cash machine?'

'I'm not letting you out until you've paid.'

'I don't have enough money.'

'Should have thought of that before you got in.'

Adam waited a minute and said, 'What do you suggest?'

'Dunno. If I had ideas, I'd be an inventor, wouldn't I? Give me the fare. Six pounds thirty. I've stopped the clock and you can be grateful for that.'

'Take what I've got.' Adam handed over a fistful of change.

The driver accepted the money, then started to count it. When he was done, he said, 'You're two pounds sixteen short.'

'So let me go to a cash machine.'

'You're not getting out.'

'How am I going to get the money to pay you?'

'Can't help you there. I'm not a financial adviser.'

Adam reached through the partition and grabbed the driver by his shirt collar.

'Two people I know have died recently.' He tightened his grip on the driver's shirt. 'My patience is running low. And I think you're being bloody unreasonable. So let me out before I get angry.'

The driver ran his tongue over his lips and nodded.

Adam let go of his shirt. When he tried the door again, it opened.

'If I see you again,' the driver said, as Adam stepped outside, 'I'll kick the crap out of you.' He floored the accelerator, tyres screeching as he pulled out of the bus stop. Failing to indicate, he narrowly missed an approaching Land Rover. It slowed just in time, the driver blaring his horn. The taxi driver replied with a fanfare that didn't stop until he was out of sight.

When Adam called Dotty, there was no answer. He tried again. Still no answer. He wondered when Dotty was planning on leaving. Was this it? Would she fly down tomorrow, and not return? Was that her plan? A one-way trip to Edinburgh? What about her stuff? Would she be able to fit all her belongings into a suitcase? Was she leaving Orkney? And why was she doing this, anyway? What was the point? She didn't have to leave, not on account of their feelings for each other.

He tried her phone once more.

She answered, breathless.

'Where are you?' he said.

'Busy.'

'You sound like you've been running.'

A pause. 'What is it, Adam?'

'Please don't leave.'

'I have to.'

'Because of me?'

'I'll talk to you tomorrow. I don't want to have this conversation on the phone.'

'It *is* because of me.'

'Can't we just leave it?'

'What did I do wrong?'

'You didn't do anything wrong.'

'I must have. Otherwise you'd be staying.'

'You're a lovely man.'

'Then what's responsible for making you want to leave? Tell me and I'll fix it so it isn't a problem any more.'

'It's nothing you can fix.'

'What is it? If it's not me, what the fuck is it?'

'Please don't get upset. Can't we speak about this tomorrow? Please?'

'Tell me now.' He waited a minute. 'Tell me, Dotty. Whatever it is, I'd rather know.'

Her voice was faint. 'Okay,' she said. She said something else.

He couldn't make it out. He was waiting to cross the road that curved round the Meadows. Vehicles surged past, nose to tail. 'I can't hear you, Dotty. Hang on a second.'

He ran across the road at the first slight break in the traffic. 'What were you saying?'

'Oh, God. Adam, I don't want to hurt you.'

'You won't. But you're getting me worried. Telling me would be much less cruel.'

'Okay, I know.' She paused. Then she said, 'I don't fancy you, Adam. Okay? I don't find you physically attractive. I'll never fall in love with you and all I'll do by staying here is cause you pain.'

The silence pressed down on Adam. He felt like he was under water, a noise in his head like a train hurtling through his brain. He swallowed, trying to make his ears pop. 'I can lose weight.'

She sounded like she was about to cry. 'There's nothing wrong with your weight.'

'What is it, then?'

'It's not something tangible. I just don't think of you the way you think of me.'

Another silence.

'It doesn't matter,' he said.

'Of course it matters.'

'No, it's okay. It doesn't matter, really. I'll see you tomorrow.'

He hung up. Slid the phone into his pocket. He was standing outside Ronald Brewer's flat with little recollection of how he'd got there. He pressed the buzzer. The fuckers inside didn't answer. He pressed it again. Why weren't they answering? This was important. They were inside, he was certain. At least, Joe was. He wasn't going to be running around Edinburgh with the police looking for him everywhere. Why didn't the bastards answer? Didn't they know this was a bloody emergency? He'd just been interrogated, for Christ's sake.

He stabbed out an SOS on the buzzer. That ought to register with them. Why didn't Brewer answer the door? What the hell was his problem?

Adam dug his phone out of his pocket, found the lawyer's home number and dialled it. It rung out.

He rummaged around in the garden. Found a small stone and threw it at the lawyer's sitting-room window. It smashed. That would teach the fucker.

Joe's face appeared at the window. Then he vanished and a short time later the door buzzed open. Adam burst through the door and climbed the stairs.

Tina stood in the lawyer's doorway, holding the door open. 'You broke the window,' she said.

'Had to get your attention.' He was slightly out of breath.

'What do you want?' Joe stood behind her.

'You going to let me in?'

'What do you want?'

'I arrived at my hotel,' Adam said. 'A policeman was waiting there. He interrogated me, asked me where you were and stuff, but I didn't tell him anything.'

'So what are you doing here?' Joe said.

'I want to help.'

'That's very kind of you,' Joe said. 'Given what you thought me capable of until recently.'

'I want to make amends for that,' Adam said. 'But that's not the only reason. What that fucker did to Gemma. What he did to Ruth.' He paused. 'I need to be there, Joe. I want to see the look in his eyes when he finds out that you know.'

'You're not used to violence, are you Adam?'

'I've not experienced much, thankfully.'

Joe grabbed Adam by the hair and twisted his head back. 'How do I know you won't step in at the last minute,' Joe said in his ear, 'like you did in Orkney when Monkman and his mates were giving me a kicking?'

'Would you pay any attention if I did?' Adam panted. He

deserved this. He deserved what Joe was about to do. He screwed his eyes shut. Waited. But nothing happened.

THIRTY-EIGHT

'You didn't tell Grove I was here?' Joe let go of Adam's hair and sat down next to Tina on the settee. He caught a faint disinfectant-masked whiff wafting up from the carpet and tried to breathe through his mouth.

Adam remained standing, rubbing his head with the heel of his hand. 'If I had, you'd be under arrest by now.' With the toe of his shoe, he tapped the stone he'd thrown through the window.

'Maybe.' Joe wanted to believe him, but recent experience had strengthened Joe's belief that everybody was guilty until proven otherwise. He crossed his legs. 'Perhaps you told Grove I was here, and he asked you to find out what we were planning.'

'Why would he be interested in that?' Adam kicked the stone. It rolled a couple of inches across the carpet. He gave his head another rub.

'Maybe he knows Cooper.'

'You're the one who's wanted for murder.'

'Maybe he knows Cooper's reputation,' Joe continued. 'Knows that if he dragged Cooper in for questioning, he'd get nowhere.' Joe stroked his thumb over the point of his chin and stared at Adam. The man couldn't hold his gaze. Adam looked down at his feet, at the stone he'd used to break Ronald's window. He idly tapped the stone again with his toe.

Despite appearances to the contrary, Joe didn't think Adam was lying. Nonetheless, Joe carried on speculating. 'Cooper's renowned for his unhelpfulness. Maybe Grove decided that he'd have more chance of nailing Cooper if he let events play out my way.'

'What makes you think Grove wants to nail Cooper? Grove thinks you're guilty. He doesn't suspect Cooper.'

'Maybe Grove wants me running around. I'm what they call a loose cannon. With me after him maybe Cooper will get nervous and break down.'

Tina sounded surprised. 'You think so?'

'I'm trying to think like a policeman, not like a normal person.'

'So you don't think so?'

'Cooper isn't the type to get nervous.'

Adam said, 'Pure fantasy, Joe.' He prodded the stone again. 'And I think you know it.'

'Perhaps. Why should I trust you?'

Adam finally left the stone alone and focussed his attention on Joe. 'I came all the way from Orkney to deliver Gemma's diary into your hands.'

'You did and I'm grateful for it. But that doesn't answer my question.'

'I could have gone to the police back home. I didn't.'

'I repeat, why should I trust you?'

Adam's face reddened. For a moment it looked like he was about to choke. He pressed his fingers to his temples and muttered to himself. After a while, he lifted his head and said, 'It's what she would have wanted.'

Joe looked at the slightly podgy little man, hating to admit to himself that Adam was right. Gemma would have wanted Joe to trust him. Still, Gemma wasn't here and even if she were, it would have made no difference.

Adam seemed to know it. His face looked like an empty bag. 'Surely I can be of some use,' he said. 'You must need help with something.'

Tina said, 'You weren't so keen before.'

'I had some bad news from home,' Adam said. 'It made me

reconsider certain things.' He stared at Joe, unblinking. 'For God's sake, let me help you.'

Joe nodded. 'I suppose you might come in useful.'

Adam started to smile.

'But I'm not going to tell you what's going on. That way you won't be able to pass on any information to Grove.'

'I have no intention of doing any such thing. But if it makes you feel more secure to keep me in the dark' – Adam swung his leg back and kicked the stone hard enough to send it bouncing off the skirting board – 'be my guest.'

'You can start now,' Joe said. 'There's something I'd like you to do.'

THIRTY-NINE

Adam kept telling himself he was in no danger. No danger at all. Cooper had left for his meeting with Tina. In theory, at least. The meeting was scheduled for eight o'clock. That much Joe had revealed. It was now eight ten, so Cooper should have left his flat ages ago. Still, Adam wished he'd arranged some kind of signal. Tina could have sent a surreptitious text message, a quick OK to say Cooper had arrived at the pub. Oh, well. It was too late now.

He rang the bell.

The lawyer had wound him up. Brewer hadn't been too pleased when he arrived home. Took one look at Adam and said, 'I thought you'd gone.' Almost immediately he said, 'What happened to my window?'

Adam explained. Well, he told a bit of a fib. Said he broke the window accidentally, when, in fact, it was deliberate. He'd felt an unbearable urge to destroy something. He'd rarely been so angry. He couldn't believe Dotty was going to leave Wrighters' Retreat. Getting threatened by Joe had calmed him down for a while, but the anger had returned as the fear subsided.

Brewer said, 'You intend paying for it?'

Adam watched his eyes to see if he was joking. Didn't look like it. 'I don't have any cash on me.'

'I'll take a cheque.'

'I don't have my chequebook handy.'

'Post it, you fucking idiot.'

Adam took a step towards the boy and might have taken another if he hadn't caught Joe's eye. Mid-stride, Adam knew that he couldn't carry out this fantasy of throttling the little fucker. He had started to shake. He stuck his hands in his trouser pockets. Didn't help much.

He was okay now. Just a bit scared in case Cooper, for some reason, was still at home.

If a man's voice answered, Adam was all set to sprint back down the path.

The voice belonged to a girl. 'Yeah?'

What should he say? No point saying his name because that wouldn't mean anything to her.

'Yeah?' she said again.

'A friend of Joe Hope's.'

'Cooper's out.'

Adam clenched his fist and tensed the muscles in his arm. 'Is that Sally?'

'Yeah.'

'What it is. Well. Joe wants something.'

'Yeah? What's that got to do with me?'

'Something of Cooper's Joe wants to borrow. Can I come in?'

'What does Joe want to borrow?'

Adam lowered his voice. 'Cooper's baseball bat.'

'Oh.' She hesitated. 'Is Joe okay?'

'He's fine. He'd just feel a lot safer with a baseball bat.'

'I can understand that. Come on up.'

'There's something else.'

'What?'

FORTY

'Testing, testing. Monkman's a dickhead.' Calling Monkman names wasn't big and it wasn't clever but it was better than thinking about Cooper.

Four stubs lay in the ashtray. It had been empty when Tina sat down at the table ten minutes ago. Waiting for Cooper to arrive was as much fun as waiting for a client with a rep for liking rough sex. Meanwhile, she had to keep herself amused. She flipped open the lid of her cigarette packet and tapped out another fag. They were bad for you, but not as bad for you as getting in the same room as that bastard. She wrinkled her nose to see if it still hurt. It did.

She muttered, 'Still no sign of him.' She nearly said Cooper's name, which would have totally screwed things up. Monkman, of course, was expecting Joe to turn up.

The seats were all taken when she arrived at the pub half-an-hour ago. Before ordering a drink she'd checked that Cooper hadn't arrived, then she'd gone to the bathroom and turned on the wire. Monkman had told her to leave it until the last minute, but what did she care? The batteries would run out in under three hours, she'd been told. That was okay. She returned to the bar and ordered a drink. She kept an eye out for a free table and managed to grab a cosy two-seater in the corner the minute an arguing couple got up and left. Tina's seat faced the door. Each time she heard it swing open she looked up, hoping it would be Cooper.

Wearing this damn wire wasn't going to benefit anybody.

Monkman had taken great pleasure in attaching the little black box. He'd shown it to her first. She'd had a quick look, but she wasn't terribly interested. She commented on the fact that it was made by Sony and that was good, wasn't it, and told him to get on with it. First thing he did was get her to strip down to her bra and panties. On reflection, that wasn't necessary. The little bastard.

'It's a known fact that policemen have very small penises. You listening, Monkman?' The policeman had offered to drive her here. It made sense, since he had to be in the vicinity anyway. Restrictions had prevented him from parking directly outside and he'd been forced to park in one of the narrow side streets further along. She imagined him huddled in the front seat of his car, raging at her insults, but she was too nervous to enjoy his discomfort. 'I wouldn't let it bother you,' she said.

She'd made her Bloody Mary last well. She poured the last of the tomato juice into her glass and took a tiny sip.

The door opened. Her glass bumped against her teeth. A biker marched in and joined a group of his hairy, leathered-up mates. Almost immediately the door swung open again and three, no four, scantily clad little bimbos strutted in on dangerously high heels. Where was he? She looked at her watch again.

When she looked up, the bimbos had tottered all the way to the bar without injuring themselves and Cooper was strolling towards her on legs like tree stumps. His expression gave away nothing. He'd dressed for the occasion, though. White collar-less shirt under a navy suit jacket. Charcoal suit trousers. His shoes looked polished. A good omen. He was taking this meeting seriously.

She switched into working mode. A pout, followed by a quick flick of the tongue over her lips. 'You're late.'

'Don't fuck me off again. Where's Joe?'

She sighed. 'Not here yet. He's been held up.'

He grunted. 'Maybe I should go.'

'Stay,' she said. 'He'll turn up. Have a drink with me. I'm not completely unattractive, am I?'

'What's that got to do with anything?'

'A girl likes to think she's capable of catching a man's attention,' she said. 'Know what I mean?' She held out her nearly empty glass. 'Fill me up.' She parted her lips and let her tongue slide between them.

Cooper nodded. 'What do you want?'

'What do I want?' She looked at his crotch. At his eyes. 'Bloody Mary. With lots of Worcester Sauce. And ice. Ask for ice.'

He barged his way to the bar.

So far so good. Everything was going according to plan. Joe had even predicted that Cooper would be late. Back at the lawyer's flat, they'd tried to talk. Having sent Ronald to the chip shop, Wright spoiled their privacy by making his dramatic arrival. And by the time they'd finished with him, Ronald was back with the food. By then, she really was hungry. She ate hers and most of Joe's.

After they'd eaten, Joe said to Ronald, 'You mind if I use your bedroom?'

'You tired? Don't know how you can sleep at a time like this?'

'Did I mention sleep?' Joe looked at Tina. 'Coming?'

'Oh,' Ronald said. 'I get it. Maybe I should change the sheets.'

'Don't bother.' Joe was still looking at her.

'You'll just need to change them again,' she said.

Ronald shrugged. 'You have half-an-hour, Joe. Then I'll need to take Tina away.' He winked. He was referring to her wire fitting with Monkman. The lawyer turned to Wright and said, 'Run it by me again. You didn't realise the stone was that big?'

In the bedroom Tina and Joe had worked out the plan that was now in operation.

She looked up as Cooper returned with the drinks. He sat opposite her. 'What's all this?'

'What's what?'

'Giving me the come-on.'

'I—I—'

'I told you I'd give you ten grand.' He pointed his finger at her. 'Then I didn't. And just to make sure you really liked me, I nutted you on the fucking nose. Now you're trying to tell me you find me a turn-on?'

She ran two fingers over the rim of her glass. 'That's exactly what I'm trying to tell you.' But she could tell from his expression that he wasn't to be won over that easily. 'You find it hard to believe a woman can fancy a man who gets a bit rough sometimes?'

'I know one or two.'

'Make that three.'

He took a gulp of his beer. 'I can't wait all night for Joe. I'm a busy man.'

If he looks like he might be about to leave, talk about the kid. That was Joe's advice. 'Joe mentioned you had a little boy. Gary?' She pushed her packet of cigarettes towards him.

Cooper relaxed and lit a fag. He sank into his seat. He picked up his drink and smiled. 'Cute little bastard.' His smile broadened. 'Like his dad.' He leaned towards her. 'You do fancy me, don't you?' He didn't wait for a reply. 'His mother dotes on him, you know. She doesn't like me as much. But I don't mind. The wee man's like a kind of glue.'

She had no idea what he was talking about. It must have shown.

'He holds us together. Think about it. Why else would a man of my maturity and sophistication be having a relationship with a young tart like Sally? Huh?'

Tina wondered if Monkman was hearing any of this. Cooper was expecting a reply. She said, 'Love?'

'Well, I never thought I'd hear a whore say that.'

'I'm full of surprises. For a whore.'

'You believe in love?'

'What about Gary? Don't you love him?'

'That's different.'

'How?'

'I don't want to fucking talk about it. It's different, okay?'

She raised a hand. The guy was a nutter. If he was a client, she'd make her escape now. Before it was too late. 'You seen Joe since he came out of prison?'

'Once. He wasn't in a particularly good mood.'

'Why do you think he did it, Cooper?'

Cooper stubbed out his half-smoked fag in the ashtray. He clasped his hands and steepled his thumbs. 'Claims he didn't.'

'Wasn't he with you that night?'

'If that's what he says.'

'I'm asking.' She shrugged. 'It looks bad for him.'

'Why all the questions?' He paused. 'Let me ask you one, eh? Why aren't you mad at me?'

'You want to know?' She offered Cooper another cigarette. He shook his head. 'I'll tell you.' She tapped one out for herself. 'The work I do, it makes it hard for me to find men sexually attractive. I rarely get turned on.'

'Doing it all night, it becomes a bit tedious.' He nodded. 'I can see that.'

Sometimes she was just plain frigging sore, but she didn't tell him that. Probably wouldn't sound too seductive. It had been a long time since she'd had a boyfriend. The last one,

Dennis, was great. Didn't want sex. Happy to give her a back rub, which is what she really wanted when she got home from work. Things were going great until he decided he was gay.

'Occasionally I meet someone I find appealing.' She lowered her eyes and stared into her drink. 'It's usually someone who's in control of his life. Someone who knows what he wants and is prepared to do what's necessary to get it.'

'You like that?'

'Someone who doesn't care what other people think.'

'I don't give a fuck what any bastard thinks.'

'I noticed.'

'Including you.'

'Which is part of your attraction.'

He stared at her, not moving a muscle. His eyes remained wide open. She could tell he wasn't really looking at her. His eyes were out of focus. She had the impression that she could get up and walk out the door and he'd carry on staring into the space she'd just vacated. She was tempted to put her theory into practice. Instead, she said, keeping her voice low, 'You want to fuck me, don't you?'

His expression didn't change. 'What makes you think that?'

'Joe told me you liked whores.'

'Some. He might be right.'

'So what's wrong with me? My nose?' She grinned. 'Hey, if you don't like it, you have no one to blame but yourself.'

'Yeah. Maybe I could do a better job next time.'

Sweat made her armpits prickle. She finished her drink. 'You believe in God?'

His chin jutted forward. The muscles in his neck tightened. 'Can't say that I do.'

'When was the last time you went to church?'

'Why do you want to know?'

'You'll see. Wait for me. I'm going to the ladies.'

She went to the toilet and splashed her face with cold water. Someone had been wearing patchouli. The place stank of it. She locked herself in a cubicle and removed the black box. She untaped the wires. Then she lifted the lid off the cistern and dropped it all inside. She unlocked the door and stood in front of the wall-length mirror to touch up her makeup. When she returned to the bar, Cooper was finishing a conversation on his mobile. He hung up straightaway and tucked the phone into his pocket. His chair scraped the floor as he got to his feet.

Tina slipped her arm through his. 'Tonight's your big night.'

'What you got planned?'

'I'm going to show you God.' She steered him away from the street where Monkman was parked.

'Where you going?' he said. 'I've got my car.'

'But you only live around the corner.'

'So?'

She tried to keep the anxiety out of her voice. 'Where is it?'

'You know, I knew straightaway you fancied me,' he said and continued walking in the direction they were headed. 'Fucking knew it.' With each step, Monkman got further away and Joe got a little bit closer.

FORTY-ONE

Joe couldn't stand being in the room with them any longer. Adam wasn't helping. He was shaking like a man with pronounced Parkinson's.

Joe opened the door of the ante-room and stepped into the dark interior of the tiny church. He closed the door behind him. His finger hovered over the light switch. Bare floorboards shone in the dull orange glow of a pair of streetlights. A long line of pews, four rows deep, had been shoved against the wall on his left. A disorderly pile of exercise mats was a vague shape near the back wall. To his right, a couple of steps led to a plinth. On the plinth was a lectern. Behind the lectern, vanishing into the shadows, was a single choir stall. The other had been ripped out, dismantled, flung into a heap and forgotten about. He made out part of a leg poking through some broken panels.

He left the lights off. Switching them on wasn't worth the risk.

The streetlights' glow reminded him of late night journeys. Returning from visits with Cooper's clients, most of whom lived in housing schemes on the edge of the city. Cruising down Niddrie Mains Road at two in the morning listening to the Blue Nile. Hardly any traffic. Joe behind the wheel. Cooper laughing. Cooper saying, 'See his face?' and Joe replying, 'Before or after?'

My, oh my. How times had changed. Here he was in this little old wreck of a church waiting for his former best mate to turn up so he could . . . could what? Kill him?

Joe shivered. It was chilly in here. He guessed that once upon a time, the church's tall windows had probably boasted stained glass. Now, the glass was plain and streaked with birdshit and most of the panes were pocked with holes. He wondered how much noise leaked outside into the grave-yard.

The church was Tina's idea. These days, she'd told him, it was only used for recreational purposes. She rented it one night a week for her self-defence classes. Another night, a rock band used it for practice sessions. A caretaker came round on a Saturday afternoon and gave the floor a cursory sweep. To-night the church was empty. And Tina had a key. That was as much as she'd told Joe.

She hadn't told him it stank. Rotten wood. A stronger trace

of mildew. A vague sweaty smell that reminded him of school gyms.

In the shadows Joe saw things move. He moved into the light, looked at his watch and walked over to the door. He entered a tiny, dark wood-panelled foyer and picked up the baseball bat that leaned against the wall.

If Tina was on schedule, she should be here soon.

Come on. The nearer he got to realising this whole thing, the more nervous he was becoming. It wasn't like him to get nervous. He set down Cooper's bat and flexed his fingers. Shook the tension out of his shoulders. He started pacing. The foyer was cramped. He went back into the church and crossed from one side of the room to the other. He picked up an upturned pew. Turned it the right way round. He sat down, facing the door to the entrance hall.

Five minutes passed. It seemed a hell of a lot longer. He got up again and went to check on the others.

The little room was drenched in the bright light from a single bulb. Adam looked up at him. Sally gave him a scared look. At least she'd stopped crying now. Joe hadn't wanted to put the gag on her, but he didn't have any choice. After Adam brought her here, Joe had sat her down and told her his suspicions about Cooper. Somehow, he'd fooled himself into thinking she'd understand, that she'd take his side. When he'd finished speaking, she asked to leave. He said she had to stay. She started screaming and wouldn't stop no matter how much he begged her. He tried threatening her. That didn't work. With Adam's help, he tore one of Gary's blankets into strips. Adam pinned her arms to her sides while Joe removed one of her socks. He rolled the sock into a ball and stuffed it into her mouth, then secured it with one of the strips torn from the blanket. He had used the remaining strips to tie her to her chair.

Joe strolled over to the cot. Gary was still asleep. He tucked the remaining blanket under the little man's arms and said to Sally, 'I wish I didn't have to do any of this.'

Twenty minutes later he was standing by the church's main entrance listening for the sound of approaching footsteps.

For the first time in ages he felt a twinge where Monkman had kicked him. He touched his side, hoping the bruising wouldn't interfere too much with his swing. He tried a one-handed air shot. It was okay. He tried with both hands. A little discomfort, but nothing he couldn't live with. *Come on.*

What was keeping Tina? All she had to do was persuade Cooper she wanted a fuck. How difficult was that? Were they walking here? He couldn't imagine Cooper suggesting a romantic evening stroll. It was possible they'd been rumbled, of course. Somehow, Monkman could have found out what was going on. Or maybe Cooper had seen through Tina's charade. After all, it would take a vain man to believe that Tina fancied him. A supremely vain man.

In the dim light, Joe grinned. There was no doubt they'd be here. He'd just have to be patient.

A few minutes later he heard the car. The engine growled, then died. After a moment a door clicked shut and a man's laughter punctured the night air. Another click. A woman's voice. Tina's? He wanted to open the door and have a quick look. The compulsion was hard to resist, but his better judgement forced him to retreat inside the church. He hid behind the foyer door, flattening himself against the wall, bat raised.

They entered the foyer, talking. Tina was saying, 'Course there's no bed. There's a pulpit, though. Standing room only.'

'That'll do me,' Cooper said.

And then the door opened.

Joe stopped breathing. He let Cooper take a few strides past him, then hit the fucker on the side of the knee. Cooper yelped and buckled.

Tina snapped on the lights and slammed the door shut.

'Fuck was that?' Cooper asked.

'One of these.' Joe swung the bat again. It smashed into the same place on the same knee.

Cooper yelled. He kept yelling for a long time. He stopped only to take a breath. Then he started yelling again. When he stopped, it was only to say, 'You bastard. You've broken my leg, you bastard. Jesus Christ, you bastard, Joe. You fucking bastard.' He yelled again. Outrage as much as pain.

Over the racket, Joe said to Tina, 'You should leave.'

'I only just got here.'

'You don't want to be associated with this.'

'Too late.'

'It'll be ugly.'

'I doubt it'll be ugly enough.'

'Just piss off, will you? I don't want you here.'

'That wasn't part of our plan.'

'The plan's changed.'

'You want rid of me because I'm a woman, right?' She grabbed the bat out of Joe's hand. Cooper was on his side, writhing on the ground, both hands covering his left knee. Tina brought the bat down hard on his elbow. His yelling rose to a new level. He rolled onto his back, mouth wide open, head shaking with his screams.

Joe held out his hand for the bat.

Tina shouted, 'I'm staying.'

He nodded.

She gave him the bat. 'What do we do now?'

'Wait for that bag of shite to calm down.'

As Cooper yelled his throat hoarse, Joe kept picturing him on top of Gemma, slavering over her, drool hanging from his lips as she tried to fight him off. His whisky breath. Those words she'd written in her diary. Those terrible words. Joe beat down the urge to hit Cooper again. He wanted some questions answered first.

Adam opened the door of the ante-room, glanced around and quickly closed the door again.

Cooper's yelling eventually subsided. He moaned loudly. In between gasps of pain, he called Joe a bastard.

Finally, Joe said, 'Why did you kill Ruth?'

Through clenched teeth, Cooper said, 'Fuck off.'

'I'll hit you again.'

'Give it your best shot, you useless prick.'

Joe thought about it. He didn't see the point. Cooper wouldn't talk. He said to Tina, 'Bring the girl out.'

Cooper was suddenly quiet. He swivelled round on the floor so he could watch Tina cross to the room at the far end. She reappeared moments later with Sally. The minute Sally saw Cooper on the floor she started making mewling noises behind her gag. All of a sudden she turned and tried to get back into the room she'd just left. Tina barred her way, grabbed her shoulders and pushed her forward.

Joe said to Cooper, 'Tell me what happened.'

'Get to fuck.' Cooper made a low moaning sound.

'I'm serious.'

Tina urged Sally closer. Joe wanted to apologise to Sally, but he knew it would be fatal to speak to her.

'You want to see how serious I am?' He walked up to Sally and aimed the bat. 'Where, Cooper? Tell me where you want me to hit her.'

'Fuck you, Joe.'

'How about the hipbone? The hardest bone in the human body. Least likely to break. What do you think?'

'Do what you want,' Cooper said.

'Hold her still, Tina. What happened that night, Cooper?'

'I told you.' His voice was quiet. 'You can fuck off.'

'I don't want to have to hurt Sally,' Joe said. 'You going to give me an answer?'

Cooper's voice was a choked whisper. 'Fuck off.'

'You won't budge, will you?' Joe lowered the bat. 'He really loves you Sally. Bear that in mind.' He shouted, 'Bring him out, Adam.'

'Bring who out?' Cooper winced as he tried to sit up.

'Who do you think?' Joe said.

'Fuck, Joe. You wouldn't dare touch him.'

'No? You destroyed my family. Murdered my wife. Raped my daughter. I hold you responsible for her death.'

'I didn't do any of that, Joe.'

'Adam?' Joe shouted.

The door opened and Adam appeared with Cooper's baby in his arms. Sally tried to break free of Tina's hold. Tina grabbed her round the waist. Sally screamed behind her gag.

'Bring him over here,' Joe said to Adam. 'Put him on the floor.'

'You won't harm him, Joe,' Cooper said. 'I know you won't.'

'Like you didn't harm my daughter.'

'I swear I didn't do anything to Gemma.'

'We've read her diary,' Tina said. 'She says you raped her.'

'Mentions you by name,' Joe lied.

'She left a diary?' Cooper shook his head. 'Fucking bitch.' He shook his head again. 'Tell you what, Joe, I'm glad the fucking bitch is dead, do you hear me? And rape, for fuck's sake? She wanted it as much as I did, I'll tell you that. Fucking bitch. It's all lies, her diary. You can't believe what she wrote. She was crazy. Didn't know what she was saying. She led me on, you know. I didn't want to do it. It was her fault. She wanted it.'

Joe's self-control almost left him. For the moment he managed to hold his rage in check. 'What about Ruth? Why did you kill her?'

'I didn't, Joe, and that's the honest truth.'

'Bring the baby to me,' Joe told Adam.

Gary was quiet, despite being jostled in Adam's shaking arms. Joe moved towards Adam, intending to meet him half way.

'You won't touch him,' Cooper said. 'You wouldn't dare. You touch him, you're fucking dead.'

'Let me explain the situation.' Joe came to a halt. 'I've lost my best friend, my job, my wife, my daughter, my home, and my freedom. I have nothing more to lose. You can decide what you're prepared to risk, but neither of us is leaving this building until you tell me what happened. You want to gamble your child's life, so be it.'

Sally was wailing into the torn strip of blue blanket that served as a gag. Her eyes were wet and wide. She started making choking sounds.

'She wants to say something,' Adam said.

Joe said, 'Let her speak.'

Tina reached round and untied the gag.

Sally spewed the sock onto the floor. Her shoulders heaved. She took several sharp breaths, then said, 'He went out. After you'd gone to bed, Joe. There were a couple of calls, then he got dressed and left. He was gone for hours.'

'Is that right?' Joe smiled. 'So. What were you doing all night, Cooper?'

'I don't think he'll be answering that, Mr Hope.'

Joe turned. Park stood in the foyer doorway, a handgun pointed at Joe. The gun looked like the one he'd had in his hotel room when Joe had visited earlier. Joe thought for a moment he might throw up again.

The hitman said, 'Drop the bat.'

Joe dropped the bat. It clattered onto the floor and rolled in an arc towards Adam.

'Thought you were never going to make an appearance,' Cooper said.

'You said twenty minutes. I waited twenty minutes. You didn't phone.' 'Yeah, yeah. Help me up, will you. I'm all fucking busted up. You believe this? Leg's busted. Elbow's busted.'

Park helped Cooper to stand. Cooper leaned against Park, damaged leg dangling off the ground, arm tucked into his side. 'Sally, take Gary and get the fuck out of here.'

Sally took a couple of steps towards Adam. 'How am I going to get home?' she asked Cooper.

He stuck his hand in his pocket. 'Take the fucking car.' He tossed his keys towards her. 'Now take Gary off that fat git and get out of here.'

Adam handed the baby over. Sally hobbled towards the door with Gary in her arms, tears streaming down her cheeks.

'And when I get home,' Cooper said, 'I'm going to tan your fucking arse a deep shade of pink for ratting on me.'

The foyer door closed behind Sally.

'Give me the gun,' Cooper said to Park. 'I want to shoot this lot myself.' Park handed over the gun. 'Help me sit down on this fucking bench.' Park took a step to the side and lowered Cooper onto the nearby pew. Cooper waved him away. 'Okay, you fuckers can all kneel down.' He pointed the gun at Tina. 'Now.'

She dropped to her knees. Adam did likewise.

Cooper stretched his arm towards Joe. 'Gun's loaded,' he said. 'Cocked. Pointed at you. You scared, Joe? Am I going to see some panic flicker?'

Joe stayed absolutely still. He wondered if Cooper was

about to launch into his speech about stillness. Joe's eyes bored into Cooper's. Cooper wasn't going to see any trace of panic however long he sat there.

'I should shoot you first, but that wouldn't be any fun.' Cooper turned to Tina. 'And you, bitch. I'm going to fuck you good and proper. It's what you want, isn't it? Come here.' He smiled, encouraging her as she waddled towards him on her knees. She stopped an arm's distance from the pew. 'Closer.' She moved a couple of inches forward. He reached out, traced a line down her face with the gun. She winced as he pressed it against her nose. 'After all, you do find me irresistible. Isn't that right?' His expression hardened. 'Get back over there with your boyfriend.'

He turned to Adam. 'Now, Joe, would you look at this? We've got some serious panic flicker going on here.'

Adam was shaking from head to toe. Joe was worried he might do something stupid.

Tina brushed her hand against Joe's leg as she returned to his side.

Joe said, 'You're going to kill us all, right?'

Cooper nodded. 'Eventually.'

'Tell me what happened with Ruth.' Joe shrugged. 'What's the harm?' 'Why should I?'

'For the sake of our friendship?'

'We don't have a friendship.'

'We used to.'

Cooper shrugged. 'For the sake of what we used to have? I don't think so, Joe. You really hurt my leg, you know.'

'Good. Now hurt me back. Tell me why you set me up.'

'Get on your knees, then, like I told you.'

Slowly, Joe lowered himself to the floor.

'Good boy,' Cooper said. 'Now, where were we? Oh, yeah. Hurt you back?' Cooper looked at Park. The hitman was standing next to the bench, arms folded, face expressionless. 'Tell you what, Joe,' Cooper said. 'Before I kill you, I'll tell you something that'll really hurt.' He took a deep breath, then said, 'I'm not sure how things came to this sorry state. Looking back on it, well it's Ruth's fault, really. All I did was try to stop her screwing things up. You ask me, I've done a damn fine job. Under the circumstances. Although you probably have a different opinion, Joe. Shite. I was trying to protect you. That's all. That's how it started. You were my friend. What was the point of you finding out?'

'Finding out what?'

'Got some mouth on you, Joe. I got advice for you. Keep it closed. You can't sort out your own problems. Don't even know you have them. So don't get fucking lippy with me. This is my fucking head and it controls my fucking life. You don't see what's under your fucking nose, Joe. That's your problem. You never have. What's the matter now?'

Joe shook his head.

'I'll carry on, then,' Cooper said. After a moment he said, 'You'd agree that Ruth is a first class bitch, huh?'

Joe opened his mouth.

'Shut the fuck up. I'm talking.'

Joe closed his mouth.

'If it wasn't for her, I'd be fine, you'd be fine, everybody would be fine. We could all carry on as normal. But no, she had to go and spoil it for the lot of us.' He hesitated for a short while before saying, 'That's why she's dead.'

'Why did you kill her, Cooper?'

'You think I want to live my life cowering in the corner like some fucking whimpering gimp she just dragged out to play with on a Saturday night? You want to know what happened? You want to know why I killed her? I'm really enjoying this, Joe. Got myself a captive audience. Thanks for setting it up so nicely for me.' He chuckled. Then his eyes clouded over. 'Tell me if I'm boring you, Tina, and I'll stop for as long as it takes to put a bullet in your head.'

Tina said, 'I'd never dream of describing this as boring.'

'Well, fucking pay attention.' Cooper faced Joe. 'Jesus Christ, my fucking leg hurts,' he said. 'But I'm man enough to ignore the pain. Maybe later we'll see if you are, Joe. A bullet in each knee, huh? Look forward to that. And an elbow or two. What do you think? Still leave me with a bullet for each of your balls. Then we'll see how much of a man you are.

'Okay. Where was I? When the damn buzzer went that night I wasn't a happy chicken. Gary was awake, having a wee drink, or I'd have been even more pissed off. Not a good start, Joe.

'I got out of bed. Asked who the fuck was waking me up this time of night. And I heard your sweet voice, Joe. Kind of faint. There was a roar in the background. Like a storm. Wasn't raining that hard, though. I asked you what the din was. Football fans, you said. Came in handy, knowing that. I buzzed you in and lit a fag and waited in the doorway. The draught was blowing a gale round my legs. Just had my pants on, but I wasn't worried about being assaulted. It was only you, Joe, and I'd heard you didn't like sex.'

'Who told you that?'

'Patience, Joe. You'll find out. Anyway, when you said you wanted to talk about Gemma, I nearly shat myself. I tried to stay cool. Stuck my hand down my pants and had a good scratch. When you started blethering about pussy snorkels I knew you were in a bad way. Kept rubbing your palms together, far too enthusiastic about this new muff diving equipment. I let you rabbit on. If you wanted to tell me something about Gemma, I wasn't going to hurry you along. In your own good time, pal. I could wait. I was calm. Focussed.

'I started giving you some advice about parenting. You cut

me off. Told me Gemma was dead. Just like that. Nice, eh? You don't know what that did to me.'

Cooper scratched the side of his face with his gun. 'You have no fucking idea.' He paused for a moment, then carried on: 'Ruth called after you'd gone to bed. I was still up, drinking a last glass of whisky. She'd been drinking, too. Don't know what or how much, but enough to get shitfaced. She threatened me. Can you believe that? Under Scottish law, a verbal threat is an offence and I could have contacted the police and had her jailed. I explained that to her, but she was so drunk she just laughed. That hurt my feelings. I'm sensitive, you know. Still. Her daughter was dead and I'm a reasonable guy. I thought I'd give Ruth a bit of rope. And with any luck, maybe she'd hang herself.'

He stared at Joe. Joe remained absolutely still. His gaze didn't flicker.

Cooper rubbed the gun over his chin again. 'I put the phone down and thought about what she'd said. Well, I had to. TV was crap. Pay a fucking fortune for an LCD TV, all very well, but it doesn't improve the quality of the shite they make you watch. Anyway, I couldn't concentrate. I had a bucketful of adrenalin still shooting around in my bloodstream. By the time she rang again, I was dressed. She asked if you were there, said she was going to tell you. Said it was about time you knew.'

'Knew what?' Joe said.

'Keep what's left of your fucking hair on, Joe,' Cooper said. 'I'm telling you.' He sucked in a lungful of air and let it out slowly. 'I calmed her down. Said I'd come and see her. Told her to hang on, keep it together, I'd see her in a while. You see, I like you, Joe. If you want to know, I like you more than I like Ruth. And there's no way on earth I wanted you to find out.'

'Find out what?' Joe said.

'No fucking way. Poor guy, you'd just suffered a bereavement and there's Ruth wanting to rub salt in your wounds. Why the fuck are you two so cruel to each other? Don't know if you remember, but I asked you once why you stayed together. You just said, fuck it, she's Gemma's mum. We're married, got a kid together. It's got to mean something. Nothing else does.

'Then you'd go and bang that whore next to you. Why do you do that, Joe? She gives good head, you tell me. You think that's a good enough reason?

'Anyway, I never wanted to get you into trouble. That was the whole point. Me,' – he banged the butt of the gun against his chest – 'trying to protect you.' He waved the gun at Joe. 'You know that. But what choice did I have? It was either that, or have you find out . . .

'I'm running ahead of myself. I haven't slept much since this all kicked off. Maybe an hour at a time. When I nod off, I dream about Gemma. Believe that? I haven't once dreamed about Ruth. Sign of a clear conscience, eh?

'So, that night, I drove across town to your flat. Ruth was in a state. She was so far gone, actually, that she asked me to leave. Claimed she didn't want to see me. Didn't want me touching her. A pile of emotional stuff like that. I waited for her to calm down. I just stood there. Motionless. Like I was on a job. She didn't respond too well. She kicked me, in fact. Bruise is still there. On the fucking shin. Same leg you've fucking smashed up. She called me all sorts of unrepeatable names.

'Well, I was under pressure, you have to understand, and I snapped.'

He let out a long breath. The silence stretched. Joe heard himself breathing.

At last Cooper said, 'I hit her once. To get her to shut up. She dropped. Must have been out before she struck the floor.

Back of her head bounced. Looked a bit nasty. No way she was going to get up for a while. I checked her out. No blood. Start of a swelling, though. She was breathing. I thought she'd be well pissed off when she woke up. And then she'd definitely tell you everything.

'I wasn't thinking too clearly, I suppose. Sat down at the table. Poured myself some vodka. Knocked it back. I've always found alcohol highly inspirational. I called Mr Park here. Left a message. Gave him my mobile number. Had another vodka. Drank it slower. Ruth didn't move. She looked peaceful, bless her.

'Mr Park phoned me back within five minutes and I explained the situation. He had a handle on the whole concept before the words came out of my mouth. It was like talking to God, I swear.'

Park raised his eyebrows.

Joe said, 'What was it you didn't want me to know?'

'Fucking patience is a fucking virtue, Joe.' Cooper stabbed the air with his gun. 'All right?' After a long silence he lowered the gun and held it by his side. 'As I was saying, if I can get on with my story, I'd finished off the vodka by the time Mr Park arrived. He went on ahead to check the coast was clear. I followed him downstairs with Ruth slung over my shoulder. I'd found your car keys in her handbag. Nobody saw us inside the building and if anybody saw us outside, they haven't told the police. Anyway, I was dragging her alongside me, you know, with her arm draped over my shoulder. Probably looked like she'd drunk too much.'

'When did you realise she was dead?' Joe said.

'Oh, I knew she wasn't dead,' Cooper said. 'She was breathing. Actually, she woke up just before we reached the car. Could have been a problem. Luckily I spotted your baseball bat and had an idea.'

'Jesus help you,' Adam said.

Cooper pointed the gun at Adam. 'Interrupt me again and I'll arrange for you to put in a good word for me first. I'm just getting to the good part.'

Joe placed his hands on the floor. Park moved towards him.

Cooper swung his arm towards Joe. 'Stay where you are.'

Joe presented his palms to Cooper and leaned backwards.

'I'm fed up telling you, Joe. Don't you want to hear the rest?'

Joe said nothing.

'Well?'

He nodded.

'Say it.'

'I want to hear the rest.'

'Ask nicely.'

'Please.'

'Okay,' Cooper said. 'Just keep fucking quiet and stay still. That too much to ask? You don't hear me whining and I've got a fucked up leg that hurts like a bitch and an elbow that isn't much better.'

'I'll be quiet.'

'Right. Mr Park, myself and Ruth got in your car. Mr Park said he knew somewhere suitable. Somewhere we could dispose of Ruth. No security cameras. She moaned a bit. She was concussed, I think. Didn't know much about what was happening. We drove to a small industrial estate. Nicely secluded. No cameras. We checked to make sure. Dragged Ruth out of the car. She couldn't stand on her own. Mr Park tried holding her up, but I couldn't get a proper swing. In the end, we let her drop to the ground and I walloped her a couple of dozen times with your baseball bat. Really put my back into it. When we were sure she was dead, we put her in the boot and drove your car back home.'

The silence in the little church was total. Nobody moved a

muscle. Even Adam had stopped shaking. If Cooper wanted stillness, he'd got it.

Joe said quietly, 'What was it you didn't want her to tell me?'

'I haven't finished my story. Next day, I arranged for Mr Park to follow you. When he told me you were at the airport, I drove out to meet him. I still had Ruth's keys. Mr Park had the bright idea of getting one of the airport staff to write down your flight number. I popped the scrap of paper in your glove compartment. Took your car for a spin and left it somewhere conspicuous with the boot open. Found a phone box and told the police about the car with the boot open and the body in it and hung up. Then Mr Park drove me home. You know, I haven't had a good night's sleep since.'

'That's a shame,' Tina said. 'I really feel for you.'

'What was it you didn't want me to know?' Joe said.

'Two things, actually, Joe,' Cooper said. 'First of all, me and Ruth have been fucking each other's brains out on a regular basis since university.'

Steel fingers pressed hard against Joe's temples. But he was amazed at how little surprise he felt. 'And the other thing?'

'Ah,' Cooper said. 'That's going to really hurt.' He smiled. 'You ready?'

'Tell me. Can't be that bad.'

'But it is, Joe. It's very fucking bad.'

'Tell me.'

Cooper screwed his face up as he shifted his weight from one buttock to the other. 'You really fucked my leg up, Joe. That wasn't nice.' He glared at Joe.

'You going to tell me?' Joe said. 'Or are you just going to whinge about your leg?'

Cooper nodded slowly. 'It's about Gemma,' he said. 'She's not your daughter.' He paused. 'She's mine.'

Joe sprang forward.

'Stay there,' Cooper said, arm fully extended, gun inches from Joe's forehead.

Joe stared at the man in front of him. He didn't recognise him at all.

'You thought you had nothing to lose,' Cooper said. 'How fucking wrong were you?' He chuckled. 'Okay, Joe. Time to get down to business. You have a preference for which kneecap goes first?'

Joe heard a roar from his right and saw Adam swinging the baseball bat. Cooper turned. A shot rang out, halting Adam's forward momentum. The bat fell out of his grasp and Joe lunged for it, catching it on the bounce. In the same movement he swivelled on his knee, bringing the bat round in a curve. Cooper's eyes registered disbelief a split second before the bat struck him on the side of the face with enough power to knock him onto the floor. The gun fell out of his hand. As Park stooped to pick it up, Tina kicked him under the chin. His head snapped back and blood sprayed out of his mouth. Tina kicked the gun towards Joe. Then she booted Park in the face again.

One hand on the bench, Cooper tried to pick himself up.

Joe bent over him and hit him on the back of the head, the force of the blow causing Joe's side to explode with pain.

Cooper slumped.

Park's eyes darted from side to side. His hands were cupped over his mouth, blood dripping between his fingers. Tina kicked him again and his nose crunched.

Gingerly, Joe stooped to pick up the gun. He pointed it at Park. 'Tie him up,' he said to Tina. She used the strip of blanket that had acted as Sally's gag to bind Park's hands behind his back.

Joe turned to Cooper. 'Give me one good reason not to kill you.'

Cooper said nothing. Joe wondered if he was dead.

On his back, fingers spread over a widening red circle at the top of his thigh, Adam said, 'He's lying.'

Joe nudged Cooper with his foot. 'Are you?'

Cooper wasn't dead after all. His voice sounded like he'd drunk an entire bottle of Bunnahabhain. 'Every word I told you is true. Deal with it, Joe.'

Deal with it? Joe looked at the gun in his hand. He lifted it towards his face. He could smell the cordite. He wondered how it would taste.

'Don't you fucking dare,' Tina said.

'Don't believe him, Joe,' Adam said. 'You can get a DNA test.'

Joe knelt down and shoved the gun into Cooper's mouth. Cooper clamped his jaws together. Joe pulled the gun out, then rammed it back in again. He heard something snap. He grabbed the back of Cooper's head and shoved again. After only a few seconds of sustained pressure, Cooper's mouth jerked wide open and he wailed. As the gun slid between his parted lips, he closed his eyes and started to whimper.

Joe wondered if he should make a speech. He didn't think Cooper deserved it. Pull the trigger. Get it over with. Blow a hole clean through the fucker's head. Pull the fucking trigger. What was he waiting for? His finger tightened.

From outside, a voice cut through the silence. 'Put down your weapons and come out with your hands up.' Sounded like that policeman, Grove. How had he got here so quickly? Ah, well. It scarcely mattered any more.

The foyer door sprang open and Ronald Brewer said, 'Drop the gun, Joe. For God's sake, drop it.'

Joe wondered about this. Some people didn't seem to want him to kill Cooper. What difference could it make to them? What did they expect Joe to do? Let Cooper hang around here on this shithole planet for a while yet? Maybe have another kid with Sally? Maybe she'd sleep with someone else. Maybe Cooper would sleep with his kid. Maybe his kid would turn out to be someone else's.

Adam said, 'Gemma knew who her father was. You ought to know who your daughter was.'

Joe's vision was blurry. *Come on*. All he had to do was squeeze. Exert a little pressure. Bang.

'Gemma was your daughter,' Tina said. 'Whatever the result of a DNA test.'

Joe's cheeks were wet. The gun rattled against Cooper's teeth. His daughter? Was she?

Cooper's eyes were darting from side to side in his fear-crazed face. Blood trickled out the side of his mouth.

'Panic flicker,' Joe said. 'Think you can be still, Cooper? Stop that shaking? Think you can deal with it?'

Adam said, 'Take the gun out of his mouth, Joe.'

Joe looked at Ronald and the lawyer nodded.

'One,' Joe said. Cooper let out a pitiful moan. 'Two,' Joe said. A putrid smell hit Joe's nostrils. Cooper's left hand clawed at Joe's trousers. 'What's the matter, Cooper? You want to say something? No, I think we've heard enough from you already.' Cooper screwed his eyes shut. 'I promise you, Cooper, it won't hurt at all.'

Joe thought how easy it would be to pull the trigger. It wouldn't be like killing somebody. This grovelling, stinking thing at his feet wasn't fit to be called human. Pulling the trigger would be doing the world a favour. Joe's hand trembled. His finger twitched.

He eased the gun out of Cooper's mouth. The barrel was

covered in spit and blood. Cooper collapsed in a heap, shivering, spitting out bits of teeth. Joe said, 'Where have you been, Ronald? Adam needs an ambulance.'

FORTY-TWO

An attractive young woman was sitting by Adam's bedside, holding his hand. Joe guessed she was Dotty. Adam had mentioned her often enough when they were waiting for the ambulance to arrive.

She was a little bit shy, he'd said. Would Joe tell her he loved her?

'Tell her yourself,' Joe had said.

Joe turned and headed back down the corridor. He didn't want to embarrass her.

Adam had pulled through. Lost a lot of blood, but he was going to be okay. Joe had wanted to stop by and say thanks, that was all. He wanted to thank Adam for saving his life. If Adam hadn't taken a bullet there might be no Joe Hope.

But for the grace of God and a fat bloke from Orkney. He'd catch up with Adam later.

Outside, he sauntered over to Ronald Brewer's car.

'How is he?' the lawyer asked.

'Seems okay.'

After Ronald had stormed into the church last night, a handful of policemen arrived. Two of them Joe already knew. Adjusting his glasses, Grove wandered in as if he was about to attend Sunday service. Monkman was right behind, tugging the sleeves of his jacket.

Joe said to Ronald, 'You knew all along, didn't you?'

'I spoke to Grove about it. He'd admitted off the record that he didn't think you were guilty.'

'He knew about Monkman's involvement?'

'All done with Grove's full support.' Ronald turned to face Joe. 'Monkman isn't even a member of the local police force. No way would he have been able to get hold of a bodywire at such short notice. Grove trusted you'd come up with the goods. They were after a confession. We thought you'd get it.'

'But you didn't know I wasn't going to turn up.'

'I was sitting in Grove's car, listening to the conversation between Tina and Cooper. When the sound went dead, I realised we had a problem. Grove had had the foresight to park in the same street as Cooper, so when Cooper appeared with Tina, we tucked in behind their car and relayed their where-abouts to Monkman. We tailed Cooper to the church. Parked some distance away. Gave them a few minutes to get inside, then followed. We hunkered down outside, beneath the church's broken windows and listened to what was happening inside.

'Park's arrival caught us by surprise. He must have driven up very quietly and was heading for the church before any of us knew he was there. Monkman saw him coming up the path and we flung ourselves flat on the ground. He didn't see us, but it must have been pretty close. When the gun went off, Grove immediately radioed for the armed response unit. But by the time they arrived, it was all over.'

'A very stupid thing you did, running in like that,' Joe said. 'You could have been killed.'

'I trusted you.'

'You're a young fool, then.'

'Maybe I just know who to trust.'

'Best not to trust anyone.'

'You're not a killer, Joe.'

Joe said, 'That's something I may spend the rest of my life regretting.'

'Cooper's not worth it,' Ronald said. 'Concentrate on what's important to you.'

'I need to buy some clothes,' Joe said, after a moment. A black outfit for tomorrow. He'd finally get to say goodbye to his daughter.